Face
to
Face

Face to Face

PENELOPE FREED

Face to Face

This is a work of fiction. Names, characters, businesses, places, events and incidents are either the products of the author's imagination or used in a fictitious manner. Any resemblance to actual persons, living or dead, or actual events is purely coincidental.

Editing by Caitlin Fitzgerald
Cover design by Vanilla Lily Designs
Interior design by Stephanie Anderson, Alt 19 Creative

ISBN: 978-1-7364893-2-1

For Liz

&

Everyone who's ever been told who they love is wrong.
Love is love.

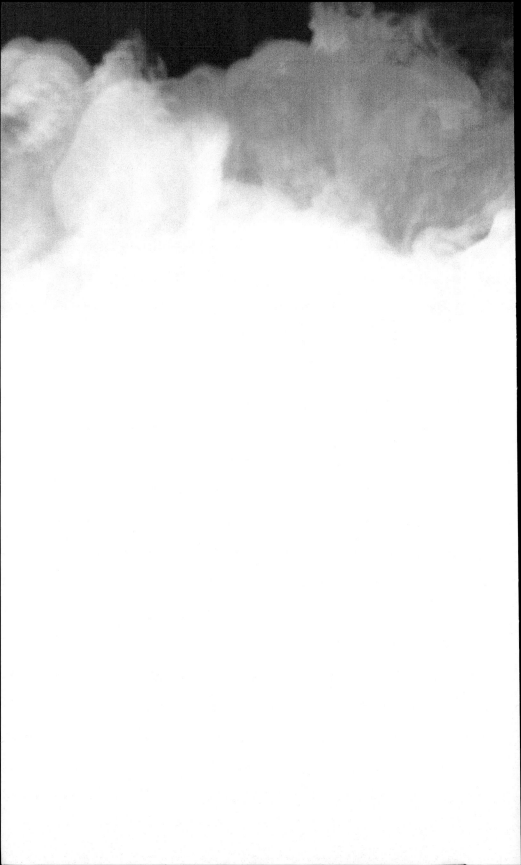

CHAPTER ONE

Hannah

"THANKS, BABE."

Jealousy burns through me as Tyler pulls Olivia to the top of the boulder, the powerful muscles in his bicep lifting her easily. It burns even hotter as Hunter does the same for Lisa a moment later. Trailing behind our little pack, I hang back as Jack hops to the top of the boulder as well, then turns back to help Katy scramble to the top. Again, I'm the odd man out—the seventh wheel. The lone sock, missing its match.

Not that I don't have a boyfriend. I do. And he's the best.

It's just that he's currently in my pocket and it's hard to hold hands with a phone.

"Come on Hannah." Jack grins down at me from his perch, holding out a hand. I've gotten to know Jack and Hunter better in the last two weeks than in the nine years that Katy and I have been friends. The seven of us have been hanging out almost every day, it's been a blast. But I wish Trevor was here too.

Scrambling to the top of the boulder with everyone else, I'm the last to take in the view. The Pacific Ocean is crashing against the rocks below us. A dull ache in my right ankle has me pausing, propping it up on a large rock so I can take my weight off it for a moment without raising anyone's suspicion. The pain has mostly gone away since the day of the show, but joining our impromptu hike at Point Mugu wasn't my most brilliant idea. For the last few days, it's only bothered me in the evening, depending on how active I've been that day. Hiding that I'm trying to rest it as much as possible without anyone noticing is exhausting. Luckily, we've spent most of our time swimming at the Quinns' house, the perfect activity for staying in shape while resting it at the same time.

Hiding my limp the first few days was the hardest, especially when Olivia insisted us girls spend an afternoon at the outlet mall shopping. But I managed. Barely. I've been doing lots of yoga and stretching to keep in shape while the studio is closed. Ms. Parker and her husband Mike got back from their annual "honeymoon" to Hawaii yesterday. Does it count as a honeymoon if you've been married for ten years?

"Are you excited?" Katy asks from near my elbow. "I can't believe you guys leave in two days."

I bump her with my hip. "Yeah, and you guys leave for your big road trip in a week. No feeling sorry for yourself." I tear my eyes off the waves below us and laugh when I see Katy's face.

Her big, brown eyes are open wide, her bottom lip jutting out, and an exaggerated tremble is quivering her bottom lip. All she needs is a big black hat with a floppy red feather to complete her transformation into a cartoon Puss in Boots. "Oh, don't give me that look. You're going to have fun. You get the studio pretty much to yourself, and you're off on a three-week vacation with your family."

"Um, yeah. Three weeks stuck in a car with these two bozos and Cole? That's going to be a real good time."

"If anyone should be upset about being left behind, it's me," Olivia says, coming up behind us. "*Everyone* is leaving me, and since you guys are going out of town, I don't even have a pool to look forward to!"

Excitement for my own trip overshadows any guilt I have for leaving Katy and Olivia behind all summer. Katy especially. Olivia has Tyler to hang out with, but Katy is going to be stuck with her brothers. She hasn't made it a secret that she's struggling with being left behind.

In two days, Lisa and I are off to the Pacific Sound Ballet's summer intensive—we're going to take ballet and dance classes all day long. Six weeks of as much ballet as my little bunhead heart can take. It's going to be perfect.

Okay, it doesn't hurt that my boyfriend, who I haven't seen since January, lives in Seattle too. When I think about seeing him for the first time as my official boyfriend, my stomach fills with butterflies. Sometimes I can't tell if I'm more excited or nervous about seeing him.

We met on a disastrous double date with Olivia and her boyfriend. Disastrous because, at the time, I had a huge crush on Tyler, and because Olivia neglected to tell me my date was Tyler's nerdy seventeen-year-old cousin and not the ten-year-old kid I thought I was babysitting.

Jack throws his arms around our shoulders, as he's been in the habit of doing. "Cheer up Bug! Once Hannah and Lisa leave, we'll be back to the original Three Musketeers. Besides, you know we'll have to keep Hunter from falling into a deep, dark depression with his lady leaving him." This is accompanied by a ludicrous eyebrow waggle, "I'm counting on you to help me out, Bug."

"Ugh, get off." Katy wriggles out from under Jack's arm and shoves him off us both. "Come on Hannah." She reaches back to grab my arm and pull me along the trail. "You can live out your little musketeers' fantasy with Hunter and Tyler. Emphasis on the *Musk*-eteers." I follow along, smiling as Katy grumbles under her breath about her brothers. I suppose growing up with Jack and Hunter as twin older brothers would try anyone's patience. And Katy is not a patient person.

As we round a corner ahead of everyone else, I tug my hand free of Katy's so I can stop. "Hang on," I tell her, pulling my phone out of my pocket. "Trevor would love this." I snap a pic of both the incredible view below us, then a selfie of me on the trail.

Having a boyfriend who lives a thousand miles away has made me an expert in documenting my activities. I'm pretty sure I've taken more photos of myself in the last couple of weeks than I ever have in my life. Olivia is so proud of me.

ME: Last minute hike at Point Mugu. Wish you were here.

A lot of my messages to Trevor say the same thing. "Wish you were here." Messages and Facetime are great, but I haven't even gotten to hold his hand yet and I'm surrounded by happy couples all day long.

Case in point, as I slide my phone back in my pocket, Olivia and Tyler come around the corner, his arm slung casually over her shoulder, her arm wrapped around his waist, their six months together translating into easy comfort with each other.

I want that.

Katy and Jack take the lead for the rest of the hike, while I fall to the rear. Between trying to go easy on my ankle and stopping to text with Trevor, I'm a good distance behind as we get back to our cars.

"Hannah, you doing okay?" Lisa asks as soon as I come into view. I wave her off.

"I'm fine. Stopped to take some pictures." It's not a complete lie. Lisa is the last person I want to tell about my ankle, she'll insist that I go to the doctor. I don't need some doctor who's never danced a day in their life telling me that I need to rest it for a month, that's not an option. It's been so much better until now, hardly aching at all for the last few days. Maybe the hike wasn't the greatest idea, but I got outvoted. I'll be fine. I'm sure of it.

Climbing into the back of Jack's SUV, I tune out my friends while I catch up on messages from Trevor.

> **TREVOR:** Looks gorgeous TT, wish I was there too.
>
> **TREVOR:** What are the odds we'll get to go on a hike like that when you're up here? I know that you're going to be dancing the whole time, so if you tell me there's no chance that's ok. But there are tons of amazing trails around here, and I'd love to show you some of my favorites, if we have a chance.
>
> **TREVOR:** No pressure though, I just can't wait to see you again.

Trevor's words calm the irritation and jealousy that hanging out with my friends seems to create. It's no one's fault, but it sucks when I'm the only one whose boyfriend can't join in. I'm sure Katy shares my jealousy, but since she currently doesn't even have the tiniest of crushes on anyone, it's not the same.

> **ME:** Only 2 more days.
> **TREVOR:** Can't. Wait. Now go have fun with your friends, you'll see me soon.

I cannot wait to get to Seattle.

"DO YOU think the food's going to be terrible?" I ask, taking another bite of my salad. "Maybe I should pack more protein bars, just in case..."

"Hannah, you already packed four boxes." Lisa points her fork at me. "They do have grocery stores in Seattle. And you happen to know someone up there with a car who I'm sure would be *more* than willing for an excuse to see you by bringing more if you asked."

"Yeah, but—" I'm cut off by a cherry tomato bouncing off my forehead. Tyler and Hunter high five each other from their table on the other side of the pool.

"NO BOYS ALLOWED!" Katy bellows across the backyard at them. "Stay on your side!" she adds, chucking the tomato back at them, hitting Jack on the shoulder.

"Hey! Tyler tossed it, not me!" Jack complains.

"Don't care. I only let you stay for the food. It's our last night together and no boyfriends or brothers are invited." Katy deliberately turns her back on the guys, shoving a forkful of lettuce in her mouth.

"Have they sent you the schedule yet?" Olivia asks while Katy chomps on her salad.

"We got an email last night with the first two days' schedule. It's just the placement days while they get everyone sorted out," Lisa answers. "For the first day we're divided by age and have placement classes all morning."

"Classes? There's more than one?"

"We have ballet placement first, then a separate contemporary placement class, and some kind of strength and conditioning class?" I jump in to answer. "I've never heard of it before but it's some Australian method I guess."

Lisa nods. "I looked it up last night. You use those big yoga balls and Therabands. It looks pretty cool." Lisa studies her hands in her lap for a moment, biting her lip. "I'm more nervous for the placement class than I was for the audition, is that weird?"

"Why would that be weird?" I ask. "I'm super nervous, too. What if we don't end up in the same group? Or what if we end up in a low level? It's not like we're going to be the youngest ones there." I bite my cheek, not sure how to say what I'm feeling. "I guess...it'd be kind of embarrassing to end up in one of the lower levels, especially after everything." I wave my hand vaguely, hoping the girls get it.

Arriving at the intensive as a regional Grand Prix winner and in the top fifteen dancers in the finals, not to mention being personally invited and given a scholarship by the director—not being placed in one of the highest levels would be humiliating. I keep to myself the fear that we'll go and Lisa will get placed in a higher level than me. It makes me a terrible friend, but I don't know if I can stomach the thought.

"Do you know how much downtime they're giving you? Obviously, you can't dance twelve hours a day. I'm assuming they give you rest time, right?"

Lisa still has her mouth full, so I answer Olivia's question. "We have a ninety-minute lunch break every day, and the classes after dinner are optional. But the first two days we have lectures after lunch instead of classes. There's a nutrition one and an injury prevention one." I shrug. I'm sure the lectures are to give us all a chance to get acclimated before diving into the full dance schedule, but I hate the idea of wasting time listening to people talk instead of getting to dance.

Katy keeps shoveling giant forkfuls of salad into her mouth, not talking. I push away my guilt for abandoning her, but I know that she'll be okay, once the saying goodbye part is over. I'm glad we decided to spend the night at the Quinn's house, even if we have to keep fighting off the boys. Katy even made me turn off my phone so that I can't cheat and text Trevor.

I guess that's one advantage over having him there, my phone is much easier to hide than the broad shoulders of Katy's brothers and Tyler. But that's what my friends get for dating athletes.

"So, are we watching a movie or what?"

"Actually." I snap out of my thoughts. "Guess what Ms. Parker emailed me this afternoon?" I almost forgot I had this surprise for them.

"No?"

"Seriously?"

"Yes!" Our table bounces on the cement from the force of Katy's happy drumming.

"Yup, I have the video of the recital. It's the preliminary proof, so it may not be perfect, but Ms. Parker figured Lisa and I would be dying to see it before we left so she sent it to me early. If we spot any major issues, we're supposed to let her know," I add, since that is ostensibly the reason she let me have the link before anyone else.

Katy and I wait impatiently at the bottom of the stairs while Olivia and Lisa take longer than necessary to say goodnight to their boyfriends.

"So, how many times have you repacked your bags?" Katy asks while we wait.

I tap my chin, making a show of counting in my head. "Only three." When Katy laughs I explain, wanting to keep her distracted. "The first time I couldn't zip my bag closed. So I had to redo it. Then the second time I'd forgotten to pack much in the way of real clothes."

"For all those dates you're going to go on with Trevor?" Katy pokes me in the ribs, grinning.

Embarrassed, I shrug. "Maybe? I don't know what my schedule is going to be like so I wouldn't let him make any real plans."

"And the third time?"

I wrinkle my nose. "Um..."

"Let me guess." Katy gives me a knowing look. "You were having a freak out and needed something to do?"

"Something like that, yeah." A blush warms my cheeks at being caught out. Truthfully, I'd repacked my suitcase, my dance bag and the box of bedding and extra stuff I couldn't fit twice more before Trevor Facetimed me, forcing me to stop.

Katy grunts in annoyance and finally snaps, dragging Lisa away from Hunter after the fourth time he pulls her back for "just one more" kiss. The only way we're going to keep the boys from crashing our sleepover is to stay in here. Mr. and Mrs. Quinn are super chill about letting everyone hang out at the house, Mrs. Quinn was overjoyed when she found out Lisa and Hunter started dating, but they have a hard rule that the boys are not allowed in Katy's room when us girls are over.

Pulling out her laptop, Katy gets the video set up while the rest of us arrange ourselves on the bed, squished together for optimal viewing. From her spot on the edge, Lisa speaks up as the opening credits roll. "You know, I'm so glad you guys planned that grand gesture with Hunter for dress rehearsal and not the actual show. I was so flustered by it, it would totally have thrown me off."

I laugh, tossing a pillow at her. "Liar! You and Hunter had already made up and started dating three days earlier. You just let us do it because you wanted to see what we had planned."

"She's not wrong," Olivia points out, fake pouting. "You guys let me do all that work for nothing."

"I still haven't figured out how you got the roses in the dressing room without me knowing." Three days before our recital, Katy, Olivia, and I had plotted with Jack to help get Hunter and Lisa together. We'd come up with a plan to have roses delivered to Lisa's bag between each of our dances, finishing with Hunter waiting for her at the stage door with the rest. It was an awesome plan, even if they didn't need it.

"We bribed MacKenzie, Anna, and Haley to do it," Olivia says. "Haley is surprisingly stealthy for a ten-year-old."

We keep chatting, laughing and pointing out the things we loved and hated about our recital as we watch. I'm going to miss this over the summer.

But I still can't wait to go.

CHAPTER TWO

Katy

I SHOULD HAVE put sunscreen on, the hot sun blazing on my shoulders already turning them crispy. When Jack insisted I come out to the backyard and act as referee, I didn't think I would be out here for this long. Craning my neck to see if the sunburn is visible, I catch a glimpse of pink. Damn it.

"I'm going inside!" I yell to my brothers as they emerge from under the water, shaking their heads like dogs. "Hunter won," I toss over my shoulder, as I slide the French door open and slip inside. The cool relief of the air conditioner sends goosebumps over my arms as I cross the open expanse of our family room to the stairs. The white walls and pale wood flooring make my mom's brightly colored decor and furniture stand out like a rainbow. I've always loved our bright orange couch and the colored throw pillows Mom changes out every season. I've heard the mutters of various judgmental girls over the years, girls my brothers invite over, complaining about the bright colors, I even heard one girl call our house a "cantina." She somehow ended up with a red Kool-Aid stain on her white shorts. Oops.

She was one of Cole's groupies. My mom wasn't even mad about the Kool-Aid that splashed on the wall as ten-year-old me "tripped" with the cup in my hand. Especially when I told her I'd found the groupie poking through Cole's room. It was the only rule my parents had—no members of the opposite sex in bedrooms. The rest of the house was fair game at all hours of the day or night.

Trudging up the stairs, I pull my phone out to see if I missed any texts from Lisa or Hannah. How pathetic am I? They've been gone for less than a day and I'm bored out of my mind. I mean, I always knew that Hannah would leave one day. You can't know her for more than a week and not see she's destined for greatness. Maybe that's why Lisa and I have always been a bit closer, not to mention that Olivia and Hannah were inseparable until recently. But that didn't make me miss her any less. And I was already missing Lisa.

> **HANNAH:** Cows. So. Many. Cows.
> **LISA:** Did you guys stop at Pea Soup Anderson's for lunch? Oh my god, so gross. Who eats pea soup? Ray. Ray eats pea soup. And then pretends to sneeze green goop onto the table. Twice.

Hannah and Lisa are driving up to Seattle for their summer intensive, each stuck in their respective cars. At least they only have two days of driving to suffer through. I have three weeks of road trip time to look forward to. Yay me. Note the heavy sarcasm.

ME: Don't get car sick. I escaped from the twin terrors after being forced to referee their little competition. They had a whole obstacle course set up. I think they're losing their minds.

ME: Why are you dating my brother again? I mean, I like that it means you're here more, but he's such a dork!!!!!

"Kaaaaty!" one of my brother's calls from downstairs. "We're going out for boba are you coming?"

"Coming!" I shout back.

Hunter drives us to his and Lisa's favorite spot, telling us about all the things that Lisa likes best about it. It's adorable and disgusting all at once. I mean, she's my best friend, of *course* I think she's amazing, but like, I don't need my brother waxing poetic about how beautiful she is. It's a little weird.

"Okay, we need a game plan for the summer," Jack says as we leave the store, ice cold cups in hand. "We've all been abandoned for the next few weeks so it's back to the old days, the three of us against the world." He grins. God, my brother is such a doofus. Sweet, but clueless.

Since I'm only fifteen months younger than Jack and Hunter, most of our lives we've been treated as closer to triplets than anything else. But I've always been the baby, always trying to keep up with them and their antics. Maybe that's why I have such a competitive streak. Being told you're too small, too slow, or too young to join in the fun is a sure-fire way to make a girl bust her ass to prove everyone wrong.

"What are you suggesting?" Hunter asks, slowly.

"Well, for starters, no sitting around mopey and depressed." Jack punches Hunter in the stomach to emphasize his point. He attempts to put me in a headlock, but I see it coming and duck out of his reach before he can get a grip.

"Seriously? Why? Always with the headlock." I huff, annoyed.

"You know you love it." Jack grins, like an ass.

"I really don't." I grump, putting Hunter between us for insurance. "So, what's this brilliant plan?"

"A terrain race." Chest puffed out, one fist on his hip, Jack stands there like a rejected superhero—I'll call him Boba Man—waiting for us to fall at his feet and worship his brilliance.

"A what?" I ask, being sure to sound extra confused. I know what it is, but I want to know what the hell he's thinking. There is no way I am running one of those muddy, messy, ridiculous obstacle course races. For starters, I don't run.

"Don't play dumb, Bug. I know you know what it is." He reaches past Hunter to poke me, but I sidestep out of his reach. "There's one at the end of August, JJ told me about it."

"JJ, huh?" Hunter teases, giving Jack a look.

"Nope, no way, I don't run," I add, deciding immediate refusal is smarter than playing dumb.

"Aw, come on Katy, it'll be fun. Besides, it's not like we can join a dodgeball team or something since we'll be gone for three weeks."

"What gave you the impression I would ever want to sign up for a dodgeball team?" This is ridiculous. "No. No way. Talk sense into him please," I beg Hunter.

"I don't know, Bug. It sounds kind of fun." Traitor. "Besides, it's something we could keep training for even on our road trip. All we need to pack are running shoes." My hope that Hunter will step in as the brains of this operation fade as a hopeful expression grows in his eyes. Hopeful eyes that he turns on me a second later, blasting my last line of defense against Jack's hare-brained idea. "Come on, Bug. It'll be fun. Sibling bonding and all."

I rub my face in an exaggerated manner, deepening my voice as much as I can. "I'm surrounded by idiots," I deadpan in as close an impression of Scar as I can.

The grins on Jack and Hunter's faces only make them resemble a pair of cartoon hyenas even more than usual. "I'll text JJ. She said she could help us come up with a training plan." Jack wanders off, phone in hand.

By dinner, I'm seriously regretting agreeing to do this stupid race. Surrounded by my family at the dinner table, Jack will not stop talking about it. He wants to get t-shirts made so, of course, he and my dad spend the whole meal tossing stupid team names back and forth.

"A la mud?"

"Like the ice cream? No."

"Mud Bugs? I kind of like that one for you Katy Bug."

I shake my head. "No, we do not need a team name of my childhood nickname, thanks."

"You're no fun."

I stick my tongue out at him.

"Band of Brudders? No, wait! Mudder Brudders!" Hunter and Jack both high five my dad for that one but I sit back in my chair, arms crossed over my chest.

"I refuse to be on a team that has brothers on the name. Last time I checked I was your *sister*."

"Aw, come on Bug, you're being a total party pooper." Jack folds his arms over his chest, faking a pout.

I shrug. Why should I make this easy on them?

My dad pipes up from the end of the table, his mustache twitching with glee. "What about…Twisted Blisters!"

When we all stare at each other, not getting it, he huffs a sigh and explains. "Like Twisted Sister? The band? But with blisters. Cause you know…Katy gets blisters from ballet and you guys are gonna get blisters from the wet socks?"

"Sorry Dad, I think that reference is a little before their time," Cole finally speaks up. He's been quiet and grumpy ever since the semester ended, but none of us know why. "What about Scrambled Legs?"

"Hmm, that's not terrible," I concede, turning the name over in my mind. "I could maybe be okay with that one."

"Wait." Jack throws his hands out, almost whacking me in the nose. "I've got it. It's the perfect name. Katy, it's perfect, you're not allowed to say no to this one. Promise me?"

"I'm not promising until I know what it is."

"Just trust me, please? It's amazing." I glance around the table, everyone's eyes on me. Even my mom's.

"Be a good sport, mija," she says, smiling at me. Ugh. That's not fair, they know I can't say no to my mom.

"Ugh, fine." I wave my hand, indicating Jack should share with the class. Always the drama queen, he pauses, looking around the table, making eye contact with each of us. My mom, then Cole, Hunter, my dad, and finally me. With a smirk, he inhales, only to choke on a cough as Cole whacks him in the stomach.

"Spit it out already!" Laughter breaks out around the table, a sound I remember well from all those nights as a kid, sitting around the table and eating dinner. I miss it when I'm busy with dance.

"Okay, okay." Jack holds up his hands. "Our team name needs to encompass pain, suffering, and our lovely sister, right?"

Shaking my head, I glance at my mom. She's smiling, enjoying the fact that all four of us are here for dinner, not something that happens often these days.

"I present to you…Agony of De Feet!"

CHAPTER THREE

Hannah

*I*THOUGHT ALL the hiking and swimming we did on our week off would have kept me in better shape. It's the first class of the entire intensive and I wanted to make a good impression, but that wasn't even close to my best. I wobbled on balances that should have been easy, my turns were all over the place, and I barely had the stamina to keep going to the end. I don't know if it's because I'm nervous, or if I'm that out of shape, but that class was a struggle from start to finish.

Fortunately, my ankle is behaving today. I'm hyper aware of it, waiting for a twinge as I'm dancing, but other than being a little weaker than my left ankle, it doesn't hurt. Fingers crossed, whatever I did during the recital is healed. I stay on my feet through sheer force of will as we curtsey to the pianist and the teacher.

My legs quiver as I gather up my shoes and clothes to clear the room. "It's Lisa and Hannah, right?" someone says from near my shoulder. I look up to see a willowy brunette tossing shoes and clothes in a bag near us. Her pale skin glistens with sweat, like ours and everyone else in the warm room. I remember her from the class—she was struggling too, maybe even more than me.

"Yeah, it's nice to meet you," Lisa pipes up from my other side. "What was your name again?" They have us all wearing name tags, but I can't see hers from this angle.

"I'm Becky," she says, twisting to show us her name tag. "Rebecca Carlson" stands out in matching print to ours. "Oh my god, that class was so hard!"

"I know, I thought I was in better shape than that," I say. "Are you coming to lunch now?"

"Yeah. Could I eat lunch with you, so I don't have to sit by myself? Somehow I ended up without a roommate, so I don't know anyone yet." Becky smiles, standing up with her dance bag slung across her chest.

Becky and I follow Lisa out the door of the studio, almost crashing into Marco Bethelo walking in. "Oh! I'm so sorry!" I back up to let him through. The last time I saw him was onstage at the YIGP competition in February where he awarded me my scholarship to be here. He is still as handsome now as he was then, silver streaks at his temples highlighting his dark hair and chiseled jawline.

"Hannah! How lovely to see you," Marco says, smiling at us. Becky freezes next to me. "How was the placement class? I'm sorry I wasn't able to watch yours, but I was leading the men's class." Marco Bethelo is chatting to us, as casual as can be. This is surreal. "Are you settled in the dorms okay?"

"Oh, um. Yeah." I stumble over my words. "The class was great. Hard, but great. We should…um. We were going to lunch." Do I keep talking? I don't know what to do. I don't want to be rude, but I don't know what to say. Flustered, I just smile, even though I'm sure I look stupid.

"Of course, of course. Please send my love to Leslie next time you speak to her," he adds with a smile, before turning to walk into the studio.

Becky is practically vibrating by the time we get into the hallway. "How do you know Marco Bethelo? Who is Leslie? And how are you both so calm right now?"

My cheeks burning, my feet stop moving while my mouth opens and closes a few times, trying to find the words to answer Becky's questions. Lisa takes pity on me, steering Becky by the elbow towards the dining hall so we can eat lunch. "Hannah won the Grand Prix at our regional YIGP. Marco Bethelo was one of the judges that weekend and was handing out acceptances and stuff on stage. I didn't think he'd remember her, but I guess she made an impression."

My face burns even hotter, but I don't say anything. What else can I add that isn't going to make me sound like a pretentious brat? Lisa doesn't mention the scholarships we were both awarded, her a half and me a full, at this year's regional YIGP competition. We talked about it before we came and decided not to mention it. If news got around, it would put a target on our backs from the more competitive dancers.

"But who's Leslie? Is that one of your moms or something?" Becky asks.

"Leslie is our teacher back home, they used to dance together at CBC," Lisa adds, turning the conversation away from me.

"Your teacher danced at CBC?" Becky asks. "Who is she?"

I take the lead to the dining hall, Lisa and Becky following close behind as we navigate the crowded sidewalk. The intensive is being held on the University of Washington campus, and it's a short walk from the studios to the dorm building housing all the dancers. Conveniently, there's a dining hall on the ground floor of the dorms, I guess they don't want us wandering off into the city. I glance around the dining hall for the crowd of other dancers to reassure myself we're in the right building. Staying on a campus this big has me anxious I'll get lost, go to the wrong building, or something equally stupid. I spot a line of girls with their hair in buns and head that way, Hannah and Becky trailing behind me.

"Leslie Parker," I say, as casually as I can, while we pull plastic trays from the pile and get in line. It's always a little weird to us when people freak out over who our teacher is, but it's a safer topic of conversation than delving into how Marco had a personal chat with me on our first day.

"No way!" Becky screeches. The girls in front of us turn at Becky's outburst, eyeing us. "Are you serious?"

"Uh, yeah?" I say, putting a sandwich and a salad on my tray, hoping to get away from the attention. "She's amazing, but we kind of forget who she is most of the time. She's just Ms. Parker to us."

"Yeah, but obviously Marco Bethelo knows her and knows who you are," Becky says, trailing behind. "Oh my God, I wonder if they were ever an item. You're not really having a sandwich, are you? I could never eat all those carbs."

"She's never said anything to us." I eye the sandwich I'd grabbed while Lisa answers Becky's question. Carbs? Aren't those good things when you're dancing? Shrugging, I keep it. I'm hungry. "Besides, she's married now. She did say he was the best partner she'd ever danced with," Lisa says. "But, I'm sure they're just friends."

"Yeah, but wouldn't it be so romantic?" Becky passes over the other food offerings, reaching for a salad. She doesn't take any dressing, gross. "What if after all these years he still loves her?"

I wait for Lisa and Becky to finish picking out their food. "Nah, Ms. Parker's husband is awesome. He was her physical therapist when she first came back to Camarillo after her accident. I think their story is the most romantic thing ever. He helped her recover from the accident and they fell in love."

"Yeah, they've been married for ten years now," Lisa adds. "He helps at all the shows and anytime one of us gets injured, he always makes time for us."

Lisa's words are like a lightbulb flicking on in my brain. Why didn't I think of talking to Mr. Mike when I was home? That was dumb, Hannah. If my ankle starts to hurt again, maybe I'll call his clinic and talk to him.

Shaking my head at my own stupidity, I can't help adding a fun tidbit to Ms. Parker's story. "Me and my friend Olivia got to go to their wedding. We were only seven, so I don't remember a lot, but it was so romantic, all soft and white and floaty. She walked down the aisle to the White Swan pas de deux music." It's one of my favorite memories.

I lead the way once we all have food and water on our trays. Most of the smaller tables are full, but I spot a long table that has some empty places at one end. The dancers are easy to pick out of the crowd in the dining hall. The girls all have their hair pulled up somehow, high buns, low buns, French twists, and even a few braided crowns. Pink tights and leotards underneath a pair of shorts or leggings with a jacket or shirt on top is the standard uniform for the girls. Most of the guys are wearing white t-shirts, in varying degrees of cleanliness, with track pants. Typical ballet hobo-chic.

"Can we sit here?" I ask the group sitting at the other end of the table. They weren't in our placement class, but two of them were in the YIGP finals last month. I have no idea if they recognize me or not, but a familiar face is a familiar face.

"Go ahead," one of the guys says, waving a hand at the empty spots. He looks about eighteen, his shoulders already broad and muscled. His dark brown eyes are friendly. "I'm Uri."

He's one of the two I recognize from YIGP, him and the girl sitting on his lap. He was the third-place winner at the finals. Gloria, the girl on his lap, won first place. I made it to the final round, but I didn't place so I have no idea if they'll recognize me. Because his teacher is Ms. Parker's good friend, I ended up hanging out with Martin Needham, who won the Grand Prix, the highest award of the competition, most of the week. Gloria and Uri spent most of the competition wrapped up in each other, not talking to anyone else.

"Hi. Um, I'm Hannah," I set my tray down on the table. "That's my friend Lisa and, uh, that's Becky."

Lisa slides into the chair next to me leaving the seat opposite us to Becky. "Hi," she says. She's fiddling with the food on her tray nervously, which is unusual for Lisa. Katy and Olivia are the outgoing ones of our friend group, but Lisa is more quiet than shy. I'm the shy and anxious one. I guess knowing that I've met these two before helps.

Uri laughs. "You look overwhelmed. First time?" His Israeli accent is lilting and friendlier than I remember from our week in New York. Maybe because this isn't a competition. His dark olive skin and tousled brown hair give him that effortless Mediterranean look. He looks a bit like Marco Bethelo.

"Is it that obvious?" I ask, unwrapping my sandwich and taking a bite.

"I went to Houston ballet's intensive last year," Becky pipes up. "The food there was pretty awful, I'm hoping it's better here."

Uri looks at his friends and laughs. "That's a valid concern," a gangly, freckled guy at the table calls out. "Don't worry, the food here is pretty decent. I'm Thomas, by the way." Thomas waves before Uri introduces us to the rest of the table. It turns out that Thomas is Gloria's twin brother. There's also Noah and a gorgeous dark-skinned girl named Elena.

"You look familiar," Gloria says, peering at me.

"I was at the YIGP finals with you last month." Was I that forgettable? The insecurity I've been fighting off since I came home from New York resurfaces, settling like a brick in my stomach. I put my sandwich down, appetite gone.

"Oh my god, yes! I knew I knew you. You hung out with Martin, right?" Well, at least my friend wasn't forgettable, unlike me.

"Yeah, our teachers are friends, so we had some extra rehearsal time together before the competition started."

Becky's stare from across the table sends heat flooding to my cheeks. Uri eyes me thoughtfully. "That's right, I recognize you now. You did the Aurora variation, right?" At my nod, Uri smiles. "You gave us a run for our money, remember babe?" He says the last bit to Gloria, poking her in the ribs. I can't relax until Becky looks away, eyeing the couple as they tickle each other. I'm not sure what it is, but Becky makes me nervous.

"Knock it off!" Gloria laughs, pushing Uri away. "So, did you guys know each other before? Obviously, I know this turd," Gloria points a thumb at her brother, "Elena is my roommate and Noah is rooming with Thomas. I think they found Uri out on the street somewhere and invited him in out of pity." Gloria winks at Uri when she says this. He tosses a balled-up napkin at her face, before reaching up to give her a quick kiss on the cheek.

"She's kidding. We met here last year, she was my partner in pas de deux class. We've been together ever since, most of it long-distance. I'm from Tel Aviv," Uri explains, although Lisa and I already knew that. "We both competed at the New York Finals, mostly so we had an excuse to see each other." He grins, explaining the story to Becky and Lisa.

Gloria laughs and smacks the hand he has snaked around her waist. "That wasn't the reason, don't be ridiculous, sweet cheeks."

"That is the sweetest story I have ever heard." Becky sighs. "I was too nervous to eat alone, so I tagged along with Hannah and Lisa after our class."

"Lisa and I have danced together forever," I add, nudging Lisa under the table. She looks up from her phone and smiles at everyone, swallowing the bite of salad she took. My money's on it being Hunter she's busy texting.

Gloria and Yuri regale us with stories from the finals while we eat lunch. Interestingly, they don't talk about the fact that they both placed. Most of their stories are about the trouble they got up to in New York City between the competition and classes. I was so busy with my parents and Ms. Parker I never noticed all the things Gloria and Uri were up to. I'm shocked that they could goof off so much and still do as well as they did. From their stories you could assume that they don't take dance seriously, but I know from class and on stage that's not true at all.

Maybe they're just better at letting go and having fun than I am.

Gloria reminds me a bit of Olivia, the kind of person who gathers people up in their circle. I've never understood how they can direct everyone else to have fun, and somehow, we find ourselves following along and liking it? It's the strangest kind of magic. I never minded it with Olivia when we were younger, because the fun was always worth it. Katy's brother Jack is another one of those people. A ringleader, the director of the show, the master of ceremonies.

Hours later, Lisa and I are waiting in our room, exhausted from the afternoon classes and lectures, legs resting on the wall next to our respective twin-sized beds when our phones buzz simultaneously. "Do you think that's Katy? Or do you think it's the class list?" she asks, I know she's afraid to look.

"Katy wants to know if we found out yet," I say from my bed.

"What level do *you* think we'll be in?" she asks, needing reassurance.

"I don't know, but I hope we end up together. Would it be better to be the best one in a lower level or the worst one in a higher level?" I'm asking her but I'm really asking myself. I want to say that I'd rather be placed in a higher level so I could prove to everyone that I deserve to be here, that I have what it takes. But I'm well-aware of the effect that too much pressure has on me, and I'm terrified of being placed in the highest level and buckling.

"I'm resigned to being in a lower level than you. We'd still get to eat together and we'd be together here. It'll be fine. I want to prove to my parents that it wasn't a waste of my summer to come," Lisa says. "I want to see where I stack up against other people my age, but I don't want to be the worst. Can I just be right in the middle?"

How is she so calm about this? I know I've been dying to go away to a professional school for years, but faced with the reality, I want my best friend to be in all my classes with me.

"Do you remember the year *after* I won the Jean Field award?" When I was ten I won the highest award for my age group at our regional YIGP competition, it's similar to the award I won this year but it's more about the future potential of a dancer than their actual skill level at such a young age. Olivia likes to call it the "child prodigy award." She's not wrong.

"Yeah, that was right after we moved from San Francisco, right?"

"Yeah." Lisa and her family had moved to Camarillo when we were nine, in the middle of the school year. The competition where I won the award was about a month after they joined the studio, so Lisa and I weren't good friends yet. "The next year—after I won—I don't know if you remember how anxious I was. I was so caught up in winning the same award again, I had it in my mind that if I couldn't win again then I was a failure."

"That's right. I remember now. That girl from Nevada won, right? That was the year you placed third, right?"

"Yeah. And I was devastated. My mom had to bribe me to keep going to dance. It was almost a month before I stopped crying in the car on the way to class," I admit. I've never told my friends this story before, ashamed of how ridiculous I'd been.

Almost as ridiculous as I was after I didn't place at the YIGP finals last month. I'd skipped dance for almost a week after getting back, unable to face my classmates feeling like a failure.

"So, you think you'd rather be the best one in a lower level?" Lisa asks, turning her head towards me so I can see her face. I sit up, reaching over to grab the charging cable draped across the desk on my side of the room. My desk is littered with pointe shoes and a couple dance magazines. Lisa's, on the other hand, is a pristine array of her laptop, some notebooks, and her rainbow assortment of pens.

I nod. "Yeah, I think so. It's my, our, first time at such a big intensive. I don't think I'm ready for that kind of pressure this summer." I trail off, my mind sifting through all the thoughts competing for my attention. "Yeah, I think I'd rather spend my summer focused on being my personal best, rather than trying to be the absolute best. That sounds like more fun." If I keep telling myself this, eventually I'll believe it, right?

"When you put it like that, I have to agree. I want to be challenged and see where I stand, that's all." My phone buzzes against the desk, a glance at the screen reminds me of the other reason why I want to be able to relax a little while I'm here.

TREVOR: Status report?

TREVOR: Ugh, why does it always sound so much better in my head than it does in writing? I swear I'm not a Trekkie.

TREVOR: I wanted to hear how the first day went, let me know when you're free to chat, okay? I have news for you. (Good news, I think)

CHAPTER FOUR

Katy

I SCROLL THROUGH the messages from Hannah and Lisa, gushing over the classes they've had so far, one eye on the time in the corner. I should get changed to go to dance.

Except I don't want to go. I didn't wake up until almost noon today, and the only reason I even got out of bed was because my room was too hot. I've been down here, stretched out on the couch ever since and to be honest, I don't want to go anywhere. Going to dance sounds like so much work.

I should go. Everyone is expecting me to go because that's what I do, right? I'm a dancer. If Lisa and Hannah were here it wouldn't even be a question, of course I would go.

"Hey Bug, we're going to go to a movie, you want to come? Or do you have dance?" Hunter's upside down head pops into my field of vision.

"Who's we?" I ask, flipping onto my stomach. "You and Jack or..."

Hunter looks at his phone. "Us, Tyler, Olivia, JJ, I think maybe Drew? Why?"

"Just wondering." I shrug. If Olivia is skipping class to go, then maybe I won't feel so bad for not being there. Besides, if she's not going, then I would be the only one of us four there and that sounds like the pits. Ballet class is fun because my friends are with me. Mutual suffering is a true bonding experience. I looked at the schedule for the summer, since Hannah and Lisa are gone, Ms. Parker combined all of our classes with the group below us. I don't know if I can take a whole summer of the younger girls' incessant chatter and stupid questions.

How many times does Ms. Parker need to go over an exercise before they can get it inside their thick skulls? Yeah, going to a movie sounds infinitely better than going to class. "Sure, when are we leaving?"

Hunter glances at the time. "In thirty minutes? I assume you can be ready by then?"

"You would assume correctly." I roll off the couch, catching myself on my hands and feet, heh, nice Spiderman move, and head upstairs to get dressed. It takes me longer than it should to decide between wearing shorts and a crop top, or a dress. Braving the overprotective "charms" of my brothers, I pull on a pair of high-waisted jean shorts and a cute striped crop top. I grab an oversized cardigan too, because it'll be cold inside the movie theater and so that my brothers don't complain about the way my shorts *just* cover my butt.

"Shotgun!" Hunter bellows the second I step out of my room. "Jack's driving," he adds, before darting outside. Grumbling, I lock the front door and follow him, sliding into the backseat, sitting in the middle seat like I always do. "We're picking up JJ, by the way." Hunter throws over his shoulder at me as I buckle in.

"Oh. Okay. I'll slide over once we get her." I slip my cardigan off as Jack starts the engine, the sweltering interior of the car too hot to stand keeping it on any longer. Hunter and Jack joke with me while we drive to JJ's house. Jack doesn't need to use the GPS on his phone to get there. How many times has he been here? And why does that make me jealous?

"Wait..." I pipe up from the backseat as we pull onto a familiar street. "JJ lives on Hannah's street? But that means Drew is like, two streets over. Why didn't she get a ride with him?" When you've had to listen to Drew go on and on and on about the running route he takes every day, it doesn't take a Lisa or Hunter-level genius to figure out where he lives, or that the house with the car covered in Marvel and DC decals belongs to Hannah's dad.

Jack shrugs. "Because she asked me, not him. Isn't that a good enough reason?" As her front door opens and JJ comes bounding outside, her thick blonde curls loose instead of braided back. I don't have a comeback other than to cross my arms over my chest and glare.

"Hey," JJ says, pulling open the door to my right. With a sigh, I unbuckle my seatbelt and pull myself over to sit behind Jack, making space. As I sit, I catch Hunter's disapproving glare—I must have given away how short my shorts are as I moved. Oh well, what's he gonna do about it now?

"Thanks for the ride." JJ smiles at me before turning her charm on my brothers, oblivious to the silent argument Hunter and I are having.

Those shorts are too short Katy.

What are you going to do about it? My raised eyebrow says.

Don't make me turn this car around and take you home, Hunter tells me with a tip of his head in Jack's direction.

Ha! You didn't drive, dummy. I smirk right back.

Hunter eyes Jack as he pulls away from JJ's house, oblivious to us and chatting with JJ. *He'd do it for me. And if he saw how much of your ass is hanging out the back of your shorts.*

I roll my eyes as his stupid protective act and shake my cardigan at him to get him off my back. With an answering roll of his own eyes, Hunter drops it and joins in the conversation.

Ugh. Stupid brothers.

HANNAH: How was class? Who came?

ME: I don't know, I didn't go. Went to a movie with my brothers instead.

I WAIT FOR the inevitable text full of reasons why I should have gone to class while I watch JJ and Jack look through the shoe display on the wall. Jack insisted that the four of us needed to go shopping after the movie to get gear for all this training they think they're going to get me to do for this race. Apparently, JJ is going to do it with us. Yippee.

Hunter is trying to hide the fact that he's texting and not paying attention to Jack's current monologue about why one pair of sneakers is better than another. From Lisa's lack of response to my text I assume that's who's on the other end of his conversation. They're adorable, but I miss my friend's instant responses to my texts.

JJ is listening patiently, chiming in with the occasional agreement. I watch from my side of the store, trying to figure out her angle. It's pretty obvious that she isn't trying to get Hunter's attention, they have a definite "friends only" vibe, despite the story Lisa told us about what she said in Chem last year, but I can't tell if she's trying to flirt with Jack or not. They have a lot in common and joke a lot, but she doesn't do that touchy thing that I notice a lot of other girls doing. You know, where they touch an arm or a shoulder. She hasn't even flipped her hair once. Granted, it's almost always back in a braid or a ponytail, but still. Not a giggle or a hair twirl in sight.

I can't figure her out and it's driving me crazy.

HANNAH: You should go to class, it'll give you something to do while we're gone.

Something to do while they're gone? Like I don't have anything better to do than sit and stare at the walls while she and Lisa are at the intensive? I know it's going to be six long weeks while they're gone but that doesn't mean I don't have anything to do without them. I'm doing this freaking race, aren't I?

I mean, I'm pretty sure I can think of something to do.

Sure, I could think of something if I tried. Dance isn't my entire personality. Is it?

I wrack my brain, trying to think of anything else about myself that is inherently "Katy." Does being a pain in the ass little sister count? Or making movie references?

I'm puzzling this over when Hunter comes wandering back over.

"How's Lisa?" I ask, needling him as he tucks his phone away.

He looks up. "She's good. They're waiting around after dinner to find out what group they'll be in."

"I hope they're in the same group. I know Lisa would be fine on her own, but I think Hannah will have a hard time dealing with the pressure if she doesn't have Lisa there with her." I finger a bright pink running shoe on the display in front of me. "Hannah doesn't always do well under pressure," I explain when Hunter looks confused.

"Lisa said she wasn't sure if they would, it sounds like Hannah looked good in the placement class and she wouldn't be surprised if she gets put in the highest level."

I shrug. Is it terrible that I don't want to talk about ballet?

"Hey," I blurt out. "How would you describe me?"

Hunter cocks his head. "Describe you? Like, brown hair, brown eyes? Or pain in my ass, goofball who somehow always gets her way and whose clothing choices leave something to be desired?" I don't bother to hide my eye roll.

"Ugh! I don't know..." I trail off, not sure what I want anymore. "Nevermind, it's stupid."

"Hey." Hunter grabs my arm before I can walk away. "You know we love you, right? Pain in the ass and all." He nods his head in Jack's direction at his words. "Is everything okay?"

"Yeah. I guess I'm a little lost without Hannah and Lisa here." It's true, I don't know what to do with myself all day. Normally I would have spent my whole summer with those two.

Hunter eyes me, his brown eyes thoughtful. "I get that. I would feel pretty lost if Jack was gone for the whole summer. But you have dance, and you have us. JJ seems pretty cool too. Maybe it won't be so bad." With a patronizing pat on the head, Hunter wanders off to answer a summons from his twin, leaving me to browse a rack of hoodies. Just touching the warm, fluffy material has sweat prickling on my upper lip.

"Do *you* buy hoodies, or do you let them buy the hoodies and steal them?" JJ appears next to me, grinning. "If I had older brothers I wouldn't bother," she adds. Is she saying she wants to steal my brothers' hoodies? That's such a…girlfriend kind of move. Right? Is that what she's after?

I'm pulled from my inner debate by a bump to my hip. "Huh? Oh. They won't let me near their hoodies. Cole sometimes gives me an old one, but usually I'm on my own in the hoodie department." Why am I babbling about hoodies? What the hell is wrong with me? This is the most interesting thing I have to say?

JJ laughs at me and pulls out an extra-large hoodie, dark gray with the logo of the surf-shop we're in splashed across the front. "Yes? No? How do you feel about logos?" Hands on my hips, I eye the hoodie.

"No logos. And not that color. If they won't let me have theirs, I'm getting the girliest color I can, but I'm telling everyone I stole it from them." Inspired, I pull a mint green and lilac-colored hoodie off the clearance rack. It's hideous but proves my point.

"Oh my god, no you can't wear that one!" JJ laughs, putting the gray one back and finding a blood red one instead. "Thoughts?"

I'm about to turn it down when another one catches my eye. Laughing, I pull it off the rack and hold it up for her to see. It'll be huge on me, the XXL tag sticking out the top guarantees it, but that makes it even more perfect. Giggling, JJ blocks me from the twin's view as I take it to the register and pay. The cashier even cuts the tags off for me.

"We'll meet you outside!" I call to the boys as JJ and I scurry out the front door, barely containing our giggles. I don't even care that it's over ninety degrees outside, I pull my cardigan off and slip the sweatshirt on. It covers my shorts, which is going to drive Hunter crazy now that it looks like the hoodie is the only thing I'm wearing.

"What the hell is that?" Jack's grunt and Hunter's growl at the sight of me has JJ bent over in a fit of laughter. Feet wide, hands on hips I wait until the gaggle of cheerleaders I spied a minute ago is in earshot before I open my mouth.

"What? You said I could have your hoodie. You didn't say anything about whether I could wear it in public." I give them both an evil grin as the pack of girls slow down enough to eye the garish tie-dye colors and the words splashed across my chest. When they pause to give Jack and Hunter disgusted looks, I know I've won. The best part is, the snarky phrase is one I have uttered myself on more than one occasion.

No need to repeat yourself, I ignored you just fine the first time.

This sweatshirt is so ugly I'll never wear it in public again, but it will be perfect for chilly nights after swimming, or at the beach. Even without this perfect moment of annoying my brothers, this sweatshirt is going to be worth the money.

Grinning, I grab JJ's arm and propel her away from the store, leaving Jack and Hunter sputtering. "I need a pretzel. You hungry?"

Laughing with me, JJ hooks her elbow with mine. "Absolutely."

CHAPTER FIVE

Hannah

I'M STUCK at the back of the crowd. Everyone is pushing forward to get a look at the papers taped to the wall next to the elevator. Squeals of happiness come from the front as a mix of happy and resigned faces move to make way for those trying to catch a glimpse of the class lists.

"Ow," Lisa groans, pulling her hand loose from mine. "You have way stronger hands than I thought." Flexing her hand a few times and grimacing, we keep navigating our way to the front of the crowd.

"Sorry, I didn't think I was going to be this nervous to find out." We push forward, the class lists looming over our heads. I gave up trying to guess where they'd place us, telling myself I'm going to be happy no matter what.

Gloria explained to us over dinner that there are eight levels of classes. Levels one through four are reserved for the eleven to thirteen-year olds and are grouped by age more than ability. The dancers in level eight are usually in their last year of training before joining a company or an apprentice program. Sometimes, a dancer in their first few years as a professional will do a summer intensive if they don't have any performances scheduled over the summer so they can stay in shape. After hearing more from Gloria and Uri, I don't want to be placed in the highest level, just saying it to myself—Level Eight—sounds so ominous.

The pressure of keeping up in class with dancers on that level... the idea of it sends my brain pinging from anxious thought to anxious thought. I fixate on the crushing weight of expectations I can never live up to, the constant need to compare myself to everyone else, knowing I'll never measure up. The burden is crushing me already.

Lisa and I finally get up to the front and look at the lists. "I'll read through six, you read through seven," I tell her. I run down the list of names, seeing *Rebecca Carlson* in the list, but I don't recognize any other names. I'm past the H's when Lisa squeezes my arm.

"We're both in seven!" she squeals, grabbing me in a hard hug. I'm so relieved we're going to be in the same class, I almost collapse against her.

"Seven? You're sure?" I ask, scanning the page over her head. There they are *Lisa Hamasaki* and a few names lower *Hannah O'Brian*. It looks like Noah and Elena are going to be Sevens with us.

We push our way to the edge of the crowd, waving to Gloria and Uri as they exit the elevator hand in hand. "So? Did you get what you wanted?" Uri asks as Gloria pushes her way into the crowd. Her thick brown hair swings against her back as she moves.

"We're both in level seven." Lisa says. "I'm so glad we'll be in the same group. I wasn't sure, Hannah is pretty amazing. I thought she might end up in eight."

"Yeah, no. I didn't want to be in eight," I interrupt. "I want to be challenged, but I don't think I'm ready for that kind of pressure. Seven is good."

Uri looks us over. "Being a Seven is more fun than being an Eight, but no one ever believes me when I say that." Gloria gives a happy shout from where she's worked her way to the front of the crowd. "What'd we get, sweet cheeks?" Uri calls over everyone's head.

"Crazy Eights, hot stuff!" Uri laughs as Gloria thrusts her pelvis in a celebratory dance before making her way back out to us. "So, you guys are Sevens, huh? That's what we were last year," Gloria says once she's reached us. The crowd is dying down, dancers milling around the common area, tentatively starting up conversations with each other. Gloria and Uri spot Thomas, Noah, and Elena already lounging on one of the couches and start walking that way.

I have no idea if they want us to hang out with them and sway on my feet, indecisive. I glance at Lisa, I'm not sure why they seem to have taken us under their wing, but it would be reassuring to have friends who have done this before. "Do you want...?" I start, gesturing vaguely towards the elevator back to our room.

"You coming?" Noah calls from the couch, waving us over.

Lisa looks to the elevator, then back at me. "Well, we wanted to make new friends, right?" With a shrug, she pulls me over to the couch to join our new gang. Noah and Thomas make room for us on their side of the couch. "You should text Trevor, I'll text Katy and Hunter," Lisa says, as we sit.

"Ooo, who's Trevor?" Gloria asks, rubbing her hands together in glee. "Your boyfriend back home?" Smiling to myself, I know Lisa did that on purpose so we both had an excuse to mention our boyfriends. It's helpful to have a best friend who's smarter than me.

"Except, he's not back home," Lisa adds. "He lives here in Seattle. They went on a date back in January when he was visiting family in California." Gloria and Uri share a calculating look at Lisa's words.

"He lives here? That's very convenient for you," Uri drags out. "Well..." He reaches across the coffee table between us to pinch my cheek. "We will have to help you find the time to see him. I am nothing if not romantic—"

"Me too!" Gloria interrupts.

Uri kisses the side of Gloria's head at that. "Yes you are, sweets. Anyway." He also rubs his hands together in glee. "Now we have a mission."

Overwhelmed by this unexpected chain of events, I manage to stammer out a thanks before nudging Lisa in the ribs. "Did you text Hunter yet?" Well, if she's going to put me on the spot, I can put her on the spot. Besides, her story is way less embarrassing than mine. "Hunter is Lisa's boyfriend. He also happens to be our best friend's older brother."

"Oh!" Gloria claps her hands. "I want to hear this story, too! But first tell me more about this Trevor. I'm super nosy, you'll have to accept that about me if we're going to be friends," Gloria adds with a grin. "Blame it on Thomas, he's a closed book and I always have to pry everything out of him. It rolls over onto everyone else I meet, and I'm not sorry." This has us all laughing and Uri squeezing her against his chest. Pangs of jealousy shoot through me. Will Trevor and I ever be that comfortable together? Technically, we've been dating for almost a month, but I haven't even held his hand yet.

"It's not important. Did you text Katy, yet?" I deflect, squirming under everyone's attention. I don't want to relive the story of how lame I was when Trevor and I met. That I'd thought I was babysitting so my former best friend could go on her first date with the boy I'd had a crush on for years. I'd shown up in ratty leggings and an oversized sweatshirt, prepared for a night of kid wrangling and sewing pointe shoes. Turns out I *was* babysitting. I was babysitting a seventeen-year-old with warm brown eyes and a great sense of humor while I watched Olivia and Tyler cozy up to each other during a movie. I may be over it now, in fact I think they're perfect together, but that doesn't make remembering that night hurt any less.

"So, obviously, Hannah doesn't want to talk about Trevor." Uri winks, taking pity on me. "It's okay, we'll get it out of her one of these days," he stage whispers in Gloria's ear, she's sitting on his lap on the couch across from us. "So, where are you guys from?"

"Camarillo, it's just north of Los Angeles," Lisa answers for us, looking up from her phone. Mine is buzzing in my pocket. I assume it's Katy texting us. "What about you guys? Uri, you said you were from Tel Aviv, right?" He nods in response, busy playing with Gloria's braid.

"Gloria and I live in Miami," Thomas offers. No wonder she has such a great tan. "Uri is on my shit list because Gloria insisted that we had to come back to Seattle for the summer since that's where he would be. I wanted to go somewhere with sunshine."

Gloria sticks her tongue out at him in response. "No one said you had to go to the same place as me," she points out.

"Yeah, but then how could we activate our Wonder Twin powers?" Thomas shoots right back.

"Don't let them get started," Noah interrupts. "They'll go at it all night." He eyes Thomas and Gloria as they fist-bump, grins on their faces. "Anyway, I'm from Nowheresville, Ohio. This is my third summer here. I almost went to CBC this year, but Thomas here convinced me I should come back to Seattle, since he was going to be here. I'm already regretting it," he adds, tossing a pillow at Thomas over my head. We all laugh at this, Lisa and I ducking down to avoid getting hit.

"I'm from Havana," Elena pipes up. It's the first time I've heard her speak. Her lilting Spanish accent is beautiful. It matches her delicate features. Her face reminds me a little of Katy, they have the same large eyes, although Katy's are darker, Elena's are more honey-colored. "It's my first time as well. My first time in America too. It's so cold here!" she adds, giving a dramatic shiver.

"You and I should be in Miami, Elena," Thomas nods. "It's too cold here, I agree."

"Ugh, quit yer bitchin'" Gloria huffs. "You'll get used to it, Elena. Besides, it's not like we're going to be outside all that much. Although..." Gloria eyes me. "If Hannah here knows a local...that could be used to our advantage."

I pull my phone out of my pocket so I can pretend not to be listening. I let the conversation move on without me as I catch up on the messages I've missed.

LISA: Hannah and I are in the same group. Level 7!

KATY: Yay!!!!! That's good you guys will be together

KATY: Have you met anyone yet? Are all the girls catty? I have so many questions!

ME: Eh. We met this girl Becky who seems like a real gossip queen, not sure if I want to be friends with her. She smells like drama. We met this other group at lunch who seem pretty nice.

I look up from my phone to catch Noah telling Lisa about his studio in Ohio. It sounds interesting, but I'm distracted by the other texts that I see waiting for me.

TREVOR: Hey gorgeous. Are we on for a movie tonight? It's your turn to pick.

TREVOR: Did you find out your placement yet? Any news on your weekend schedule?

Trevor and I had chatted while Lisa was in the shower, before we came downstairs for dinner. I haven't even had a chance to tell Lisa the exciting news he had for me, distracted by the rumbling in my stomach on our way to eat.

"No way!"

Looking up from my phone, Noah, Gloria, and Thomas all staring at Lisa and me. What did I miss?

"Leslie Parker is your teacher?" Gloria says, loud enough for several heads to turn our way. "Oh my god, what is she like? No wonder you two are so good."

Lisa elbows me hard, so I tuck my phone away. "She's an amazing teacher. I mean, sometimes I forget that she's *Leslie*

Parker. She's just always been Ms. Parker, ever since I was six."
I shrug. It always weirds me out when people get starstruck
over Ms. Parker. Most of the time, I forget that she was a huge
star a few decades ago. She got hit by a motorcycle crossing the
road in front of Lincoln Center when she was twenty-four and
came home to Camarillo to recover. Her doctors weren't even
sure she would ever walk again, going back to her career as a
principal dancer at The Classical Ballet Company was out of
the question. When her old ballet teacher wanted to retire, Ms.
Parker took over the studio and has been teaching ever since.
Olivia and I have vague memories of Madame Dubois, but she
was only around for a few years when we were little before Ms.
Parker took over. Ms. Parker used a cane when I first met her,
but she doesn't need it anymore.

"Is she super tough?" Noah asks.

"She has high expectations of us, but she's one of the nicest
teachers I've ever had," I tell him. I let Lisa take over the conversation while I put Trevor out of his misery.

> **ME:** First day was good. I'm so tired my yawns are
> yawning. Lisa and I got put into level 7. I'm super happy
> with that.
> **ME:** Finding out about the weekend now, will keep
> you updated.

Shifting my legs on the couch, I discover they've turned heavy
and stiff from sitting. No matter what position I try I can't get
comfortable, so I slide onto the floor and fold over into a butterfly
stretch. "Aren't you guys sore?" I ask. "I swear, my legs weigh a
hundred pounds each."

Elena joins me on the floor. "Si, my legs feel terrible."

"Drink lots of water," Gloria says. Plenty of other dancers are lounging on the floor and stretching. "Supposedly eating blueberries helps, but I'm pretty sure my mom told me that once because we had blueberries in the fridge that were about to go bad." We all laugh at this, Uri stretching his legs out and dumping Gloria on the floor next to Elena. These seem like easy people to be friends with, maybe this won't be so bad, especially if Elena and Noah are going to be in our class.

"I noticed we didn't have any classes scheduled for Saturday afternoon and Sunday," I start, hoping to get the answer to Trevor's question. "What are we supposed to do over the weekend?"

"Ahhhhh, this is where your Trevor may come in very handy for us." Gloria grins. "Technically, if you're under eighteen, you're supposed to stay in the dorms and relax." I can't help my disappointment at this news, I was hoping to get a chance to see Trevor. "If you're over eighteen, you can sign out of the dorms and do whatever you want. They don't like it, but they can't stop you either. And..." She pauses for dramatic effect. "If you have someone who's an 'adult' with you, they can sign you out to go off campus with them. Aren't you guys lucky that Uri, Thomas, and I all happened to turn eighteen a couple of months ago?"

"Do you think your Trevor would be willing to play tour guide?" Uri interrupts. "Even better if he has a car," he adds with a wink.

"Actually, starting in two weeks he's going to be staying on campus too. I just found out he's doing a training camp here for the next three weeks as well." My news is met with cheers and grins, even from Elena.

"Lucky girl," Thomas says, slapping me on the back. "What is he training for?"

"He runs track and cross country. He qualified for state this year but missed placing. Next year is his senior year and he's hoping he can qualify and podium at state so he can get a spot on a college team."

Gloria leans forward, almost falling off Uri's lap, glancing from side to side, then grinning as she whispers, "So, I'm proposing that Hannah's Trevor be our tour guide this weekend. We…" She waves a hand at herself and Uri. "…can sign you guys out, Trevor can show us around and Hannah gets to see her boyfriend. It's perfect!"

Lisa looks doubtful. "You're sure we won't get in trouble? I'm pretty sure I read that minors are supposed to stay on campus unless signed out by an adult…" Lisa barely managed to talk her parents into letting her come, getting in trouble is a sure fire way to make sure she's never allowed to leave the house again.

"We *are* legal adults." Gloria shrugs, then nods at the phone in my hand. "Text your boy, see what he thinks." I glance at Lisa to see what she thinks. The way she's biting her bottom lip tells me she's not sure if this is a great idea, but she isn't objecting so I type out a message to Trevor.

ME: Would you be willing to play tour guide for me and some friends? It looks like Sat we have class until lunchtime but then we're free. Sun we have the whole day off.

TREVOR: All I I want is to see you. If that means playing tour guide, I'll do it happily. As long as I get to spend time with you, I don't care what we do.

CHAPTER SIX

Katy

*T*HEY HAVE got to be kidding me.

"Three miles? You think I'm going to run three freaking miles? Is a bear chasing me? Is there macaroni and cheese at the end? The good kind, not the blue box kind. No wait..." I interrupt myself before either of my brothers can get a word in. "No amount of mac and cheese is worth running three miles. Why am I doing this?"

"Because sibling bonding, dear sweet sister." Hunter laughs at me. I should add, laughs while he runs in literal circles around me. Backwards.

I hope he trips and falls on his ass.

Crossing my arms over my chest, I shift my weight front to back on my feet, debating if it would be too mean to stick a foot out and trip him, or if I should go with the direct approach and punch him in the face.

Not only have my brothers dragged me out of bed at seven in the morning—hello summer vacation—to the park down the road from our house, but they didn't even have the decency to provide any kind of caffeine first.

"Hey Katy," a decidedly feminine voice calls from behind me. "You ready?"

JJ is crossing the grassy field toward us, the early morning sun almost as bright as her smile. Am I allowed to hate her for looking this pretty so early, and without any makeup on? Surely that's in the Girl Code Handbook somewhere. Her curly blonde hair is pulled back in another French braid, this time with a wide fabric headband added to it, I assume to keep any stray hairs off her face. Like me, she's dressed in spandex shorts, a sports bra and a tank top, but her running shoes look far more used than mine.

"Are you running too?" JJ's grin has me groaning at my stupidity. "I'm sorry, I'm real dumb before nine in the morning. Ignore me." Just as I finish removing my foot from my mouth, Jack comes loping up to join us, stuffing the keys to his truck in a pocket of his athletic shorts.

Instead of saying hello like a normal person, Jack bends down and scoops me up over his shoulder, spinning me in circles with my butt in the air. "Hey JJ, glad you could make it. You awake now, Bug?" I'm going to kill them both. I'm going to kill them dead, then beat them to death again for good measure. God, they are so embarrassing.

"Put me down, idiot!" My voice rings out over the empty field. This early we're the only ones here. My fists rain down on Jack's back for a few moments longer before he puts me down. I waver on my feet, determined not to land flat on my back in front of JJ. So much for them not treating me like a baby anymore. Of course, Jack hasn't done that particular move to me for years, although when I was little, he and Cole used to take turns scooping me up and tossing me around. They claimed it was practice for football, but I think that was their way of roughhousing with me without getting in trouble with Mom.

I used to love it, especially when Hunter would join in or we'd do it in the pool. All my memories of summer vacation revolve around being in the pool or at the beach with my brothers, being tossed in the air, carried on their shoulders or saved from the giant waves of the Pacific. They may drive me crazy, but I've never doubted for a second that they would keep me safe. And ever since I can remember, I've done my best to return the favor, even if all I could do was keep their hearts safe from the girls who weren't worthy of them.

I still haven't figured out JJ's angle, but you can bet I'm keeping a close eye on her. No one messes with my brothers, *or* my besties. Except me.

"So, what's the plan, JJ?" Standing with his feet planted wide, Jack stretches his arms over his head, like a sad imitation of an eighties Jazzercise video. "Are we just running? And do you and Hunter get a handicap or something, so Katy and I can keep up?"

"That's where I recognized you from!" I blurt out. Now that Jack said something, I remember seeing her at the track meets. Her long legs must be a huge advantage in her races.

"Uh…yeah," JJ drawls, now I feel like even more of an idiot. "So, I figured we could start with an easy three miles and then do some practice over there." JJ points to the jungle gym off to the side of the park.

Hunter grins and rubs his hands together, eyeing the field. "Sounds good to me."

"Sound good to you, Katy?" JJ asks me. Is that a glint of fear I see in her eye? It better be.

"First of all. Three miles and easy do not belong in the same sentence. And second of all, you do realize that if we run in a circle…" I point my toe at the dirt track ringing the field. "You and Hunter, okay and Jack too, are going to keep lapping me. And I will eventually be unable to suppress my need to either clothesline or trip you." I eye JJ up and down, she looks like she can take it, she's taller than me after all. "And don't think you're immune just because you aren't related to me."

Holding her hands up in front of her, JJ grins. "Wouldn't dream of it."

"You're obviously not afraid enough if you thought that dragging me here at seven in the morning—in the middle of summer vacation—was a good idea." I grunt and cross my arms over my chest, daring her to argue.

JJ points to the sidewalk leading away from the park. "We're going to run a loop on that trail over there. I tested it yesterday. We start at that tree." She points to a large tree at the edge of the field. "To the main road and back is a perfect 5k loop."

"I thought you said *three* miles. Five and three are not the same."

Laughing, JJ squats down to re-tie her shoe. "Five *kilometers*. It equals three-point-one miles."

"Whatever." It's not my best comeback, but it's still early.

The three of them ignore my crankiness and get ready to take off. JJ fiddles with her watch and I shake out my legs in a half-hearted attempt to prepare. I still have my doubts. My body is made to dance, not run, but there's no way I'm going to let my brothers make me look like an idiot in front of her, so I keep my groans inside as we take off.

As I expected, Hunter takes off ahead of us, his legs pumping beneath him in an easy cadence. Jack sticks next to me for a while, but it doesn't take long for my slower pace to have him doubling back to keep next to me. I wave him off with an irritated growl. God, the only thing worse than struggling to run is to have my brother running extra and *still* having more energy than me.

I last about three quarters of a mile before I have to drop down to walk. Surprising me, JJ drops to a walk next to me. She's been keeping pace with me the whole time, but wisely didn't say anything, letting me stew in silence.

"You okay?" she asks, as I suck air into my lungs.

"You do this for fun? What is wrong with you?" I manage to get out around my heaving breaths.

JJ laughs, the fact that she can laugh annoys me further. "I dunno, I've always loved to run. You can't cheat at running, you either put in the work to be better, or you don't."

Huh. I can get behind that sentiment. "Dance is kind of like that too." Our feet hitting the sidewalk is the only noise in the cool morning air. I suppose I should be grateful my brothers dragged me out of bed early enough that it's not too hot. "Yeah, there are people who are naturally talented, like my friends Hannah and Lisa. But if you put in the work it shows, and if you don't, well, it shows too."

We walk along in silence for another moment, before I speak up again. "Can I ask you something?"

"Yeah?"

"You think my brothers are obnoxious too, right?" At JJ's confused look, I laugh and take off running again, knowing she'll catch up. I need to figure out a way to see if she's hanging out with us because Jack asked for her help with training for this terrain race, because she wants to be friends with us, or if she's just another member of the Quinn Brothers Fan Club. I can't help wishing it's because of me. At least a little.

"*T*HAT ONE looks like a crocodile," Hunter says, pointing to one of the fluffy clouds overhead. Grass clippings are already sticking to my sweaty back, tickling and itching my skin, but I'm too tired to care. Three miles running, then JJ had us climbing over and under all the different parts of the playground equipment. I'm glad there weren't any kids coming to the park to play yet, since I'm sure their parents would not have appreciated us climbing over the sides of the walls and running suicide sprints back and forth over the little chain bridge. *I* didn't appreciate it.

Although, crawling across the top of the monkey bars was pretty fun, a little scary the first time, before going back the other way hanging from my arms the normal way. My hands already have blisters. "Did you talk to her last night?" I ask. Jack is walking JJ back to her car, but I'm too tired to take another step so here I am, flopped on my back, staring at the sky, while my irritating brothers are perfectly fine.

"For a bit, yeah. Do you remember the girl who won first place at YIGP, Gloria?"

Laughing inside at my brother's casual mention of the ballet competition we watched together, I nod.

"I guess her and her boyfriend are there and have adopted Lisa and Hannah into their little group. Lisa said her twin brother is there, plus their roommates." There's an odd tone to Hunter's voice, I twist my head to the side so I can look at his face.

"Are you worried?"

He turns to look at me. "Worried? About Lisa making new friends?"

"About Lisa making new friends with guys," I clarify.

"Oh. No. I trust her." A handful of grass clippings flies at my shoulder. "We talked about it before she left. I know they're going to be dancing together, and like, touching each other, and stuff. But I get that it's part of dancing. It's not like they'll be rehearsing in private, it's all in a class with other people, right?"

I shrug, I don't know for sure. "As far as I know, yeah." Not wanting to sound like I doubt my friends, because I don't, I add, "This is Lisa, the most loyal person I've ever known. I trust her too. I just wanted to make sure you were okay."

"I'm good. I miss her, that's all. We hardly had a chance to be together before they left."

"But at least she's coming back in a few weeks. I feel worse for Hannah and Trevor. They're going to get to see each other for the next six weeks and then who knows when they'll be in the same place at the same time again?"

Hunter's thoughtful for a moment. "I hope these new friends are good people, you know? Do we trust them with our girls?"

"Come on you lazy bums, let's get breakfast, I'm starving!" Jack's voice calls from near my feet, accompanied by a foot tapping my leg before I have a chance to answer.

Groaning, I roll to sit up but that's as far as I'm going. "Help, please," I moan, my muscles aching and protesting the movement. Each grabbing one of my hands, my brothers pull me to my feet. "Why is the car so far away?" It's at least fifty yards to Hunter's truck. Fifty yards I don't think I can walk at this point. So much for being in great shape.

"Come on, Bug." Jack laughs, bending down and pulling me onto his back. "You get a piggyback this once. We gotta toughen you up."

"But I'm a delicate flower. Your sweet and precious baby sister." I pout. "Maybe I don't want to be tough."

Setting me down next to the passenger side door, Jack pulls it open for me so I can crawl in. Squished between them, their broad shoulders don't leave a lot of room for me, but I don't mind, not even now when we all smell ripe. Okay, I mind that a little. But being squished between them? That's my safe place, my home. Challenges don't scare me, trying new things doesn't scare me, because I've always had this. When you throw Cole into the mix, us Quinns are an unstoppable team. For all that I complain about my brothers, I love them fiercely.

"Let's get some grub," Jack commands, as Hunter pulls out of the parking lot. "Man, that JJ is something else. That wasn't even a hard workout for her, she said she was going to go home and run another three miles. That is a badass chick." The admiration in his tone is obvious, and I have to admit I understand it. JJ did the entire workout with us, everything she told us to do she did herself, and did it better. I may not have her figured out yet, but I am officially signing up to be a member of the Jordan James Appreciation Club.

"Well, since she stayed with me and my slow ass, instead of taking off like you two..." I poke them each in the side for good measure. "I'm sure that three mile run-slash-walk wasn't a challenge for her."

"She's hot."

"You're not allowed to date her." The words pop out of my mouth before I know I've even thought them. Why did Jack's declaration rub me the wrong way like that? I'm like a cat with its fur raised, prickly and irritable in a flash, because Jack said she was hot.

"Didn't you learn your lesson from last time?" Jack pokes me in the ribs. "I thought you said you weren't going to interfere with who we date?"

"I never said that. When did you hear me say that?"

"I thought it was implied when you guys came up with your grand plot to get Lisa and I back together," Hunter chimes in.

"First of all, you and Lisa are perfect for each other, so don't pretend you aren't grateful. Second of all, I haven't finished vetting JJ. You've dated so many stupid, annoying girls and they *suck* to hang out with. I've decided that I need to approve of all your girlfriends from now on, Jack." Crossing my arms over my chest, to protect my sides in case they decided to start poking me again, I nod my head. "If they can't hang out with us," I indicate the three of us, "*and* my friends, then they're no good."

"JJ hung out with us the other day and she was cool," Jack points out. He has a point, but I still can't shake my gut feeling that Jack and JJ would be a terrible couple.

"She's still on probation." The possessiveness that takes hold of me must be because I don't want to share my brothers with some groupie. Yeah. That must be it.

I'm not jealous that JJ has more in common with my brothers, or that she probably wants to hang out with them more than me. It's definitely not that. I swear.

CHAPTER SEVEN

Hannah

*T*HE STARES of everyone else in my class dig into my back like daggers as I demonstrate the exercise. I do my best to ignore them as my feet quiver underneath me, the million tiny steps of my bourres taking me across the room as my arms sweep overhead and then down. They cross in front of my chest, as if holding a bouquet of flowers, before I step out into an enormous arabesque.

I balance on one leg for three beats, the other extended behind me, both arms reaching forward, as if towards an invisible partner. Gently, I bring my leg down to join the other, holding as still as I can while standing on pointe. Listening to the music, on the high note I picked out the first time we tried it as a class, I lift my eyes and release my front foot before doing a controlled fall onto it and sweeping my arms from side to side. A few counts later, I finish with a series of small jumps, my feet crossing and fluttering underneath me each time.

This exercise reminded me of Giselle Act Two from the moment our teacher set it. When he added the iconic crossed hands of the Wilis and mimicked the same slow and quick pattern of the traditional choreography, it was obvious. I've been picturing myself in the long white tutu and flower crown that's the signature look of the ballet, letting the heartbreak and yearning of Giselle guide my movement.

I know it's just class, but I always dance best when I picture what I'm doing as if I'm on stage.

This is the fourth time today I've been singled out to do something on my own, to demonstrate it for the class. Normally, I'd be over the moon and honored to be noticed by the teachers like this. And I am. At least, I was the first two times it happened yesterday. And the day before.

While I'm not the only person who's asked to demonstrate, Elena has too, and so have a couple different guys, word of how Marco Bethelo knows me painted a target on my back. And when you're in class where one whole wall is made of floor-to-ceiling mirrors, there's no getting away from the glares and whispers.

"Thank you, Hannah," Mr. Popov says as I finish. His thick accent is a little hard to understand sometimes, but he's not the scary Russian teacher I was expecting when I saw his name listed as one of our teachers. For starters, he's Ukrainian, not Russian. "Ladies, did you see? Hannah moves her feet fast, so very fast. Like sprinting. Some of you do more like walking, yes? Now. We try again."

I roll my ankle to release the ache building up, glad our class is supposed to finish in five minutes before taking a place in the second row of girls, frozen while we wait for the pianist to start. Since this is a pointe class, the guys are in a separate men's class right now, working on the explosive jumps and turns that are the signature of men's dancing.

As we try again, the click of the door behind us distracts me for a moment and I risk a quick glance in the mirror. Marco Bethelo is leaning against the doorjamb, watching our class. It's not the first time he's done this, he pops in to watch our classes at least once or twice a day, but he hasn't taught any of them yet.

We hold the ending position for a moment as the music fades away, waiting for the signal from Mr. Popov that we may relax. With a nod, he smiles at us before turning to Marco. "I believe you have an announcement to make?" I wonder what this is all about. Confusion and eagerness are etched on all the other girl's faces.

"It's nothing too exciting, don't worry," Marco assures us as he walks through the class to the front of the room. "I have two things to announce. First, because of the numbers, we are going to have the Level Eight guys join your pas de deux class, that way each of you girls will have your own partner and the guys don't have to double up."

An excited murmur runs though the class. We had our first pas de deux class yesterday, but there are twice as many girls in our class as guys, so two of us were assigned to dance with each guy. Since it was the first day and we weren't doing much more than getting used to working with a partner, it was fine. But it meant that each of us girls only got half a class worth of practice. Having twice the number of guys is going to be a real treat.

Marco holds his hands up for silence and we quiet down. "Secondly, after this weekend there will be another camp sharing the same housing with us. They are also athletes who share your passion and dedication, albeit to a different art. They will be housed on different floors to you, but they will be sharing the dining hall and the common areas with us. We expect you to be welcoming and courteous when in the common spaces, but they will not be allowed on your floors or in your dorm rooms. And as always, the rule stands that guys and girls may not enter each other's dorm rooms under any circumstances."

My eyes find Lisa's in the mirror as excitement runs through me. Could he be talking about Trevor's camp? I knew that they would be on campus, but I never dreamed that his camp would be housed in the same dorm building as mine. Is Trevor even going to be staying in the dorms? He lives here, maybe he's going to commute in every day? I need to text him.

"Understood? Thank you, ladies. Reverence and then you may go," Mr. Popov says turning to us. We get into position and wait for the pianist to play a chord before stepping away from the piano, then back, opening our arms towards the pianist, a silent, age-old motion to thank her for the music. We repeat the movement the other way gesturing towards Mr. Popov and Marco, since he's still standing there, holding the end pose. At his nod, we relax and clap briefly before gathering up our bags and shoes so we can go to lunch.

"Do you think that's Trevor's camp he was talking about?" Lisa asks as we pull on our leggings. I'm so sweaty from class I debate whether to put on the tank top I was wearing this morning, but knowing we have to walk outside to get to the dining room, I slip it on.

"I don't know. I'm going to text him in a minute."

"How perfect would it be if it is?" Lisa stops to sip from her water bottle, waiting for me to finish zipping my pointe shoes into the bottom compartment of my dance bag. The ventilated bottom is perfect for letting them air out between classes. I have a second pair in my room that I've been swapping out with each day, trying to let my shoes dry out so they last longer.

> **ME:** So… we just got told that another camp is sharing the dorm building with us starting next week. Do you think it's your camp? Are you even staying in the dorms or are you staying at home?

I follow Lisa down the walkway that leads from the arts building to the building that contains our dining hall and dorm rooms.

> **TREVOR:** I am staying in the dorms. We start at 6am every day and there's no way I'm getting up early enough to drive the 30 minutes it takes me to get there. I don't know what dorm building it is, I guess I'll find out on Sunday when we move in.
> **TREVOR:** But how awesome would it be if we were? Can I tell you how excited I am for tomorrow? I might even be more excited than when I was ten and we got to go to Disneyland on Christmas Day with Tyler's fam.
> **TREVOR:** We've been in the same city for almost a week and I haven't been able to see you yet. I'm dying a slow death here TT.

Picturing ten-year-old Trevor and Tyler running around Disneyland together has me smiling as we walk into the dining hall.

ME: Same. This is the closest we've been since January and it feels like you're as far away as ever.

Chatting about the class while grabbing sandwiches and some sliced fruit, Lisa and I make our way into the downstairs lobby, eyeing a pair of overstuffed chairs with a coffee table set between them. The tables in the dining hall have a definite 'you can't sit here' vibe as we walk past. I'm happy to sit away from everyone else and give the dagger wounds in my back a chance to heal.

"Are you sore? I'm dying today," Lisa says, dropping her dance bag on the floor. "You would think that after four days I would be *less* sore, but no. My calves are killing me."

I drop into the cushy chair, groaning. "Ugh, yes. My calves are so tight. And my back? I don't know why. Maybe it was from that contemporary class yesterday. "

"Can I join you?" I look up to see Elena standing awkwardly in front of us. I guess the Eights haven't finished yet because I don't see Gloria anywhere. Elena was getting her share of icy stares in class as well.

"Of course," I say, looking around for an extra chair. She plops down on the floor by my chair when Uri, Thomas and Noah join us, flopping on the carpet around us. I guess no one else wants a chair.

"Did Marco come tell you guys about the pas de deux classes?" Noah asks, taking a bite of his salad.

"Yes," Elena answers for us. "I am glad to have one girl for each guy. It's hard to keep switching."

"Well, since we've never done any proper pas de deux, Hannah and I are happy to get to do anything," Lisa says, swallowing her bite of food.

"It's way easier for us to have one girl to figure out in each class," Thomas adds. "Hey," he turns to Lisa. "Rumor has it, you guys had private coaching from Marco Bethelo?"

"What?" I almost drop my sandwich at Thomas' words.

"Where did you hear that?" Lisa asks. "And that's one hundred percent not true. We met him at YIGP, when he awarded the Grand Prix award. We've had exactly one conversation with him here when he asked us about our teacher, that's it."

"Oh, I remember that," Uri pipes up. "That one chick, Becca or something, said something."

"I bet that the rumors could all be traced back to Becky," Lisa mumbles around her bite of sandwich.

"I heard that some of the girls in Six are pissed that they aren't in Seven," Thomas adds. "One of the guys in our class goes to the same studio as some of them. He was bitching about it this morning."

"Great, I might as well paint a bullseye on my back, make it easier for everyone to find me," I mutter, more to myself than anyone else.

"It'll be okay, Hannah. We got you," Uri surprises me by saying. "Gloria and I can sympathize," he adds. I guess they do, walking into the intensive with big wins at YIGP. They placed first and second, and even though I didn't place, I still made it to the finals. That puts us in the position of being the dancers to beat, the ones on top of the pedestal ready to be toppled off.

"What do we have, babe?" Gloria appears, sandwich and soda in hand.

"Hannah's back from the whiny girls in Six," he explains, pulling her down to sit between his legs.

Gloria groans. "Oh god. It's always the Sixes that cause the drama, especially if they're older. They're good enough to know they're decent, but also old enough to realize that they may not be as good as they think they are." She reaches out to pat me on the knee. "It happened to me last year. Once you're an Eight the drama tends to die down, everyone in there is working too hard to care about anyone but themselves."

As if to prove Gloria's point, at that moment Becky and a group of girls walk past us on their way to elevators, throwing dirty looks to our whole group on their way, one of them muttering something about "holding court" as she passes me. I sink down into the chair, wishing I had taken my lunch up to my room and eaten it there. When I imagined my summer, I didn't picture this.

CHAPTER EIGHT

Katy

*S*HOULD I tell him about the drool? Or let him discover it when he wakes up? Equal parts fascinated and disgusted, I'm mesmerized by the string of drool running from Cole's bottom lip to the sweatshirt he has balled up against the car door. It sways with the movement of the car, threatening to break with each bump on the road.

A finger snakes its way over the back of the seat, aiming for Cole's ear. "Don't!" I whisper-hiss, smacking it away before Jack can stick his finger in Cole's ear. "Let him sleep."

"You're no fun." Jack pouts, crossing his arms over the back of our bench seat, resting his chin on his arms as he eyes me. The empty landscape of southern Nevada flashes past us, we left Las Vegas an hour ago after stopping there for a second, late breakfast. "You know, JJ was surprised at how fast you've been catching up in the training sessions."

"Why is she so surprised that I'm awesome?" I snark back, grinning. No way am I going to admit that I've surprised myself with how much I've enjoyed the training sessions, once I got over having to get up at the crack of dawn four mornings a week. Running is a lot like getting through a long petit allegro exercise, there's the same satisfying exhaustion at the end of it. Since JJ helped me figure out how to keep to a steady pace, I've been able to run almost a full mile before needing to take a quick walking break. And the other training, the obstacle course stuff, makes me feel like a badass, especially when I can do something faster than my brothers. Being smaller has its advantages in some things. But there's no way I'm going to give Jack the satisfaction of knowing I'm having fun doing it.

"Come on, Bug. You know you like it." Jack elbows me from his perch. "JJ told me you snuck in some extra reps over the monkey bars when Hunter and I went to get donuts yesterday." My gut twists at the mention of JJ. It's obvious from how often Jack talks about her that they're in touch more than I thought. He mentions her name every other sentence. It has to mean something, right? But when we do our training sessions, she stays by my side, giving me a little extra encouragement. I can't tell if it's because she thinks I'm the weakest link on our team, because she doesn't want me to feel like everyone is ganging up on me, or because she wants to impress Jack.

But maybe they're hanging out together without me? Jack is always in and out the house, the boy just can't sit home and relax. He talks about her a lot, but he talks a lot in general and I've never seen him truly interested in a girl so it's hard to tell. With Hannah and Lisa gone, I've been spending most of my free time with Hunter. Weirdly, Cole has been hanging out with us a lot too. I thought he would be spending his summer hanging out with his college friends or maybe working, he is going into his junior year after all, but he's either been in his room, swimming laps in our pool, or playing Mario Kart with me and Hunter. I know something's wrong but I haven't gotten to the bottom of it yet.

So far, this summer has racked up a never-ending list of questions in my mind and very few answers. I hate it.

"Why are you so surprised that I'm more badass than you? Hunter knows how tough us dancers are." I crane my arm over the bench seat to poke Hunter in the knee, distracting him from scrolling through his phone.

"What?"

"Jack didn't think I would be awesome at the terrain race training because he doesn't have the same respect for ballerinas that you do."

Hunter shakes his head at us. "Never doubt the ballerinas, dude. They're tough. And devious."

Jack laughs at that. "*Katy* is devious. Olivia too. Your girlfriend doesn't have a devious bone in her body. It's just that she's smarter than anyone except you, so none of us see her coming."

That earns Jack a smack upside the head from me, very convenient of him to leave his head right there where I can reach it. "I am *not* devious."

"Says the girl who planned our 'accidental' run in with you girls before your dress rehearsal?"

"That wasn't devious, that was good directing." I huff.

"God, you guys are noisy." Cole's gravelly voice interrupts us. "I'm trying to nap."

"We noticed. You got a little something…" I point to the puddle of drool decorating Cole's cheek and get a menacing glare in return.

"Go back to sleep, Grumpypants." Jack pushes Cole's head against the window. "You need a nap." Cole growls and swipes at Jack's head. He dodges by leaning back into his seat, before turning to face me, leaning an elbow in the space between our oldest brother and me.

"Hey Bug? Why'd you let Allyson and her girls hang around? I kept waiting for you to find a way to drive them off."

Not sure where this random question is going, I hesitate to answer. "Well, they were Olivia's friends. And since Olivia was the only one worth talking to, I didn't want to piss her off by driving off her friends. Besides, you managed to get rid of them just fine without me." I settle back into my seat, arms crossed over my chest.

"After what they said about Lisa, there was no way I would let them anywhere near our house again." Hunter growls, thinking back to that day. "But weren't they competition?"

"Competition for what?" Now I'm confused.

"For the other guys, Bug. " Jack blurts out. "Drew and the other guys," he elaborates when I still don't get it.

Competition for the other guys... The second it clicks, a deep blush heats my cheeks. I did have my fair share of crushes on Cole's friends when I was a lot younger but... "Um, no. I have seen and heard way too many of them farting, burping and being disgusting to ever be attracted to any of them." I shudder, trying to keep the revolting memories tucked away in the back of my brain where they belong.

"Besides," I add. "Why would I be dumb enough to have a crush on any of them when I hear the way they talk about those same nasty bitches? They can have each other."

"But back to JJ." Jack pokes my arm. I swear I'm going to end up with mental whiplash from the way this conversation is skipping around. Jack and Hunter must be having an entire mental conversation that I'm not aware of because they seem to be on the same page and I'm barely keeping up. Stupid twin ESP.

"*Back* to JJ? Were we *on* JJ?" Somehow, I manage to restrain myself from rubbing my temples.

"Is she cool with you?"

I pretend to think, just to get under Jack's skin. I get the feeling that he may like JJ, given how insistent he is and how much he talks about her. And for some reason, it doesn't sit right with me. "I'm not sure yet. I can't tell if she hangs out with me during training because she's smart enough to know that I'm the one that needs buttering up, or if she has a keen sense of smell and self-preservation. I don't know her that well yet, but so far she seems cool."

I'm sure Jack is blinded by the brightness of her smile and the way her face lights up anytime we talk about food or music. Or running. Or pulling pranks on her younger brothers. We've had a lot of time to chat while I huff and puff beside her on our runs. Huh. Maybe I do know her better than I thought.

"Here." My phone buzzes with an incoming message, Jack's contact name lighting up my screen. "I sent you her number."

THING 2: JJ's number. You should try to get to know her better, I want to know if she meets your standards.

Why does the thought of getting to know JJ better for my brother's sake fill me with dread?

ME: In case I ever need to blackmail my brothers. Guard it with your life.

I ATTACH THE photo I took of Jack and Hunter before sending it to Lisa and Hannah. Hunter's face is squished against the window, his mouth hanging open. But the real reason I took it is because Jack has somehow wedged himself behind Hunter's shoulder, his head resting in the crook of Hunter's neck. The wet spot on the shoulder of Hunter's shirt is the crowning glory of this masterpiece of blackmail.

Not sure if I'll hear back from my friends right away, it's late Saturday afternoon and I don't have their intensive schedule memorized, I put my phone down to look out the window. I'm pretty sure they're off exploring Seattle with Trevor and their new friends, but since I don't want to think about them making friends that aren't me, I push it from my mind. Instead, I stare at the landscape passing by my window. We've been in the car for hours upon hours, the desert transforming into mountains, and now back into plains.

I'm so bored.

Turning my phone over in my hand, I weigh my options. I could play a game, but that's going to chew up my battery and it's my dad's turn to charge his phone. Same with a video. Music it is. Popping my earbuds in, I flip to my favorite playlist and go back to gazing out the window, but after skipping two songs in a row I know that just listening isn't going to cut it.

I wonder what JJ's up to.

Face to Face

Before I can second guess myself, I send her the same text and picture I sent to my friends. I guess seeing her reaction to this is as good a way as any to get to the bottom of her motives.

> **JJ:** That's adorable. Saving it in my super-secret "for blackmail purposes" folder on my phone.

My quiet chuckle has Cole looking at me funny. I flash him the conversation and grin when he mouths "send it to me please."

> **ME:** I knew I liked you for a reason. I'm bored out of my flipping mind. Ten hour drives suck.
> **JJ:** Wanna play I spy?
> **ME:** That seems a little difficult, since I'm in the middle of Nowhere, Utah and you're in CA...

While I wait for JJ to respond, I flip back to see that Lisa is typing something in our group chat.

> **LISA:** I realize that I'm biased, but that is utterly adorable. Just for that, here's this.

A picture pops up beneath her text and it takes everything in me not to squeal with delight. It's a photo taken from behind of Hannah and who I must assume is Trevor, walking down the sidewalk holding hands. It's so sweet, I want to kick my heels up and celebrate. They're looking sideways at each other, oblivious to everything around them, the shy smiles on both their faces so genuinely happy that if I didn't love Hannah so much and know everything they've gone through to get this moment together, I'd be sick with envy.

Instead, I send Lisa a barrage of heart eye gifs and every heart emoji I can find.

> **JJ:** How about 20 questions then? I'll go first. Animal, vegetable, or mineral?

She's a quick thinker, I appreciate that. I think for a moment, then fire back a response.

> **ME:** Vegetable

A text from Lisa pops up while I wait for JJ's response.

> **LISA:** They are so cute together. I'm not sure who was more nervous, Hannah or Trevor. But I managed to distract everyone else so they could have a minute alone and they've been like this ever since. Don't know what he said, but it worked. And it turns out, he's pretty fun. Kinda dorky, but fun. He and Hunter would get along.

In our separate text thread, I dig a little more into their first week of classes.

> **ME:** So how was the first week? Anything I need to know? People I need to murder?
> **LISA:** They're definitely singling Hannah out in our class and there's a pack of Sixes out to get her. I swear, I caught one of them eavesdropping on our conversation at dinner the

other night. But Gloria and Uri caught onto it and started making up some outrageous stories from YIGP (at least, I don't THINK they're true. I hope they're not true) and she got all offended and backed off.

ME: Hahahaha! Are they bothering you at all? Have you been deemed guilty by association?

LISA: Not too much. I've been hanging out with Elena too. She's cool. She seems as overwhelmed by everything as I am.

ME: Good overwhelmed or bad overwhelmed?

LISA: Definitely good overwhelmed.

The last two hours of the drive pass quickly, between Lisa's updates on Hannah and Trevor and playing multiple rounds of twenty questions with JJ. Jack and Hunter wake up with groans and a few choice words about an hour before we arrive and, of course, Jack has to butt in on my game with JJ.

As we pull into the parking lot of a motel in Green River, Utah, my phone buzzes again.

HANNAH: while I agree with all the above sentiments, you guys know I can read this whole conversation, right?

HANNAH: But thank you for that picture, it's very cute.

CHAPTER NINE

Hannah

"I FORGOT HOW tall you are," was the first stupid thing to come out of my mouth as Trevor approached our little group in the downstairs lobby of our dorm building earlier this afternoon.

He'd laughed and stuffed his hands in the front pockets of his jeans. "I forgot how short you are," he'd said, rocking back on his heels. "It's good to see you," he'd added, his eyes roaming over my face. We'd stood there for a moment, staring at each other—the butterflies in my belly tripling in number, not knowing where to look or what to do with my hands. The dress I'd changed into after showering the sweat of morning classes off didn't have any pockets so I twisted my hands around the handle of my purse instead.

Lisa had let the silence drag on for a moment before clearing her throat, reminding me that everyone else was there. "This is Lisa," I pulled her up next to me, holding her arm like a security blanket. Trevor had smiled at her and everyone else while I made introductions, then suggested we head to the nearby train station since his car wasn't big enough for all seven of us.

Gloria and Uri led the way, laughing and goofing off with Thomas and Noah, while Lisa and Elena joined in from time to time, leaving Trevor and I to bring up the rear of the group. I didn't know if it was on purpose or not, but I had been glad for a moment to regroup. Walking so close to him, and yet, on display in front of my friends had sent my nerves into overdrive.

Finally, Trevor had broken the silence between us by reaching around my shoulder and pulling me against his chest for a hug. The second his arms wrapped around me, my brain stopped whirling. A few seconds after that, I'd relaxed against him, my arms snaking around his waist, the weight of my head resting against his chest. Trevor's heartbeat in my ear, even though it was racing like mine, grounded me. "Hi," he'd whispered above my head, giving me an extra squeeze. "I can't believe you're here."

I'd pulled back far enough to look up into his face, giving him a shy smile. "Me too. Are you as nervous as I am? 'Cause I am more nervous right now than I was backstage at the finals."

"God, yes. I'm trying so hard to be cool right now." The giggle that escaped me at his pained expression was cut off by Uri, his shout sweeping down the sidewalk toward us, shattering the remaining awkwardness between us.

"Come on lovebirds, the train's almost here!" With a laugh, Trevor had taken my hand and pulled me down the sidewalk to catch up to everyone else.

Now that we're all walking around the streets of Seattle, laughing and chatting, Trevor's hand holding mine is the most natural thing in the world. The sun is out and warm enough that Gloria and Elena haven't complained about it being cold once, while the breeze off the sound is keeping it from being too hot. We've explored Pike Place Market, wandering through all the little shops, stopping to watch the fishmongers put on their show of tossing enormous fish.

Thomas and Uri put on a competing show by tossing Gloria between them, she's so tiny she weighs less than the biggest fish those guys are tossing, earning the applause of some scattered tourists and the fishmongers themselves.

"I can't wait for pas de deux to start next week." Gloria waggled her eyebrows at Uri as we wandered down the street. This time, Trevor and I are in the lead, since he's the one who knows where we're going, his hand warm in mine.

"Hannah and I have never done pas de deux," Lisa says, "well, not *real* pas de deux. We've tried to partner each other in class, but it's not the same." We don't have any guys at Ms. Parker's at all, well, unless you count the under ten crowd, then there's a few.

Uri and Noah both turn to face us. "Seriously? Here," Noah holds out his hand to Lisa who takes it gingerly. "Pique into an attitude, I got you." Lisa does, stepping onto her right foot, left lifted and bent behind her. "Ok, now brace your arm and I'll promenade you." Noah pulls Lisa around in a circle while the rest of us laugh. It's a bit of a disaster since Lisa's shoes keep sticking to the sidewalk, and she has to swing her leg up high to the side to avoid kicking over a display of knickknacks outside the store we were passing.

"I'm sure it works better on Marley," Lisa says, laughing as she falls over.

"Pas is much easier in pointe shoes, less sticky," Elena says.

"What do you think?" Trevor says in my ear. "Are you excited to try it next week?" Is he asking because he's curious or because he's jealous of the guys who'll be touching me in class? I study his face for a moment before I answer, trying to find a hint of what he's thinking in his eyes.

"I'm excited to learn new things, yeah." Feeling brave, I ask, "You're not worried, are you?"

Trevor looks over at the other guys. "Should I be?"

"No?" Wait, that's not a question on my part. "I mean, no. Definitely not. I just…"

"Hannah?" Trevor squeezes my hand.

"Yeah?" His face is sincere and a tiny part of me relaxes.

"I've done my research, I know what pas de deux is. I thought we established I'm not a Neanderthal. Dancing with the guys in your class is important to you, right? Important to your training?"

"Yeah."

"Then it's important to me. Besides…" He raises his voice enough for the rest of the group to hear him. "These guys will keep an eye out for me, right?"

The guys chime in with assurances that they'll keep an eye out for both me and Lisa, putting my mind at ease. It's not that I don't trust Lisa or myself, but we can only defend ourselves so much, if we have the other guys running interference for us it will make me feel better.

We have a blast wandering around Seattle, exploring and being led around by Trevor. There's a cool underground tour that we all decide to go on next weekend since we miss the last tour of the day by the time we get there. Trevor always finds some excuse to touch me, whether it's holding my hand as we walk, or a hand resting on the small of my back. My favorite is when he runs his fingers down the back of my arm before twining our fingers together. It tickles and sends goosebumps down my spine, but not in a bad way. It's like the scared feeling you get in the pit of your stomach right before you get on a roller coaster. Terrifying but also promising an exhilarating rush. I could easily become addicted to this feeling.

"We should get back, curfew is in an hour," Gloria reminds us as the sun starts dipping in the sky. "We don't want to miss dinner." She pokes Uri in the stomach. "Gotta keep this one fed or else he gets hangry." The feeding Uri jokes last the entire train ride back to campus, not stopping until we get to the dorm entrance.

"Thanks for showing us around man." Thomas reaches out to shake Trevor's hand. "Hopefully we'll see you soon." With a nod, he heads inside, Noah and Elena following after saying their goodbyes as well.

"We'll grab you some dinner, see you in a bit," Gloria adds as she pulls Uri through the doors, waving and winking.

"You okay?" Lisa checks with me before leaving. "I'll save you a seat. It was good to finally meet you Trevor." With that Lisa takes off inside, leaving Trevor and I alone for the first time all afternoon. The setting sun casts a golden glow around us, even if the front entrance of the glass and steel dorm building isn't the most romantic setting I could have imagined.

Nervous, I grasp my purse handle with both hands, rocking on my heels. "So you, uh, move into your dorms tomorrow, right?"

Rubbing a hand on the back of his neck, Trevor looks almost as nervous as me. Everything had been easy once we got used to having everyone else around, now that we're alone, an awkward silence descends between us. "Yeah. I still don't know which building, but I'll text you when I find out. I think for sure we're sharing the dining hall here with you guys, I looked and it's the only one that's open right now. So we'll at least get to eat together, if our schedules match."

"That'll be good." I wrack my brain for something else to say but come up empty. "Why is this so awkward?" We both laugh, breaking the tension between us.

"Come here." Trevor pulls me in for another hug, just like he did earlier. I don't know what it is about his hugs that put me at ease, but they do. "Don't worry about it, I'm not going anywhere. You put up with my million and one texts a day, I think we can handle a little awkwardness now."

"I guess that's true." I say into his chest, trying to memorize his woodsy scent and the feel of him against me. The steady thump of his heart in my ear, the evenness of his breaths—they ground me. When we were a thousand miles away he could calm my anxious thoughts with a few words. I had no idea how much more powerful that sense of security would be in person. I tuck the feeling away in my heart, saving it for a rainy day. Something tells me I'm going to need it before the intensive is over.

Trevor's arms squeeze tight before he pulls back to look down at me. "You should go eat. I'll talk to you later, yeah? Maybe even see you tomorrow?"

I nod. "Yeah. Fingers crossed for tomorrow."

We stand there for a moment, neither of us wanting to be the first to let go. Trevor's eyes drop to my lips when I unconsciously lick them, his eyes dark in the waning light. He unwraps one arm from around my waist, his hand cupping my cheek. I don't want to move, enjoying the moment, the tension between us too much to break the spell. "Night Hannah," he says softly, leaning down to drop a kiss on my forehead. Then, before I can say anything he steps back, releasing me.

"Bye, see you later," I manage to say, my mouth dry. That's it? A kiss on the forehead? That was not as magical as I was hoping. Then, I guess this isn't the most romantic place in the world.

With a wave, he turns and leaves me standing in front of the building, happy but a little disappointed.

CHAPTER TEN

Katy

"TO YOUR left is the student union building. The main dining hall is there on the bottom floor, you're welcome to eat there while you're here."

Mom asks about meal plans and dining room hours as the tour guide continues to lead us across campus. I trudge along behind my family with Cole—neither of us interested in the tour. Cole's already in his junior year at UCLA and I'm not interested in moving to Boulder for college. We're here for Jack, one of the CU scouts got in touch with him and asked him to come check the campus out. They tried to convince Hunter as well, but he has his heart set on staying in California, determined to get an internship at SpaceX or JPL. It doesn't hurt that it would keep him near Lisa.

"How come you decided to come with us?" I ask Cole as we trail along. "Don't you have anything better to do?"

"Why? You didn't want me to come?" He grins at me, not quite the carefree grin I remember from when we were kids, but it's better than the grumpy scowl he's been sporting since he came home for the summer.

"Of course I wanted you to come. Geez, can you imagine the torture I would have to put up with if it was the Wonder Twins and me? Ugh." I give a dramatic shudder, hoping to get another smile out of Cole. I don't know why he's been so grumpy since he came home, but I'm determined to find out. "It's just that this is more of a 'college tour for Jack and Hunter' than family vacation kind of trip."

"Feeling left out?" Cole's question cuts to the heart of my own inner grumpiness. Not that anyone else has noticed. "I needed to get out of my routine. It was a tough year."

"You want to talk about it?" I'd wondered if something had happened at school. Maybe it was a girl? Or his old shoulder injury? "I'm good at keeping secrets you know."

That gets a real laugh out of Cole, loud enough to have my dad looking back over his shoulder at us. I wave him off with a grin. "You mean, like how you didn't tell anyone about me kissing Natalie Lay behind the bushes?" I shrug, it had been worth Cole's revenge dunking when my dad turned the cold hose on them. Natalie was a bitch, she called our mom "the help" when she brought out some snacks. And her friends had told me to "go play with Barbies" when I tried to teach them how to play Quinn Ball. It was their own fault when a stray ball gave that one girl a bloody nose.

We follow the rest of our family across campus, the green trees overhead giving us plenty of shade from the warm sun. I appreciate how nature-y the campus is, but I'm already short of breath and all we've done is walk around.

"Still not sorry." I dance out of Cole's reach when he tries to put me in a headlock. Why do they always go for the headlock? "I've only shared secrets when it was for your own good. Was it a girl?" Sometimes I can pester the info out of them, the advantage of being the lone girl.

"No, it wasn't a girl," Cole growls, his face going dark. My brothers all share the same square jaw and defined cheekbones, Jack and Hunter may be identical, but Cole could pass for an older version of either of them. I know that dark look well, I've seen it on all three of their faces over the years. It's the look that says, "Quit prying Katy, I don't want to talk about it." Experience has taught me that right now is not the time to push, but that he'll tell me eventually—once I've sun shined the answer out of him. I just need to bide my time and wait for the right moment. Some stupid Katy antics and twin jokes will wear him down.

Jack does some of the work for me a second later when he walks face-first into a tree, too engrossed in his phone to look where he's going. His flailing arm takes Hunter down with him. "Uh-oh. Looks like Jack can't wait for *fall* semester to start in Sep-timber!" I call out once I catch my breath from laughing.

"Hey Katy, why was the weeping willow so sad?" Cole's wink sets me off again.

"I don't know Cole, why was it so sad?"

"It was watching a sappy movie!"

Hunter can't help grinning at that one, even as he helps Jack up off the ground.

"Hey Cole, what's a tree's favorite dating app?" I can't help myself, it isn't often the twins make it so easy for me. It's been ages since Cole and I have ganged up on them, when he's away at school I have to do it all on my own.

"I don't know Katy, what is it?"

"Timbr!"

Jack and Hunter's groans at that one are echoed by my parents' laughter.

Once the boys are up and dusted off, the tour guide herds us along towards the athletic department, our real reason for visiting. I sidle up to Jack, peering over his shoulder at his phone. "So, what, or should I say who, was so very interesting?"

Hunter throws his arm over my shoulder and stage whispers in my ear. "My money's on JJ."

And with those four words, big black clouds roll in to dim my sunshine. JJ's texting Jack. And he's engrossed enough in the conversation to walk into a freaking tree. I guess she really is buttering me up to get close to my brothers. Just like every other girl at school.

This is why Hannah and Lisa are my best friends. Even Olivia, who I know was my friend first, was more interested in my brothers than me. I don't know why I'm surprised, I should be used to this.

It happened with Jenny Bastian in first grade.

And Ayushi Sharma in fourth grade.

Can't forget Millie and Danielle Chapman, the reigning queens of our fifth-grade class. Silly Katy had thought we'd shared a bond since they were also twins, somehow equating them to the sisters I always wanted. I even fell for it *again* in sixth grade when I got a highly-sought after invitation to their birthday sleepover. It was only once the other girls had me in tears when I couldn't tell them which boy I had a crush on—newsflash there was no boy—and they suggested I call my brothers to come defend me, that I realized what had happened.

Instead, I'd called my mom to come pick me up, even though it was after one in the morning. It had taken me years, and I'm pretty sure some intervention from those same brothers, to get them to stop calling me Baby Quinn.

"Do you not like JJ?" Hunter asked, misreading the change in my mood. "We thought you'd given her the stamp of approval?"

"No, I like JJ. She's cool." The truth of my words hits me square in the gut. I do like JJ, I like hanging out with her, whether or not my brothers are there. Am I so disappointed because I wanted her to want to be my friend more than I wanted her to be interested in my brother?

I'm so stupid.

Once again, disappointed by my own expectations. This is why I let Hannah and Lisa be the ones to aim for the stars. I'm happy to be their cheerleader and bask in their success, just like my brothers. Always the cheerleader, the sidekick, the support staff. I'm happy when I stay in my lane, it's when I forget and imagine for a moment that it's about me that I'm disappointed.

I'll have to thank JJ for the reminder.

As if she can read my mind, my phone buzzes in my back pocket. One glance tells me it's a text from the exact person I'm torn up over. Dragging my feet, I follow my family through the athletic complex, paying enough attention not to trip and give my brother's the satisfaction of karmic payback, but not paying attention to the tour guide at all.

JJ: Animal, vegetable or mineral?
ME: Animal

JJ: 4 legs?
ME: No
JJ: 2 legs?

"Is that Lisa?" Hunter asks over my shoulder. "I thought they were in class right now?" It's a little after three in the afternoon, I haven't heard from Hannah or Lisa since their lunch break.

"Back off Lover-Boy, it's not Lisa. I have other friends you know." Do I? "Even if it was, she was my friend first, do your own texting." I shrug him off and retreat to Cole's side. Cole may be grumpy, but at least he never steals my friends.

ME: Yes
JJ: Male?
ME: No
JJ: Famous?
ME: Only to me
JJ: Someone I know?

The brand-new, state-of-the-art gym is reserved for the student athletes, but the world-class sports medicine facilities and half dozen other things the tour guide points out go right over my head. If I was an athlete, I would be impressed.

ME: Intimately
JJ: ?????

Her accompanying gif of a confused cartoon bunny starts pulling me from my funk. I can't help giggling as I realize how my one-word response must have looked.

ME: Not like that! Just...if you don't know this person inside out by now I'll have to rethink our friendship.

JJ: You?

"Katy?" Dad's voice startles me enough that I walk into Cole's back. Panicking, I stuff my phone back in my pocket. Am I blushing because my dad is calling me out or from the idea of JJ knowing me...intimately? What did I even mean? Why did I type that? What is wrong with me? JJ must think I'm a world-class idiot.

"What?"

"Did you want to see the dance department, Katy?" My mom's voice snaps me from my moment of self-loathing.

"Oh, um. I guess? I hadn't thought about it." Cole pulls me under his arm and holds me in front of his chest. I'm tempted to kick his shins, but don't, because Mom will see.

The tour guide's eyes light up at the mention of touring the dance department. "I didn't know you were a dancer! I'm a dance major. Come on, I'll show you around." Before I can object, she's hooked her arm through mine and is leading me down the stairs and out the door. The looming athletic complex dominates the sky behind us as she leads us west towards another bunch of red brick buildings. "So, we don't have quite as fancy a building as the athletes, but it's still nice." I don't have the heart to tell her that I'm not interested in the school while she drags me down hallways showing off the various studios, talking a mile a minute about the classes and performance opportunities they have.

"Sound great," is all I have to say when she asks for my email so they can start inundating me with information about the school. I was going to give her a fake email address, but my mom is standing at my shoulder and gives it for me. Guess I'm gonna be deleting a bunch of emails in the future.

It's almost another hour before she waves goodbye and leaves us to wander back to the car. I completely forgot about the text from JJ I never answered until I see all three of my brothers pull out their phones while we wait for our order at the campus coffee shop.

> **ME:** Sorry, got pulled into a tour of the dance department. I can't even remember what I was thinking of anymore so I guess you win.

JJ's answer is almost immediate.

> **JJ:** No worries, Jack kept me updated. Are you considering going there for dance?
> **ME:** Not really. I don't know what I want to major in. I haven't thought about it much.

That's a total lie, I have thought about it, but I don't know if it's realistic. For the last year, I've been thinking about becoming a physical therapist, like Ms. Parker's husband, but I don't know if I'm cut out for everything it would take to make that happen. The idea of signing myself up for all that extra schooling on top of getting my bachelor's is daunting. But between all my brother's injuries, and the dance injuries me and my friends have had over the years, let alone knowing what Mr. Mike did for Ms. Parker when they first met, it seems like it would be a pretty rewarding job.

JJ: Well, whatever you decide to do, you'll be amazing.
ME: Thanks. But it won't be here in Colorado. The altitude here is killer. I'm out of breath and all we've done is walk. Also, I swear, everyone here is white. How am I going to find decent Mexican food in a place like this? No thank you.
JJ: Good Mexican food is an absolute must. I'll have to take you out for tacos when you get back. Altitude is a bitch. But that's why they train so many great athletes, because when they come down off the mountain, they have better oxygen capacity. Speaking of, did you run this morning with your brothers? Jack never said if you guys did your training…

This is followed by a gif of a little girl pointing from her eyes to the camera. I grin.

ME: There was only one treadmill at the hotel, so we let Hunter have it while Jack and Cole lifted weights and I gave myself a ballet barre. We took over the whole exercise room, Quinn style.
JJ: Cheater
ME: You say cheater, I say self-sacrificing sister
JJ: Po-tay-to, po-ta-to

This time I'm the one responding with a gif, Samwise Gamgee and his beloved potatoes.

ME: They are my favorite vegetable

JJ: Have you heard from Lisa or Hannah today? How's ballet camp?

I laugh under my breath at JJ's text. Hannah and Lisa would be mortally offended at it being called ballet camp. I can picture their outraged faces—mouths hanging open like goldfish, Hannah's pale skin turning beet red and Lisa's brain working overtime to formulate a response. Man, I miss them.

ME: Sounds like they're having fun. They got to start pas de deux today. I think they were both pretty nervous about it. I haven't heard from them since lunchtime though.
JJ: Is that dancing with a dude? Hard pass for me.
ME: You don't want to dance with a guy? What about at homecoming? Or prom?
JJ: Nah. I'd rather go with my friends than a date. Besides, girls smell WAY better than guys. I'll take a girl over a stinky dude any day.
ME: This is 100% accurate. We had to open the window when Jack took his shoes off in the car. New Quinn family rule: shoes must be worn at all times while in the car.
JJ: 100% on board with this rule.

JJ adds a sick face and thumbs up emoji before following it up with an appropriate retching gif.

Yeah, JJ is pretty awesome. It doesn't replace the loneliness of being left behind by Hannah and Lisa, but maybe I have room in my life for another bestie. Even if she isn't a dancer. *Especially* since she isn't a dancer.

CHAPTER ELEVEN

Hannah

NOAH'S MUTTERED curse is too quiet for anyone else to hear over the general chatter in the room. "I'm so, so sorry. Are you okay?" I don't want to touch him, I think I've already done enough damage. Instead, I hop from foot to foot, peering at his face, well, what I can see of it between his cradled fingers. We've been practicing partnered pirouettes, I'm turning while Noah has his hands on my waist, guiding me and keeping me on balance so I can do extra turns.

Unfortunately, we seem to be having a bit of trouble.

I maaaay have been a little cocky when we tried the first one, I am a pretty natural turner and doing four to five pirouettes on my own isn't that unusual for me. What I didn't realize was that with my long legs, if I place my toe at my knee like I normally do, that leaves my knee sticking out at just the wrong spot. Yes, I kneed my partner in the, ahem, on my first try. What an accomplishment, right?

Once we figured out how far away from me Noah needs to stand, and how I need to adjust the height of my leg, we had a bit more success. Once we'd done several successful turns to the right, we'd switched so that I was standing on my right foot and turning to the left.

What I hadn't anticipated was my right ankle giving a sharp reminder that it's not healed. The shooting pain knocked me off balance, and my flailing response landed us here. Me, gingerly trying to roll my ankle and Noah clutching his face, blood dripping from the end of his nose.

I gave my partner a bloody nose.

This is so embarrassing.

"Are you okay?" I whisper again. "Let me go get you some tissues." I scurry across the room to the tissue box in the corner, grabbing the whole thing and bringing it back to Noah.

"Ahhhh, I see we have our first casualty," Mr. Bethelo's voice booms across the studio.

Did I forget to mention that not only did I give my partner a bloody nose, but that our teacher for pas de deux is the director of the whole school? When Marco Bethelo walked in the door behind the guys, the crescendo of excited chatter rose and then crashed into silence as he clapped his hands for attention.

So yeah.

Now I'm the girl who punched her partner in the face, and it's being pointed out by the man who controls whatever shot I have of a future dancing here.

Great.

"Please keep practicing with your partners." Mr. Bethelo instructs the room as he crosses towards Noah and me. "What happened?"

Since Noah is busy taking care of his bloody nose I speak up. "I fell as I was turning and accidentally hit his nose with my elbow." Crossing my fingers that he doesn't pry into why I fell, the last thing I want is to admit my ankle may not be one hundred percent okay, I wait for Mr. Bethelo to yell at me.

"The perils of partnering!" His laugh booms across the room, the rest of the class freezing at the sound. He waves them away and chuckles to himself. "It happens to the best of us. Noah." His tone turns a little serious, "You're okay, right?"

"Yeth, thir," Noah lisps, pinching his nose and grinning at me. "I tried to tell her."

I shrug, my anxiety still bubbling away in the back of my brain, making it hard to concentrate on anything except the fact that my partner is bleeding and it's all my fault.

Mr. Bethelo eyes us for a moment before gesturing me to come closer. "Come, try again. The best way to get over the fear is to get back on the horse." He waves a hand to the patch of floor in front of him, indicating I should prepare for my pirouette. "Are you a righty or a lefty?"

"Ummm," It takes a moment for my brain to process what he's asking me. "A little better to the right." Also, that means I'd be standing on my left foot and not worried about my ankle.

"Well, then, let's give it a go. And don't worry about falling, all you need to worry about it holding your body in the position, the falling bit is my job." I place my feet on the floor, my left foot about twelve inches in front of my right, in fourth position. My right arm extended in front of me, my left reaching to the side. Mr. Bethelo is standing behind me, his fingertips lightly touching my waist. For once, having someone's hands on my waist doesn't make me twitchy. Maybe because Marco Bethelo knows *exactly* what he's doing. How many times have I heard Ms. Parker say that he was the best partner she'd ever had, and how all the principal ladies used to want to be cast with him. And not just because of his handsome face.

As I'm about to push off the floor, he steps back. Confused, I look back over my shoulder at him. "Do one pirouette for me on your own, I want to see something." Turning back to face the mirror, I bend my knees, then snap up into the turn. As I turn, I focus on holding the correct position, right toe stretched and touching my knee, arms rounded and held in front of my chest. Back straight, hips level, right thigh supported and turned out, leave my eyes to the front of the room as long as possible. The list of corrections is long. But, I don't think all these things individually anymore, I've spent so many hours training that my mind and body know what my "pirouette position" feels like without having to think of all those things one at a time. As I go into my third rotation I have to work a little harder to hold the pieces in place. Choosing to end the turn, I whip my head around one more time and finish the turn, shooting my right leg behind me to the floor in a deep lunge, my arms stretching out to arabesque.

"Good, good," Mr. Bethelo says. "Did you adjust your knee height with Noah? You've got very long thighs…" At my embarrassed nod, Mr. Bethelo smiles. "Go ahead and cross your wrists while you turn as well, instead of holding them out in such a big first position." Oh. Yeah. I knew I forgot to do something. He did tell us that at the beginning of class. That instead of turning with our arms out like we would do on our own, we should drop our elbows and cross our wrists to bring our arms closer and have less chance of hitting our partner. Oh god. I'm the worst partner ever.

"Did Leslie ever tell you about the time she gave me a black eye and a bloody shin at the same time?"

Like a record screech, the whole room falls silent, staring at Mr. Bethelo.

"Um, no?" I manage to squeak out, aware of everyone in class staring at us, listening.

He grins, glancing around to make sure the whole room was listening to his story. "It was in the middle of a Nutcracker season, before we were principals, thank goodness. We were cast as Spanish Chocolate together and there was this one quick turn at the end. I don't know if you have ever seen CBC's Nutcracker, but in that version the Spanish girls dance with castanets. Anyway, she was doing that last tricky turn, it was a supported pirouette and she had to switch her arms as she was turning, clicking the castanets as she went. We'd done it a hundred times without ever having a problem."

"Somehow, during a Sunday matinee show, something went wrong in that turn, we never figured out what. Maybe I was too close to her that day, maybe she was tired from the two shows the day before, but she managed to clock me right in the eye with a wooden castanet *and* the heel of her shoe caught my shin. Our Spanish wasn't on pointe, the ladies had heeled character shoes. I've never bowed or gotten off stage so fast in my life. My tights had to be trashed since there was a huge hole down the front, not to mention they were covered in blood, and I had a massive shiner by the time the ballet was over." Mr. Bethelo grins at the memory. "The makeup team *did not* appreciate having to cover that up for the evening show."

"Oh man, dat's rough." Noah's nasal exclamation takes me by surprise, so does the murmur of chatter and giggles around the room. Even more so when I realize that they're not directed at me. I make eye contact with Lisa across the room, she's partnering with a guy from Eight who I don't recognize, and she smiles. I guess it's not the end of the world after all.

"Come Hannah, try with me while Noah goes to clean himself up." I get back into my pirouette preparation, and once again Marco freaking Bethelo places his hands on my waist. I press up into the turn, doing three rotations on my own before I feel Marco's left hand give me a slight push, and then suddenly, one hand is sliding along my waist, keeping me balanced, while his other hand is pushing me into more and more turns. I lose count at ten but keep whipping my head around and trying to hold my body as steady as I can.

And then he grips my waist tight, stopping me at the end of a turn. I grin at myself in the mirror as I hold the position, triumph surging through me. Mr. Bethelo's face in the mirror reveals his own smile, before he releases me and steps back.

"That was so much easier." The shocked words are out of my mouth before I think about Noah's feelings. Fortunately, he hasn't come back from the bathroom yet.

"Yes, a good partner should make it *easier* to dance, not harder. That's true in life as well as ballet," Mr. Bethelo adds with a smile. "Come, no more life lessons for today. Let's try again while we wait for Noah."

After several more successful turns, thankfully my ankle doesn't give me any more twinges, Noah is back and Mr. Bethelo steps back to let him try. As soon as I prepare for the turn, all my confidence melts away. I swear everyone is watching, waiting for me to screw up again. I'd forgotten about the target on my back for a few precious moments, but it all comes rushing back the second I catch some girls staring at me in the mirror. Noah's hands on my waist make it hard to hold myself still, my skin twitchy at his touch, I'm struggling to trust that he's going to support me like Mr. Bethelo did. It's as if Mr. Bethelo were a solid wall and Noah is a set piece. It looks like a solid wall, but wouldn't hold you up if you leaned against it.

Maybe I need more practice.

The last ten minutes of class Mr. Bethelo has three different couples demonstrate the combination we've been working on to the class. I'm relieved when he doesn't pick me and Noah. When he asks Lisa and her partner to demonstrate, I can't help bouncing on my toes and clapping silently for my friend. They're an excellent team, already doing a beautiful job, I can tell she trusts her partner more than I trust Noah. I'm glad at least one of us is doing well in this class.

Following Lisa out the door to head to our contemporary class, we both pull out our phones to check for messages. Lisa's grin tells me that she's got messages from Hunter to match mine from Trevor.

TREVOR: So apparently Thurs nights are movie nights in our dorm? We've all been told to pick up our dinner and bring it up to our floor for whatever it is they have planned. Bummed I won't get to see you tonight.

We discovered on Sunday night that Trevor's running camp is the one sharing our dorm building. He's joined us for dinner every night this week, and he and I managed to have lunch together a couple of times. Breakfast is not an option since they start their day at six in the morning, and me and my bed have a standing date at that hour. Unfortunately, both of our programs have a nine thirty curfew during the week, so we haven't been able to do much more than dinner and hanging out in the lobby afterward. Gloria and the gang are always around, so I still haven't figured out how to spend time alone with Trevor. I was hoping he might have some ideas.

> **ME:** It's fine, you have fun. I'll have a girl's night with Lisa. Are we still on for this weekend?

Of course, Trevor's reply is almost instant.

> **TREVOR:** Absolutely, wouldn't miss seeing my girl for the world. I have our tickets already. Tell everyone to wear closed-toe shoes, there's a lot of dust and rocks and stuff. Also, I don't want to see those ballet feet.
> **TREVOR:** That sounded better in my head. You know what I mean.
> **ME:** Yes, I know what you mean. Gotta go, class in a few.
> **TREVOR:** Dance good!

That's the goal.

"*L*ISA IS totally teacher's pet in pas de deux," I tell Katy as we walk down the sidewalk. The gang is up ahead of us, leading the way to the train station, Trevor's hand is holding mine while Lisa keeps pace next to me, holding up her phone so I can see Katy's face on her screen.

"I am not!" Lisa pulls the phone away from me, but I grab her arm, pulling it back so I can see Katy's face, Hunter lurking over her shoulder. "She totally is. She got partnered with one of the guys from Eight and he happens to be from Japan. So when she started explaining things to him in Japanese, the other girls in our class who are also from Japan heard her and got her to explain it to them too. So now she's become the official translator for our class and all the teacher's love her for it."

It's faint, but a tinge of pink is creeping up Lisa's cheek at my words. "It's not a big deal, and it doesn't make me teacher's pet. I'm just helping. They were all struggling to follow, you would do the same if you spoke Japanese."

"That's my girl," Hunter's voice booms from behind Katy before she elbows him out of the screen.

"Anyway." I grab the phone from Lisa. "Lisa is kicking butt in pas de deux while I am sucking hardcore at it. But it's okay, I'll just have to practice more."

Katy grins. "Is Trevor there? Maybe you should practice with him?" Trevor's laugh answers Katy's question as my cheeks go up in flames.

"I'm here," he answers for himself. "If the guys will show me what to do, I'd be happy to help Hannah 'practice.'"

Yes, he makes air quotes with his fingers and all, swinging our joined hands up to do it. Katy's squeal of delight at the sight has me glad that the phone is in front of me and not next to my ear.

Lisa plucks her phone out of my hand and hurries away, I'm guessing to talk to Hunter. Trevor is smiling down at me, his grin crinkling his eyes a smidge. His hair is tucked inside a baseball cap today, the way his curls stick out from underneath it is adorable. He was so proud of me when I recognized the abstract spider shape on his t-shirt as a Spiderman logo. I was smart enough to throw a cardigan over my jean shorts and plain green t-shirt, hopefully I won't freeze tonight in the chilly air off the sound.

"You're struggling with pas de deux, huh? Do you really think I could help? You know I will if you want me to try." Letting go of my hand, Trevor slides his arm around my waist, tucking me into his side. I slide my own arm behind his back to grip his waist, his lean torso warm under my palm.

Shrugging, I struggle to find the words to explain why I'm having such a hard time. "It's just...I get anxious about it and then it's hard to think while I'm dancing. I gave Noah a bloody nose—how do I come back from that?"

Suddenly, Noah is walking next to me. "Dude, Hannah, it's not a big deal. It's not the first time it's happened. Last year, Gloria kicked Uri in the face and gave him a fat lip that lasted for a week."

Gloria adds to it by piping up. "I punished myself since he couldn't make out with me for *days* afterwards. Learned my lesson!" To emphasize her point, she pulls Uri's face down and kisses him thoroughly. They don't go in for much PDA, at least not on campus, but seeing her kiss him sends a strange, swooping heat through me.

"See, T, it's fine. But I'll still help you practice if you want." Trevor emphasizes his words with a squeeze of his fingers against my waist. The fabric of my shirt slides up enough that his fingers brush against my bare skin and a giddy nervousness washes over me. For a moment I wonder what it would be like to have his whole hand resting against my skin. What it would feel like to touch his.

A confusing tangle of excitement, nervousness, and warmth settles in my gut, worse than any stage fright I've ever experienced. If I was backstage, I would close my eyes and picture the scene, tell myself the story I was about to dance, but I can't do that here. Besides, the visions in my head are closer to a jumble of sensation than an actual story. The comfort of Trevor wrapping his arms around me, holding me tight. A flutter of anxiety that I have no idea what I'm doing. Streaks of triumph and nervousness when Andrew Park's hand caressed my skin at Katy's house that day at the pool. While Andrew Park touching me made me more and more uncomfortable each time he did it, until I forcefully distanced myself, right now, I'm imagining those same touches from Trevor and it's anything but unwelcome.

"Hannah?" Trevor's question pulls me from my thoughts. Looking up into his face, it's all I can do to smile back at him, hoping that the happiness in my eyes is enough to dispel the doubt I see in his.

"Yeah. Practice would be great. Maybe not the pirouettes though, I don't want to give you a bloody nose like Noah." Trevor's grin sends flutters through me.

"Hey Noah!" Trevor calls over everyone's heads. "Think you can show me how to help my girl?"

"Yeah, I can show you a thing or two. I'll do anything to make sure I keep all my teeth in place."

"We can help too!" Uri calls from the front of the pack.

The rest of the walk to the train station and the train ride are filled with ribbing and laughing from everyone on how they're going to teach Trevor some basic pas de deux and some good-natured advice for me from Gloria and Elena. Trevor takes it all in good fun, laughing with them, his arm slung over my shoulder.

During the entire fascinating Underground City tour, Trevor and I find little ways to touch each other. Holding hands, Trevor guiding me through the narrow spaces with a hand on the small of my back, leaning close to whisper in each other's ears. All of it has me wound tighter than a tutu. It isn't helped by Thomas and Noah sneaking up to scare us girls every time we stop to explore one of the cavernous rooms that hang out under the city of Seattle. Lisa and Elena stick together after the guys attempt to scare them one too many times.

"Dude, come here," Noah calls Trevor over as we near the end of the tour. I wander over to the other girls rather than stand awkwardly alone in the room we're exploring.

"I don't think so?" Lisa is saying as I approach. "What do you think, Hannah?" She turns to ask me.

"What do I think of what?"

"I wanted to know if she was worried about her boyfriend getting jealous," Elena explains.

"Hunter? Of her being here? Or are we still talking about pas de deux?" My eyes are trained on Trevor, even as we're on opposite sides of the room. I'm glad that the other guys have pulled him into the group. It would be easy for them to exclude him since he's not a dancer, but I guess they don't care. Trevor *is* pretty easy to like. "I don't think Hunter would be jealous. He's too smart for that."

"I don't think smart has anything to do with it. We know that it doesn't mean anything. I imagine it would be hard for a guy to trust that nothing is happening if he knew some other dude had his hands all over their girl," Gloria pipes up from the other side of Elena. She's so tiny I hadn't seen her there. "I'm lucky that Uri was my partner, but, it can be hard when we're not dancing together, because he knows what we got up to last year." Gloria grins. "We did a lot of 'extra' practice." She winks and we laugh, but worry creeps into my gut. Is Trevor going to get jealous? He seemed like he was okay with everything earlier, but is he just putting on an act in front of the other guys?

Once again, my inexperience leaves me unsure of what I'm supposed to do. "I'm sure Hunter is fine. Katy will knock sense into him if he does anything stupid." Lisa smiles at my words, the tiny worry lines in her forehead relaxing.

By the time we emerge from the labyrinth hiding beneath the streets of Seattle, we're all hungry. Heading to a nearby coffee shop, I find myself sandwiched between Noah and Trevor. With an empty expanse of sidewalk in front of us, Noah stops me with a touch to my arm. "Shall we?"

"Now?" I glance nervously at Trevor. He nods his head, his Adam's apple bobbing with a hard swallow.

"No pirouettes though. How about tombe pas bourre, yada, yada, yada." He demonstrates with his hands, so I know what he's planning. With a last glance at Trevor to make sure he's okay with this, I turn my back to Noah and he rests his hand against the small of my back. Pulling a deep breath into my lungs, I take off, stepping out with my right leg, then pulling my left leg into a little running step beneath me, Noah echoing the step behind me, his hand on my back telling me where he is. As I do a little preparation spring from one foot to the other Noah's hands wrap around my waist and then I leap as high as I can, splitting my legs in the air. Noah lifts me easily, our joint momentum translating into lift as he propels me higher than I ever could have gone on my own, lifting me above his head. Defying gravity, he lowers me back to the ground, I shift my weight forward so he can set me down on one leg, the other lifted straight behind me as I hold the same position, one arm reaching forward, the other slightly back.

Someone takes my back hand, tugging on it. Keeping in character, I step back on my lifted leg, spinning into whoever's arms pulled on me, expecting to come face to face with Trevor. It's not Trevor.

I'm wrapped up in Thomas' arms, chest to chest, staring at his mischievous grin. "Um." I stumble backwards, my ankle giving an angry twinge, and bump into someone behind me. Strong hands grip my upper arms, stopping me from falling. "Sorry." I whirl, pulling my arms against my chest, praying it's Trevor who caught me and not someone else.

Relief floods through me at the Spiderman shirt almost touching my nose. Trevor isn't looking down at me, but glaring at Noah and Thomas. "Dude," is all he says to them before looking down. "You okay?"

"Yeah. Um. yes. I'm fine. I thought that was you." I stammer, jerking my thumb over my shoulder at Thomas. "Are *you* okay?" I want to slide my arms around him but I don't, unsure of what he's thinking.

"Yeah. Maybe I'll help you practice later. Without the peanut gallery." His voice doesn't have the usual carefree sound to it that I'm used to. Is he angry at me? Pulling away, I nod and hurry to catch up to Lisa.

Did I do something wrong?

The worry that I've done something to hurt Trevor gnaws at me for the rest of the afternoon, especially since Trevor is keeping his hands firmly to himself. No little touches of my arm, no hand on my back guiding me through the crowd. Every moment that passes with Trevor being distant sits like a rock in my stomach, my heart racing and not in the fluttery excited way.

We stop for coffee and the whole time, Trevor is distant, sitting beside me, but chatting with Uri and Gloria while I chat with Lisa and Elena. I can't help eavesdropping on their conversation, Uri and Trevor comparing notes on his running camp versus the intensive. Uri sounds impressed by what Trevor has to do. I know I am.

Lisa and I get Elena to tell us more about her, she's been a bit of a mystery until now. Elena's description of her hometown in Cuba is fascinating. I had no idea she moved to Havana from a much smaller town in the country to live at the ballet conservatory there when she was ten. I can't imagine leaving home so young.

Eventually, we head back to the train and ride it back to campus. Something changed in the group dynamic this afternoon leaving us split into two groups—Trevor, me, Lisa, and Elena sit together, while Noah and Thomas laugh and joke with each other. Gloria and Uri flit between the two groups, Uri is definitely the friendliest of the guys to Trevor, which I appreciate.

Walking back to campus, Gloria and Thomas are deep in conversation, her whispered words sounding angrier than teasing. As we get to the glass doors of the dorms, Thomas taps me on the shoulder. "Hannah?"

"What do you want?" Trevor growls, tugging me closer by the elbow. It's the first time he's touched me since our botched bit of pas de deux practice. I should be relieved, but it sends a wave of anxiety through me instead.

Startled at his tone, I allow myself to be pulled away, but turn to face Thomas, curious what he wants. "Yeah?"

"Sorry for startling you…earlier." He jerks his thumb behind his shoulder. "I was just messing around."

I'm glad he's apologizing to me and not to Trevor. I may be inexperienced, but I'm not naive enough to not have noticed the way Trevor's been glaring at Thomas ever since the incident, but I'm the one he scared. "It's okay. I thought you were Trevor, so you took me by surprise. No hard feelings." I elbow Trevor in the stomach with my words, intending them as much for him as for Thomas. With the way the Six girls are gossiping about me, the last thing I need is for any more fuel for their venom.

Thomas rubs a hand on the back of his neck. Is that the universal boy gesture for when they need to say something and aren't sure how? "Gloria will kill me if I don't," he mutters to himself. "Um, yeah. It's just that the rest of us were all a little jealous of Noah, that he gets to be your partner. Being your partner means a pretty good shot at being cast in a lead for the end of workshop performance. Just shootin' my shot." He shrugs.

What is he talking about?

Gloria interrupts, shoving her twin out of the way. "He was an ass, he's sorry. To both of you," she adds, eyeing Trevor. "What he was trying to say, was that all the guys were hoping to get to be your pas partner because that's one of the ways they cast for the workshop performance, and level seven and eight are the only ones that get to do a pas. Since everyone is pretty sure they're going to want to cast you, being your partner was a hot topic of conversation."

Knowing I was being talked about has my skin crawling. Now I have to worry about my friends talking about me too, not just the level six girls? I'm not sure how much more of this I can take.

She glares at him again. "What he's forgetting is that they wouldn't have cast him anyway since he's an Eight with me. Ignore him. We're gonna go. See you at breakfast."

With a wave, Gloria leads everyone except Lisa inside. Lisa hovers near me, looking like she has something on her mind. "What's up Lisa?" I ask, no idea what she wants to say. I haven't managed to make her mad too, have I? "Did you know about that?" I jerk my head at Gloria's retreating back.

"That they were talking about you? Yeah." Lisa shrugs. "They weren't saying anything bad, so I didn't think you'd want to know."

"Can't I hide in the back and wave a flower back and forth?" I whine, rubbing my arms, goosebumps prickling my skin as clouds start rolling in, blocking the sun.

Lisa eyes me. "Is that really what you want?" Groaning, I shake my head. It's not and we both know it. "Yeah, I didn't think so." She smirks, punching me in the arm.

"Are you going to stay for a while? I was hoping to go call Hunter." Her cheeks go pink. "And I, um, wondered how long you'd be gone?"

Trevor regards me thoughtfully. Is that regret I see in his eyes? "I think we'll hang out a while longer." I don't even notice when Lisa leaves, I'm so lost in the look in Trevor's eyes. He's pulling me away from the door, his warm hand finally twining with mine again. The second our fingers lock, the bands around my chest loosen and I can draw a full breath again. I follow Trevor around the corner of the building to a small courtyard, large concrete planters and patches of grass occupying the space between our dorm building and the empty one next door.

Leaning against one of the planters, Trevor pulls me towards him, his hands on my hips guiding me to stand between his legs.

Nervous and unsure of what to do with my hands, I fiddle with a stand of hair, not able to meet his eyes. I keep my gaze trained on the graphic on his t-shirt, tracing it over and over, anything to stop from seeing the look on his face. Is he upset with me? Jealous at the idea that apparently everyone wanted to be my pas de deux partner? Am I supposed to apologize?

"Hannah?" I can't help the way my shoulders droop when he uses my name. If he's not using his nickname for me he must be mad, right? I can't stop the tears that prick at my eyes. "Hey," gently, he pulls the strand of hair from between my fingers, tucking it behind my ear before sliding his fingers along my jaw to pinch my chin. Tipping my face up, I blink and the tears I didn't want to cry spill down my cheeks.

"I—" I start to whisper but can't get any farther, my throat closing up.

And then I'm being enveloped in Trevor's arms, my face pressed against his chest, the familiar feel of him washing away some of my fear. "I'm sorry Han, don't cry. I didn't mean to upset you, I swear I didn't."

He upset me?

With my ear pressed against him and Trevor resting his cheek on top of my head, his shaky breath rattles in my ear. "I'm sorry," he whispers, tightening his arms.

I pull back a little so I can peer up at his face, his arms sliding back to my hips. "I thought I made you mad…" I don't get any farther before Trevor is shaking his head.

"I was mad, but not at you. You didn't do anything wrong, T. I was pissed at Thomas. And a little at myself." Again, he touches the hair he just tucked behind my ear, his chocolate eyes searching mine. The hand still on my hip slides to the small of my back, drawing me closer until there's less than an inch of space between us.

My breath quickens before I manage to get words out. "Why were you mad at yourself? You didn't do anything wrong."

That gets me a smile, Trevor's fingers still playing with the strand of hair he seems to have taken captive. He can have it, if it means he's not leaving me.

"I wish I could help you with this the same way I help you with math." I smile at that. "I hate that I can't be the one to help you with this, T. I know how important it is to you. It kills me that I have to let some other guy help you when that should be my job."

Swallowing down my fear and embarrassment, I reach up to cup Trevor's cheek, my thumb lightly grazing the corner of his lip, before resting my hand on his shoulder. I pull up to my toes, using him for balance, his hand on my back steadying me. "Working with a partner, letting someone touch me like that...I'm not used to it. It's going to take me awhile to be more comfortable." Trevor's thumb slides under the fabric of my shirt, sending sparks of awareness dancing across my skin.

"I don't know how comfortable I want you to get with other guys touching you," Trevor admits, his eyes going dark. He keeps talking before I can argue. "But I know you need to do this, that it's important to you. And I trust you." His eyes search mine for a long moment. Not sure what he's looking for I hold still, waiting for him to say more. His hand on my back tightens, holding me firmly. "How can I help?"

"You are helping me. More than you know," I whisper, unwilling to break the quiet surrounding us with my voice. My voice, my words, aren't going to reassure either of us right now. Instead, locking eyes with Trevor, I guide his other hand to my back, then lift my arms, holding them high and rounded above my head. Still balancing on my toes, I pick up my back leg, releasing it low behind me. "I'm going to lean back, will you hold me?" I ask, waiting for his nod of assent before I lift my eyes and bend back, arching towards my lifted leg. Trevor's arms brace to take my weight as I look up to the clouds in the sky. The green leaves of the tall trees near us dance across my vision, contrasting with the patch of blue sky peeking between the buildings. Closing my eyes, I trust that Trevor is going to hold me as I lean back even farther, my hips counterbalancing me, Trevor's hands reassuring and strong. Bone-deep, I know, I trust, he won't let me fall.

Slowly, I straighten, opening my eyes to meet his, smiling when I see the happiness in Trevor's face. With a grin, he bends his knees, wraps his arms around my torso and spins us both in a circle. I can't stop the joyful laugh that bursts out of me. Setting me down on my feet, I take Trevor's left hand with my right, then duck under his arm, switching hands as I straighten, stepping into another arabesque, grasping his left hand with mine, my right hand resting on his shoulder. A classic pas de deux move.

"What do I do now?" Trevor's voice echoes in the quiet.

"Lock your arm and walk in a circle." I instruct, jerking my head in the direction I want him to go. Using my inner thigh muscles, I pivot my foot on the ground to turn with him. This is a million times harder on concrete and in tennis shoes than in pointe shoes. I barely manage to keep myself from falling. "That's a promenade. They're harder than they look." I continue with my lesson. "Stop there," I add when we've made a somewhat complete circle. I let go, opening my arms to the sky, balancing on one leg for as long as I can before collapsing with a grin.

Before I can instruct him again, I'm being swept up in Trevor's arms, one arm beneath my knees, the other supporting my back. I throw my arms around his neck. "I don't know any lifts from here," I tease.

"Me neither. But I couldn't help myself." Taking long steps towards one of the benches, Trevor sits down with me on his lap. "Hey, are we good?"

Happy to stay here, I nod. "Yeah. We're good. You're a pretty good partner, you know that?" The shy smile Trevor gives me has my heart rate picking up, but it's the way his hand brushes my cheek before softly griping the nape of my neck, drawing me closer that has it racing.

Our first kiss is perfect.

Soft.

Sweet.

Trevor's lips press against mine, new and familiar, safe but wild.

I pull back with a gasp, my hands finding their way to his cheeks without any guidance from me before I lean back in for another, silencing the words he was about to say. For once, my mind is still. The hundred worries and thoughts that never leave me, the second-guessing, the anxious surety that whatever is wrong is somehow my fault, disappears.

There's just us. Just Trevor's arm tight around my waist, our fingers tangled in the hair at the back of each other's necks.

Lips tasting and exploring, tentative at first, and then with more confidence. Eventually, I have to come up for air, although I'm not sure if I'm gasping from the lack of oxygen or because kissing Trevor is that breathtaking.

This space, where it's just us, just me and Trevor, feels like home.

CHAPTER TWELVE

Katy

GPLUTTERING AND pushing my wet hair out of my eyes I come up for air, already reaching out to return the favor. Nothing says "welcome home from your long and boring road trip" like being tossed in the pool. My brothers do it so often it's a habit to toss my phone on the nearest chair as soon as I walk outside.

What I wasn't expecting?

For JJ to be the one to grab me around the waist and jump in, dragging me with her.

Geez, she and Jack are perfect for each other, that's exactly the same thing he would do. As I wipe the water away from my eyes, I swim in circles looking for her. She bursts out of the water to my left, flipping her hair back in a decent imitation of a mermaid before her laughing eyes find mine and she grins.

"You are so dead!" I laugh, pushing off the wall to swim towards her, arms already reaching out to grab her.

"You have to catch me first." JJ's longer arms and legs make it hard for me to catch up, every time I get close, she manages to slither away again. Her arms and legs are slippery smooth under the water, making it difficult for me to get a grip. I have her by the ankle when she swims down, a direction I wasn't anticipating, then wraps herself around my waist, like a human floatie. Between the ridiculous way she's hooked her arms behind her own knees so I can't shake her off, her hair tickling my sides and the pure fun of being silly with her, I'm laughing so hard I snort. And not a cute delicate little snort, nope, this is a full on, phlegm rattling, piggy snort.

Which of course makes us both laugh even harder.

"Truce, truce," I gasp as JJ comes up for air. Laying back on the water, I float away, staring at the sky. My wet sports bra and shorts aren't an ideal swimsuit, but I've been tossed in this pool in far worse. Let's just say, the time they tossed me in wearing full denim overalls when I was ten and the Christmas they tossed me in in my fancy velvet dress still live in infamy in our house.

"My arms are noodles. You're sadistic, you know that?" I add, letting the cool water soothe my aching shoulders and clean the sticky sweat off my face. "We only got back late last night. Would it have killed any of you to let me sleep in for once?"

"It was Jack's idea, don't blame me. He saw this terrain race where you have to carry a bucket full of rocks for fifty yards or something and wanted to try it. Buckets full of water was the best I could do on short notice."

The mention of Jack's name sends my stomach sinking to the bottom of the pool. How often do they talk? I'm dying to know but afraid to ask. JJ and I were texting so often it felt like she came on the trip with us, keeping me company and teasing my brothers with me. Was she texting him the same amount? She couldn't be, right?

With nothing else to do but look out the window and stare at the landscape passing me by, I've a lot of time to think. Is it too much to ask to have a person who's mine? That I don't have to share with my stupid charismatic brothers?

Not just any person—JJ.

I float over to the edge of the pool, letting my legs sink down as I hook my elbows backwards over the edge. The cement is hot on my skin, but the contrast between the heat on my back and shoulders and the coolness of the water soothes my tired body. "I can't believe I ran a full five miles with you today. If you'd asked me in June, I would have said never, but here I am, running five miles without thinking twice. What have you done to me?" Tipping my head back to rest against the cement, I close my eyes against the bright sunshine that's already beating down on us at ten in the morning.

There's a small splash of water near me, but I don't open my eyes, basking in the sun like the lizard I am. "Well, you were already halfway there with all the dance you do, and all the work you guys did on the road. It's not like you took those three weeks off." JJ's voice comes from right next to me. I smile, keeping my eyes closed, picturing the two of us. "All you needed was the motivation."

"Ha! You realize dancers don't run, right? It's supposed to be bad for your knees."

"Do your knees hurt?"

"Well, no. But I'm not the real dancer in our group. I leave that up to Hannah and Lisa."

A finger pokes my cheek. Turning my head and cracking one eye open, JJ's face is closer than I expected, her head pillowed on her elbows. "Why do you do that?" she asks, irritation in her voice.

"Do what?"

"Write yourself off. You work just as hard as everyone else, but you say Hannah and Lisa are the 'real dancers' and your brothers are the 'real athletes.' Granted, I've never watched you dance, but Jack's told me how many hours you dedicate to it every week. And you can't tell me you aren't determined to kick your brother's asses every time we train. Sometimes I have a hard time keeping up with *you*."

JJ sees all that? In me?

Not knowing what else to do, I slide off the wall and dunk my head under the water, needing a minute before I have to face her again. JJ's words leave me exposed, no one has ever *seen* me like that before. But I'm also aware of the warm glow her words stoke in my chest. No one's ever seen me like *that* and appreciated it.

With my lungs burning, I push myself up out of the water and rest my elbows next to JJ's, pillowing my head to match hers. "No one ever notices me," is all I can say. I would shrug, but my shoulders are already up around my ears.

"Well, I notice." JJ's smile has the warm glow in my chest building to a blaze, until her next words quench it faster than a bucket of ice water. "Jack notices too. I think you should give your brothers more credit. They love you, you know?"

"Yeah, yeah. I think they love you more." The truth of my words sends my stomach sinking to the bottom of the pool. Once again, I'm the afterthought, I helped them get what they wanted—Lisa in Hunter's case and now JJ—and they took it without thinking about whether it was something I needed too.

I need a friend. And I guess JJ isn't going to be the one I hope for.

"WHY HAVEN'T we done this before?" Olivia asks as I slide into the passenger seat of her car.

"We have done this before?" In all the years we've known each other, Olivia and I have definitely gone shopping together before.

"No I mean, why haven't we hung out, just you and me, this summer? It seems like we should have." We stop at a red light and Olivia pulls her sunglasses down to peer at my face. I shrug in response. All I know is, I needed to get away from my house and my brothers.

"I don't know. You've been busy hanging out with your girls, I've been hanging out with my brothers and JJ. We've been training for that terrain race at the end of summer." How many more excuses does she need? Although, I'm glad Olivia doesn't mention anything about me ditching dance all summer. I get enough guilt from Hannah and Lisa whenever I talk to them.

"Honestly? I haven't seen the girls from the squad much at all. Since they were such bitches to Lisa at your house that day, I've been keeping my distance." She blows out a deep breath. "Of course, I'm going to have to deal with them eventually. Did I tell you that Coach made me co-captain for next year?"

"Congrats Olivia, that's awesome. Are you excited?" We're circling the parking lot of the outlet mall, looking for a spot.

"Yeah, I'm excited. I'm a little nervous because it's a lot of responsibility. But I'm glad that Coach picked me because her other choices were Allyson or Megan. And that would have been a disaster."

"Why would that be a disaster?" I ask, curious.

"Because while those girls are *my* bitches, they're still bitches. How they acted towards Lisa and Hannah? They're kind of like that to everyone. It wouldn't have been good for the squad. Captains are supposed to be fair, not the leaders of the mean girl clique."

I can't think of anything to say to that as Olivia parks. I never thought she noticed how awful those girls were.

"What?" she asks as we climb out.

"And here I thought wearing pink on Wednesday's was your idea," I tease. "I'm kind of surprised you saw how awful they are. I didn't think you cared."

Olivia gives me a look, well, I assume so since her sunglasses are hiding her eyes from me. "I wasn't completely oblivious to them. I know they've been rude to you, I just..." She pauses to open the door to the clothing store, letting me go in front of her. "I'll admit that I was so busy being mad at Hannah and everyone who was on her side, that I didn't say anything when I should have. I should have called them out on their bitchiness ages ago."

Wow. I was not expecting this conversation at all. When I'd called Olivia to see if she was busy, all I wanted was a chance to hang out with someone instead of moping alone at home, and I'm so mixed up about JJ that hanging out with her wasn't going to be the relaxing afternoon I needed. "It's okay," I mumble, unsure of what else to say.

"It's really not. But thank you."

"I'm not hugging you in the middle of the store or anything," I add. "Apology accepted. It's nice to have a friend who isn't using me to get to one of my brothers." I don't know where that came from, I barely stop myself from clapping my hands over my mouth to bring the words back in.

Instead, I busy myself flipping through racks of clothes, hunting for anything that catches my eye. I haven't been back to this mall since Jack and I kidnapped Hannah and forced her to tell Trevor she liked him and we schemed to get Hunter and Lisa together. Was that only two months ago? It feels like longer.

"What about JJ? I see her hanging out with you guys all the time. Tyler said she's helping you train for that race." Olivia pulls out a flimsy-looking lime green strapless dress with the most hideous design splashed across the front. It looks like an abstract version of a package of Cheetos.

"That's hideous. You have to try it on." I laugh. "I'm pretty sure JJ is there for Jack," I add, sadness tugging at my chest.

Olivia eyes me over the pile of clothes in her arms. "You know, whenever I see her, all she does is talk about you. I was surprised when you called me and not her to hang out today."

"What?" I nearly drop the pile in my arms at Oliva's words. "That's, um...oh." Why am I so tongue-tied, isn't this what I wanted? Proof that JJ wanted to be *my* friend, not to flirt with my brothers? I ignore the little spark that ignites in my chest at Olivia's words.

We take our clothes to the dressing room to try on, laughing at the ridiculous lime green dress when Olivia puts it on. It's even more hideous than it looked on the hanger. We fall into easy conversation, talking about everything and nothing. Olivia's been babysitting her younger siblings in the morning most of the summer, she's saving up her money to go on a trip to Europe after graduation with Tyler. Two years should be enough time to have a decent chunk of money to travel with.

We're standing in line at the food court, waiting to get some Chinese food, when my phone starts buzzing in my pocket. Tapping to accept the call, Olivia and I smoosh our faces together so we can both see the screen.

"Hi!" we call, as Lisa and Hannah's smooshed faces appear on my phone.

"Oh my god, hi!" Hannah's bouncing with excitement, good thing it looks like Lisa is holding the phone still. "What are you guys doing? I'm so happy to see you both!"

Laughing, Olivia flips her hair over her shoulder. "Just having a girl's day, doing a little shopping. How are you guys? How's PSB? Is it intense?"

Hannah fills Olivia in a bit, but I can tell they have news to share. After a minute I interrupt Hannah's description of all the classes they're taking to ask, "Do you have news? Wasn't the casting for the end of intensive performance going up today?" At least, that's what Lisa told me last night when I wrestled Hunter's phone away from him long enough to say hi to her.

Hannah's squeal is loud enough to have everyone around us in the food court looking our way. Turning the volume down on my phone with an apologetic look, I try to focus on what Hannah is saying.

"We're doing excerpts from Swan Lake for the performance and Lisa is doing Cygnets!" Hannah says quickly, talking over whatever it was Lisa was trying to say.

Lisa pulls the phone away from Hannah's smug face. "And Hannah is doing the Black Swan pas de deux with Noah!"

"What?" This time my yell is the one drawing eyes and disapproving glares from the people around us. "That's amazing! Both of you! Cygnets? That's so freaking cool. Dude, Black Swan pas? That's *epic*, Hannah."

Olivia manages to pull the phone away from me, dragging me out of line and around the corner by the elbow. She talks over my shoulder as we walk. "Cygnets is amazing Lisa. I hope you can do it better than when we tried." That has all four of us laughing, remembering the summer we convinced Ms. Parker to teach it to us, the famous Dance of the Four Little Swans. For starters, it's an exhausting dance, all that jumping while holding hands with three other people is *hard*, and with all the super precise head and footwork, if one person gets off it not only messes everyone else up, but means you end up turning your head to look straight into the eyes of the person next to you and in our case, that meant instant giggles. I don't remember if we ever got all the way through it without someone screwing it up.

"You have to promise me something Hannah." I smirk. "Don't pull a Natalie Portman, okay? No going crazy with the Black Swan business."

"Or making out with Mila Kunis!" Olivia yells from behind me.

"I dunno." I fake a thoughtful expression. "Mila Kunis is pretty hot..."

Once she stops laughing, Hannah promises not to pick imaginary feathers out of her skin or stab herself with a broken mirror. "We both got cast in a contemporary piece as well," Hannah says. "They picked four Seven's and four Eight's to be in it. We don't know who's choreographing it yet, the casting sheet didn't say."

"Tell us about you guys though, how's dance? How's Ms. Parker? Any of the younger girls get moved up into our class? Has Katy finally shown up for class?"

I know Hannah is teasing, but her words set my teeth grinding. I don't need her reminding me that I've been skipping class. Olivia takes the phone from me so she can answer. "Anne, Jaime, and Grace all got moved up into the senior class, you know they're all freshman this year, right?" I let Olivia keep talking, filling Hannah and Lisa in on the gossip.

I could use the excuse of the online driver's ed class I've been taking, and the three weeks I was out of town with my family, but really, I don't have an excuse other than I haven't wanted to go. Plain and simple, when given the choice of going or staying home I've chosen to stay home every single time. And now, I definitely do not want to think about what that might mean other than I needed a break. I'm not ready to think about whether this means I can still call myself a dancer. I know JJ gave me a hard time about it, but it's true, Hannah and Lisa are the 'real dancers' in our little squad. Olivia and I do it for fun, no big goals for us.

"Bye!" Hannah and Lisa's voices call out from my phone.

Scrambling to catch them, I stick my nose over Olivia's shoulder. "Bye!" I take my phone back and stuff it in my back pocket. "I didn't know those girls had moved up."

"Yeah, Ms. Parker had them join in for the summer. They're alright, I guess. Kinda giggly and young, but we already knew that from rehearsals." Olivia shrugs. I'm waiting for her to point out that I've been missing class, but she keeps walking towards one of the smaller clothing boutiques.

"Is Ms. Parker mad that I'm not there?" I finally blurt out, unable to keep the question inside any longer.

"I don't think so. She asked if I'd seen you the other day, but..." Olivia trails off. "*I miss you in class though, the other senior girls aren't as much fun. You should come tomorrow.*" I hadn't thought about Olivia missing me in class, things got so weird between us when I thought she'd hurt Hunter's feelings last year that I'd kind of written off our friendship.

"I'll try." I do miss it, even if I'm having fun doing other things as well. But it's hard without Hannah and Lisa there. "Will you give me a ride?"

"Of course I will, then I can guarantee I won't have to share a barre with Jackie. She's a barre hog and she keeps taking Hannah's spot. It irks me." Laughing, we pull open the door to the boutique and start flipping through racks of clothes.

CHAPTER THIRTEEN

Hannah

MY JAW aches from clenching my teeth, but I'm not going to let the sharp pains shooting up my ankle stop me from nailing this step. Noah and I have been struggling with this lift all evening.

Gripping his right wrist with my right hand, I'm supposed to step into a jump, brushing my left leg forward before flipping my body in the air to face him, holding my leg up as he eases me down, defying gravity like the bird I'm playing. The problem is that I'm taking off for the jump on my right foot, and every time I try to jump, shooting pain sears up my leg and I lose power. As much as Noah is trying to help me by bracing the wrists we're holding and using his other hand against my hip to push me higher, I can't seem to get high enough in the air.

"I think is enough for today, we try again tomorrow." Mr. Popov claps his hands before I can try again. Noah steps back from me, shaking out his arms. We gather up our things and head to the dining hall to join our friends. I walk slowly and deliberately, my ankle angry with each step.

"Is there something wrong? I can feel you twitch every time you take off," Noah asks as he holds the door open for me to duck through. We wave to our group, before going to pick up our own dinner and join them.

"No, I'm fine. Just tired." I lie. Ignoring Noah in the hopes he'll drop the subject, I eye the pasta and chicken on offer for dinner tonight. A body bumping into my back knocks the cutlery on my tray to the floor. "What the..." I whirl to see a pack of Six's retreating, Becky's waifish body in the middle. She looks back over her shoulder at Noah and I, eyeing us speculatively.

"Hope your partner can lift you after eating all those carbs," Becky says with a plastic smile. "Wouldn't want to injure him." Laughing, she leads the group of giggling girls away.

No longer eager for the pasta on offer, I turn to grab a salad instead, almost bumping into Noah as he reaches for the serving spoon I dropped. "Don't let those bitches get to you. They're jealous."

"Easy for you to say, they didn't call you fat," I murmur. I've never worried about my weight before, trusting my natural thinness and the hours I spend dancing to keep me in shape. As long as I could see the defined muscles of my thighs in class, I didn't worry. Ms. Parker doesn't ever comment or judge us on our bodies. I hadn't realized how different that was until I got here and suddenly *everyone* talks about it. Besides, the conditioning class they have us doing three times a week has had me feeling more toned than ever, not to mention the eight or nine hours of dancing a day. My stomach growls.

"Just eat the pasta Hannah. I don't want my partner passing out on me." With a wink and a laugh Noah walks away, leaving me to debate between satisfying my hunger and easing the anxious voice in my head telling me to eat the salad instead.

"Hey," Trevor says in my ear, sliding his arms around my waist, his chin resting on my shoulder. "You should have the pasta, it's pretty good. Also, I'm still hungry so I'll finish anything you don't eat." I relax against him for a second, giggling when he presses a quick kiss to my cheek. This is what I'll be missing when I go home, the little things, the tiny moments. "How was rehearsal?" Trevor reaches past me to scoop up a pile of pasta and veggies onto a plate.

As usual, Trevor's dressed in jeans and a t-shirt, smelling like soap and mint. More than once over the last few weeks I've regretted that he only sees me after I've come straight from class or rehearsal, with shorts and t-shirts thrown on over my leotard and tights, my hair in a bun, still sweaty and stinky. The only time Trevor has seen me in "normal" clothes has been on our weekend excursions.

"It was fine. We're having a hard time with one of the lifts though, that's why we were so late finishing." I skirt the truth—that my ankle is throbbing and that's why we were struggling.

"Anything I can help with?" Can he invent invisible ice?

"Probably not. I think I'm just tired and sore." It's not a complete lie, only a minor rearranging of the facts. Trevor takes the tray from me, leading the way to the table where our group is sitting. Noah and I are the only ones who haven't eaten yet, our rehearsals running longer and longer this week.

"So," Gloria says the moment I sit. "How's Black Swan? Is it as much fun to do as it looks? I've always wanted to do that one."

"It's so much fun," I say, swallowing the bite of pasta in my mouth. Okay, Trevor was right, it's pretty good. "That big, dramatic backbend right as the music changes is my favorite part. It's just so over the top." I laugh.

The other girls laugh with me. "Yes! I know exactly which part you mean." Gloria demonstrates her own dramatic drop into a backbend, throwing her arms and head over the back of her chair. The chair tips back and she yelps as Uri scrambles to catch the chair and Gloria before they fall backwards.

"Watch it!" A chorus of voices exclaim from behind her. Our table's laughter at Gloria's near miss chokes off at the sight of a table full of girls all looking down their noses at us. By their perfectly made-up faces and curled hair, it's clear they're not from our intensive. They eye our table with barely concealed sneers. I shrink down in my chair, chewing my dinner and avoiding eye contact with them.

"Sorry," Gloria says, straightening up. She leans a little closer to Uri, letting his arm over her shoulder shield her from view. The brash and confident Gloria I've come to know over the last few weeks dissolves in front of my eyes under the scrutiny of the table full of girls. I wince in sympathy, I guess it doesn't matter where you're from or how good you are, being a serious ballet dancer automatically makes you uncool to the wider world.

Flashbacks of my confrontation with the cheer girls at school sends my shoulders up around my ears. Lisa slinks down in her chair next to me, eyes down on the table. When she and Hunter started dating, more than one girl at school had it out for her for daring to take one of the school's hottest guys off the market. It was ugly.

"Trevor?" One of the girls asks. "What are you doing over there?" And there it is.

Trevor spears a piece of chicken off my plate, leaning closer than necessary to do it. Deliberately, he bumps his shoulder against mine. Startled, I look up to find him grinning at me. With a wink, he pops the fork in his mouth, then puts an arm around my shoulder while he chews, ignoring the girl's question. Only once he swallows does he look at them and answer. "Having dinner with my girlfriend."

Several of the girls at the other table narrow their eyes, assessing me. I want to shrink even lower in my chair, but the weight of Trevor's arm resting on my shoulder stops me. What would Katy do? What would Olivia do right now? Instead of disappearing into the floor, I sit up straighter and stare right back.

"Your *girlfriend*?" The pretty brunette who said it is staring at our table. "Or do you mean your *boyfriend*?" She titters along with the other girls at the table. The second her words register, Noah, Thomas, Uri, and Trevor are on their feet, glaring at the table, us girls a half second behind.

"Did you just...?"

"I'm sorry what?"

"Excuse me?"

"What the fuck did you say?"

"Seriously?"

"What the hell?"

"What the hell is wrong with you?"

"You did not just say what I think you said."

We all yell at once, outrage and anger competing with shock at her words. Even some of the other girls at her table are looking at her, shock, and disgust on their faces. The brunette puffs up, opening her mouth to speak but Trevor interrupts her.

"You want to take that back? Because I think you just called my girl a dude and then insinuated that if I was gay I should be ashamed of it?" Trevor's voice drops as he leans his hands on the table, staring her down. "For starters, my girl here is a thousand times more beautiful than you without even having to try. And secondly, if you think that calling someone gay is an acceptable insult, or that they should be ashamed of it, you are dead wrong."

Trevor takes my tray, walking away. We've only gone a few steps when a combination of cheering and shrieking stops us in our tracks. I pull on Trevor's arm, stopping him so we can see what's causing the commotion. Noah is gripping Thomas by the shoulders, kissing him soundly on the lips. Half of the girls table is cheering, the pretty brunette and her tittering friends the ones shrieking in disgust. Lips still locked, Thomas and Noah flip middle fingers to the table of rude girls, earning them another cheer, plus more cheers from around the entire dining room, before taking a theatrical bow and following the rest of us out the door.

"You didn't have to do that man, we're kind of used to it." Thomas says after we've returned our trays in silence and gone outside. It seemed like an unspoken agreement that we all needed some fresh air after the ugliness inside. "We know how to handle idiots like that," he adds, shrugging.

Gloria rests a hand on her twin's shoulder. "Just because you're used to it, doesn't make it okay. Besides, I'm pretty sure you made your point," she adds with a laugh. "It's such a lazy insult anyway. If you're going to insult someone, at least have the decency to be creative!" Her joke breaks the tension and has us all laughing as we settle around the outdoor space beside the dorm building. She's sitting on Uri's lap on a bench, Lisa, and Elena on a bench opposite them. Thomas and Noah are pacing up and down the narrow space, while Trevor is on the ground, leaning back against one of the giant concrete planters. He pulls me to sit between his knees, my back resting against his chest.

"Call me a hobo, point out my biscuits, or that we can't dance like normal people all day long and I'll laugh with you. But seriously, she went straight for the gay? I'm disappointed," Noah says. "Pun one hundred percent intended," he adds with a wink. He stops walking with a jerk, pointing at Thomas. "Dude, you know that was just to prove a point, right?"

Thomas laughs, and points right back. "Yeah dude, I know. You're not my type, I like them tall, blonde and handsome."

"Biscuits?" Trevor asks in my ear, as Thomas and Noah get into a good-natured tussle over Thomas' comment.

"Bad feet. Bananas are good, biscuits are bad." Stretching my legs out in front of me, I toe off my flip flops to illustrate by pointing and flexing my feet.

"Hannah's bananas are to die for," Lisa points out, helpfully. "I've been offering to trade feet with her for years."

Laughing, I keep pointing and flexing, until a familiar sharp pain catches me off-guard. I can't control the hiss of pain it triggers or the way my fingers dig into Trevor's arm wrapped around my waist.

"What was that?" Trevor asks, concerned. "Are you okay?"

Angry at myself for being stupid and giving it away, I shrug. "I'm fine, a little sore from rehearsal." Glancing up, Lisa is eyeing me across the space, half-listening to whatever Elena is saying. She raises an eyebrow at me and tips her head to the side, a question clear in her eyes.

"**S**O, WHAT'S really going on?" Lisa asks as soon as we're alone in our room. "And don't tell me it's nothing. I saw you wince." I open my mouth to protest but Lisa cuts me off. "You were wincing when we went shopping with Olivia, and I saw you limping on our hike weeks ago. I'm not stupid, Hannah."

"It's just a little sore." I shrug, maybe if I keep pretending it's nothing it will go away. Manifesting and all that jazz.

"Is it your ankle? Your foot?" Lisa doesn't let it go. Knowing she's going to keep at me until I spill, I might as well get it over with.

"It's my ankle. It started hurting during dress rehearsal. I was trying to rest it over the break and it was fine. Maybe a little twinge now and then. A smidge achy at the end of the day, but it's not a big deal." When Lisa doesn't speak, I fill the silence, adding in a quiet voice. "This week has been worse, though."

"Hannah! Why didn't you tell Ms. Parker? Or at least Mr. Mike?" Lisa starts rummaging around in her drawer, hunting for something.

"What if they told me not to come?" I explain. "It was okay until now. Mostly."

Lisa pulls a tube of cream out of her drawer and brings it over to sit next to me on the bed. "I get it. It was still dumb, but I get it. Here, rub this on, I'll be right back." She hands me the tube before heading to the door. Turning it over in my hand, I can't read any of the Japanese characters covering it.

"What is this? Where are you going?" Panic that she's about to go report me flares in my chest. "Wait, I'll come with—"

"Hannah," Lisa interrupts me. "It's ibuprofen cream and I'm going to go get some ice. Relax, I'll be right back."

I hold out a hand to stop her from leaving. "You're not going to tell anyone are you?"

Opening the door, Lisa turns back to look at me. "No, *I'm* not going to tell anyone. But *you're* going to call Ms. Parker and talk to her and Mr. Mike while I'm gone. Okay?" When I hesitate, Lisa raises an eyebrow at me. "You better do it, or I will." She doesn't leave until I nod my head.

I squeeze out a nickel-sized drop of the cream and rub it gently into my ankle. The pressure of my fingers is painfully cathartic as I press into the tender spots. It doesn't take long to rub in, leaving me with no choice but to talk to Ms. Parker before Lisa gets back. Lisa doesn't make empty threats. With a sigh, I pick up my phone, ignoring all the notifications on it to open the messages app so I can text Ms. Parker.

> **ME:** Hey Ms. Parker, do you have a minute? I'm sorry, I know it's late but I need to talk to you.

My phone rings almost immediately, startling me. "Hello?"

"Hannah? Are you okay? What's wrong?" Ms. Parker's voice is anxious, making me regret my choice of words.

"I'm okay. Lisa's fine too," I add before she can ask. "I didn't mean to scare you."

She mumbles something to someone nearby, hopefully that's Mr. Mike. "That's okay sweetie. What's up then? Are you having trouble with your Black Swan pas?"

"Kind of?" I hedge. "Please don't get mad at me for not saying anything sooner, but during dress rehearsal my ankle started hurting. Just the odd twinge every so often and kind of achy at night. I tried to rest it as much as I could over the break so it would be okay once I got here, and it was okay until the other day."

"Sweetie, Mike is right here, I'm going to put you on speakerphone so he can hear," Ms. Parker interrupts me. I wait until she speaks again. "Okay, go ahead."

"Hannah, can you start over for me?" Mr. Mike says gently. "When did it start hurting?"

"During dress rehearsal."

"So that was about five or six weeks ago? Did it hurt at all while you were in New York?" I hadn't thought about that.

"No, it didn't. I noticed it the first time after dress rehearsal and it wasn't that bad, mostly aching."

"Got it," Mr. Mike says. "So, what's happening now?"

"I rested it as much as I could before I came and it was getting better. It only hurt when I went hiking one day and walked around the mall a lot. But I was trying hard to rest it, I promise." The more I talk the more panicky I am about the situation. What if it keeps getting worse? "It hadn't gotten any better or worse until this week. It's mostly achy after class with the occasional sharp pain."

"When do the sharp pains occur? When you jump? Taking off or landing? When you relevè? Does it hurt when you pliè?" Mike asks his questions in a gentle, methodical way. I guess he's pretty used to us dancers and knows how to ask the right questions.

"Tonight, I started getting sharp pains when I took off for a jump. Pliès and stepping onto pointe isn't too bad, it's jumping and going up on relevè that hurts."

Lisa tiptoes back into our room holding an ice pack while I listen to Mr. Mike. Gingerly, I wrap it around my ankle. Moments after I put it on, the cold starts drawing out the pain I hadn't even noticed. It was so constant I forgot what it felt like not to have the tight, dull ache in my ankle. Grabbing one of my leg warmers, I wrap it around the ice and tie it so I have my hands free.

Sliding my feet up the wall next to my bed, I lay back, patting the space next to me in invitation. Lisa doesn't hesitate before joining me.

"Without looking at it and maybe an X-ray, I can't tell you what's going on, but hopefully it's just a strain and a few days of rest will be all you need," Mr. Mike says, sounding concerned. "But you need to go see the therapist there, this is in no way an official diagnosis young lady."

"Hannah," Ms. Parker says, "you need to go to whoever PSB has on staff. It's important that they know you're having an issue."

I chew my lip, fighting Ms. Parker's words. If Lisa wasn't here beside me, I would be tempted to pretend this conversation never happened. But Lisa has been listening to each and every word. There's no way she'll let me get away without doing what Mr. Mike and Ms. Parker are telling me. No matter how much I want to fight it.

Lisa's already giving me the stink eye for hesitating to answer. "Yeah, I'll go tomorrow morning."

"Promise?" Mr. Mike and Ms. Parker say in unison.

"Yes, I promise." I sigh, dreading going. Almost always, the solution to an injury is to rest. I don't want to rest—I came here to dance, not waste time here sitting on my butt.

"Is Lisa there?" Ms. Parker asks, not letting me wriggle out of it.

"I'm here, I've been listening. I promise to make sure she goes to the physical therapist in the morning," Lisa answers for herself.

"Good," Mr. Mike says. "Hannah?"

"Yes?"

"I want to know what they tell you to do, okay?"

"Okay. I promise." It's late and we're all tired but there's one last thing I need to ask Ms. Parker. The thing that scares me more than anything else right now. "Ms. Parker?"

"Yes?" The concern in her voice has tears pricking at my eyes. "Do you think this is going to ruin their opinion of me? What if this makes them think I'm unreliable or injury prone?" I don't voice the last part of my thought—what if this ruins my chance at being invited to stay year-round?

There's a long pause before Ms. Parker speaks. "Sweetie, I'm not going to sugar coat this. Depending on what you do next, there's a chance that it will." I knew it. I knew I shouldn't have said anything. Too fast to sort out, half-formed thoughts crowd my brain, drowning out Ms. Parker's words. "Hannah, listen to me. Take a breath." The sharp words cut through the fog building in my mind. "I know this is difficult to hear but listen to me. What you do right now is going to be more important than the fact that you have an injury. When they tell you you're not allowed to take class for the next few days, because that's the most likely scenario, you're going to go to class and be present. You are not going to touch your phone. You are going to bring your yoga mat and do the barre exercises laying down. Do them as much like the class as possible, but modify it to slow down as needed. We've done floor barres before, you know what to do. If you can do any of those strengthening exercises you've learned…"

"The Progressing Ballet Technique ones?"

"Yes, those ones." Ms. Parker's voice is insistent. "Do as much of them as possible without being a distraction to the class. When they get to center, sit up and do all the upper body to each exercise. You're going to show that even though you have to rest your ankle you are still engaged and taking class with everyone else. Do this for every class. That's how you're going to show them that you're there to work, not get sympathy."

"Okay." I swallow hard, adjusting the ice to a different spot. "I can do that. Thanks Ms. Parker. I'll let you know what they say tomorrow."

"Please take care of yourself sweetie." She calls out a little louder. "You too Lisa! I'm glad you called. I'm going to pester you tomorrow until I hear from you," she adds with a laugh. "Lisa, you keep an eye on her, okay?"

"I will!" Lisa says, sticking her tongue out at me. "I'll try to keep her from doing anything too stupid."

CHAPTER FOURTEEN

Katy

"ARE YOU texting my girlfriend?" Hunter leans into my field of vision, blocking my phone.

"No." I don't bother to hide the annoyance in my voice. "And she was my friend first so back off." I shove at his chest so he quits looming over me. Annoyingly, he just stands up straight, arms crossed over his chest, like the freaking Iron Giant or something, blocking the sun from warming my skin. Ass.

"Are you texting *my* girlfriend?" Jack's face pops up on the other side, grinning stupidly before taking up a matching position on my other side.

Raising an eyebrow at him with a dash of "I don't care" attitude, I pull a face, desperate to keep my real feelings hidden. "What girlfriend? All the gorillas at the zoo are accounted for."

Hunter cracks up at this, which is good. I can laugh with him and cover up the very real anger that simmers in my gut and the panic I'm fighting. Don't say JJ. Please don't say JJ. I can't take losing one more person to these clowns. "As a matter of fact, no, I am not texting Lisa or JJ." I fight the wave of nausea that hits me and keep talking. "I was texting Olivia about going to class tonight."

Jack's easy grin is replaced by confusion at my words. "Bug, JJ isn't my girlfriend."

"Whatever, 'girl you're talking to' doesn't have the same ring, but you know what I mean." I grump. Putting my phone face down on my lap, I collapse back into my lounge chair. It's been unbearably hot all day, so I've come outside for a dip in the pool after lunch. For once, we are taking a rest day from training with JJ and I am determined to relax and enjoy it.

Jack shakes his head at my words. "I'm serious, Bug. We're not dating, she's *just* a friend. I'm pretty sure she has a crush on someone else, she mentioned something about liking someone but them having no idea." I open my mouth to say something, but Jack claps his hand over it before I can make a sound. "And no, it wasn't in that subtle but not at all subtle way that girls do it. She meant it was someone else."

Hunter nods in agreement. "She said something similar to me the other day, and I know she wasn't fishing for compliments from me. She likes Lisa. She stood up for her when the other girls on track were talking shit about us dating."

None of this is easing the sick churning in my stomach. Why am I so upset at the thought of JJ having a crush on someone? "Huh, and here I thought she was another one of your groupies using me to get to you." The words are out before I can stop myself.

"Groupies?" Hunter says slowly. "What do you mean, Bug?"

Do they not know? I swear we've had this conversation before.

"I mean, that for as long as I can remember, girls have been coming over here vying for my brothers' attention. It's like living in the Bachelor sometimes." Jack grins and holds his hand out for a high-five from Hunter. "The smart ones pretend to be nice to me to get in good with you knuckleheads."

Jack's offended look would be hilarious if it wasn't because of my words. "Bug, you can't be serious. They're being friendly. That's what normal people do."

Oh, my sweet summer child. Pulling my legs up to my chest, I wrap my arms around my knees to make space for them on the lounger. Hunter is the first to sit, one hand resting on my knee. "We know you've always tried to vet the girls for us, but what do you mean? Care to elaborate?" he says, jerking his head at Jack to sit down.

"When Cole was a freshman, and the girls started coming over more, I always wanted to hang out with them. I thought they were so pretty, so cool. What other fifth grader could brag that she spent the weekend hanging out with high school girls, right?"

This time Jack high-fives me. "Hell yeah! We get it, we had the same thought. Why do you think we invented Quinn Ball? So we had an excuse to hang out with Cole and his friends."

My brothers aren't giants, but they've always been super athletic, the bastards never went through that horrible awkward stage in middle school. Nope, they went from gangly kids to muscular teens overnight. I, sadly, was not blessed the same way.

"Anyway," I say, trying to get back to my point. "Most of the girls would tell me to go away, go play with my Barbies, or what-ever, and it would piss me off. So, I would find ways to get rid of the ones who made me mad. Like, telling mom who was kissing

Cole behind the bushes, or which ones I caught trying to sneak into Cole's room when they went 'looking for the bathroom.'"

"I remember a few of those," Hunter says, smiling. "I begged Dad to let us put a lock on our door after a girl walked in while I was changing. And I don't think it was an accident."

Hugging my knees tight I keep going. "I doubt you guys ever heard about them, but there were girls at school who would pretend to be my friend for a while, they'd hang out with me at recess, sit with me at lunch, until I finally invited them over after school. A few of them were dumb enough to make a beeline for you guys the second they walked in the door, some of them were smarter and would come over a few times before asking where you were. In the end, it didn't matter how long it took—they were all just tricking me into thinking we were friends so they could make a pass at one of you." I finish with another shrug and scrunch down into the cocoon of my arms and knees, my stomach roiling. "I thought JJ was different, but I guess I was wrong," I whisper into the safety of the darkness between my chest and my legs.

"Seriously, Bug?" Jack's indignant snort has me looking up at him. I'm not sure if the snort is because he doesn't believe me, but the second I see his expression I know it's because he's angry on my behalf. "I wish you'd said something. You know we wouldn't have hung out with anyone who would use you like that. Quinns stick together. You know we'd have your back."

Silent, I shrug. It wouldn't have changed anything, but I appreciate the thought. "It's okay, Jack. I thought that JJ was better than that, but I guess she was just smarter than the rest." I move to sit up, but Jack puts a hand on my shoulder, stopping me.

"Bug, I'm serious, we're friends. That's it. She hasn't flirted with me once. I assumed she had a boyfriend until the other day, she was so hands off. But she said something about being single and wishing she had someone to go out with. But," he says before I can interrupt. "She didn't say it like she was wanting *me* to ask her out." Jack falls silent and eyes me for a second. "She was looking at you when she said it. Well, you and Hunter, but we all know Hunter is happily taken and oblivious to every other girl on the planet."

"Can you blame me?" Hunter asks, grinning.

"Nope, you got the best girl out there. You and Trevor," I add. It's only after I say it that Jack's words sink in. JJ was looking at me when she was hoping for someone to go out with?

"Wait..." I trail off, my brain shorting out. Like a goldfish, my mouth opens and closes several times as I try to find words to process what I think Jack just told me. "Me?"

Jack shrugs. "Maybe? That's what I thought at the time."

"Either way, the important thing is," Hunter interrupts my frazzled thoughts. "JJ isn't in it to get to me or Jack. She wants to hang out with *you*." He pokes my forehead with a finger to emphasize the word. "So I guess there's only one question left to ask. Do you like her or not?"

Record scratch. "Do I...?" I snap my mouth closed, my mind turning the thought over. "Why are you guys so interested?" I turn it back on them, hoping to get out of the conversation.

"We figured it was our turn to make sure your crush passed inspection. Like you do for us." Hunter reaches out to punch me on the arm.

This conversation did not play out the way I was expecting. I need space, need to think about what they're asking.

I stick my tongue out at them both, playing at my usual self even if the old Katy feels a million miles away. "Can you go away now?" When shooing them away doesn't work, I push at their broad chests until they give up and head inside. It's about two in the afternoon, I can't call Lisa or Hannah, they'll still be in the middle of classes for the afternoon. And, I don't want to talk to Olivia, it's too weird.

JJ and me. Me and JJ. I turn the idea over in my mind. I've had my fair share of girl crushes over the years, but I took them as seriously as my crushes on various celebrities—fun in theory but never going to happen in real life. But why not?

I'm still staring blankly at my phone when someone sits down on the edge of the lounge chair. "I told you guys to go…"

"You want me to go?" Looking up, it's not the Weasley twins grinning at me, it's Cole. "And here I thought you'd want to hear all my deep dark confessions." With a shrug, he starts to stand but I stop him with a hand on his arm.

"No, wait! I thought you were the Wonder Twins. Stay?" I tug on his arm, pulling him back to sit with me. "Please?" I add my patented puppy dog eyes. They only work on Cole, but they work one hundred percent of the time. "I'd much rather hear about your drama than think about mine."

When he hesitates, I tuck my legs under me so I'm kneeling, hands clasped in front of my chest, batting my eyelashes. Laughing, Cole sits back down, clasping his hands between his knees, head dropping as his smirk fades. Sensing he needs comfort more than he's letting on, I move to sit next to him, wrapping my hands around his bicep and resting my cheek on his shoulder while I wait for him to speak.

"You wanted to know why I've been so grumpy."

"Yeah?" I draw the word out, not wanting to pressure him, but dying to know what he's going to say.

Cole heaves a sign, dislodging my head from his shoulder as he runs his hands through his hair. "I hate my team."

"You hate playing?"

Cole shakes his head, still not looking at me. "Maybe? I dunno. I can't stand my teammates, Katy Bug. It gets harder and harder to keep playing with them. But I have to, I can't afford to lose my scholarship."

Wrapping my arms around his waist, I worm my way under his arm so I can hug him. "I'm sorry, Coley. Why do you hate them?" He squeezes me back, resting his cheek on my head. The scruff on his face catches my hair as he talks, but I don't protest, he needs someone to talk to and I'm glad it's me.

"It's a freaking testosterone overdose, all the damn time. Everything is a dick-measuring contest. How'd you score, who you score, what shoes you wear, what you eat, what you drink, how much you drink, how hard you can party, how long you can party. It's exhausting, Bug."

"It sounds awful, Coley. But can't you just play and ignore them? There must be one or two guys on the team who aren't like that?" I have no idea. We went to as many of Cole's basketball games as we could last season, but you don't know what a person is like just from watching them play. There was a lot of what looked like friendly shoving between teammates though.

Cole's shrug tickles my cheek. "Not really. They're my teammates, Bug. It's supposed to feel like we would do anything for each other, that's how a team should be. But I swear, every time I turn around one of them is in my face, wanting to get the ruler out. It's not that I don't want to have fun, I totally do, but maybe

I was spoiled by all our years of having everyone always coming here, going to other people's places to party is so tiring, god, they are so loud and obnoxious."

That has me laughing. "Seriously? Do you not know how loud and obnoxious your entourages have always been? Why do you think I always tried to sneak downstairs to see what was happening? There is no way to drown it out in my room and do anything else." I pull away from Cole and poke him in the chest. "There must be one or two guys you can stand?"

"There are a couple of guys who I think..." Cole trails off. "But Marcus lives with them, so it doesn't matter."

"Who's Marcus? And why does it matter that he lives with them?"

"Marcus Church, our team captain. It matters because he's the worst of everyone. He's like a fucking cartoon villain—has a new girl every night, never even knows their names, barely goes to class, always has to be tough, will jump on you the second you show weakness. Total homophobe. God, I hate him." Cole's hands fist and clench as if by reflex at the sound of this Marcus' name.

If the fists weren't a giveaway for Cole's feelings, the clenched jaw and hard look in his eyes would be. "Did he..." I swallow, not wanting to make Cole feel worse, but curious. "Did he do something in particular to you?"

Dark eyes snapping to meet mine, I know I've hit the sore spot. Dislodging me, Cole hops up and starts walking away. Scrambling to my feet, my own worries gone, I follow. "Cole?"

"Bug..." He stops with a jerk, like he's hit a wall. I do hit the wall of his back, with an "oof" before stepping back. Whirling to face me, Cole wraps me up in his arms and the words tumble out of him, like he can't keep the words inside any longer, but he can't look at me while he says them either.

"There was a guy on the team my freshman year, Henry. He was great. He didn't party, didn't tolerate the ball bunnies, he was so chill, you know? An all-around cool dude. He was the captain, actually, and he was good at it. We started hanging out and got to be good friends, best friends even. I liked him." Cole's shrug trembles against me, all I can do is squeeze him back. "Turns out he...liked me too."

"Did you..." I have to stop and think about how I want to ask this. "Did you...?" My already frazzled brain can't come up with the words I need.

"Did I like him in that way?" Cole supplies the words for me. At my nod, he sighs sadly and keeps talking. "Not at first. But I couldn't stand the thought of losing him as my best friend. So, we stayed friends. He was super respectful and never made me feel uncomfortable or anything, just kept being my best friend. And I don't know, by the end of the year he was...my Henry." The shift in Cole's body language is subtle, but hugging him like this makes it easy to feel the way he stands a little straighter, less defeated at the mention of Henry's name. "Going from loving him as my best friend to loving him completely was as easy as breathing."

Was? I don't like the way Cole keeps saying his name in past tense. I pull back far enough to look up and see the far-away look in my brother's eyes. "Neither of us wanted to broadcast our relationship to the rest of the world. Henry's family is super conservative and he knew they'd never accept him."

"But Cole, why didn't you tell *us*?" I have to interrupt, not wanting him to think for a second that any of us would love him less no matter who he loved. "You know Mom and Dad wouldn't care, we'd all have your back."

"I know, Bug. I wanted to tell you guys, but Henry asked me not to because he couldn't come out to his family. And I would have done anything for him." He's still talking about Henry in the past tense and it's starting to worry me. "Marcus was his roommate. The night before school started last year, we thought he'd be gone all night—he'd been bragging about the chick he was going to bag at this fraternity party—but he came home early and, well, caught us making out on the couch." With a jerk, Cole lets go of me and walks away, scraping his fingers through his dark hair. I let him walk away, sure he'll come back in a moment. He gets to the corner of the pool and turns to pace towards me, the hurt and anguish on his face breaking my heart.

"Cole...what happened?" I ask quietly, scared of the answer.

"The asshole starts yelling and screaming about how he won't live with Henry, won't play with either of us, called us every slur you can think of plus more I won't repeat. It was ugly, Bug." I want to hug him again but he stalks away from me, so I wait until he comes back.

"Anyway, the fucker goes to Coach and rats us out. Henry gets called into Coach's office after practice the next day. Next thing we know, Henry isn't team captain anymore, Marcus is."

"But that's discrimination, he can't do that!" I growl, incensed. "There's no way that's legal, Cole."

"It's our word against Coach and Marcus. There's no way to prove it. Henry told me afterwards that Coach never said a word about being gay, just that he didn't feel that Henry was capable of 'uniting' the team, that he would be divisive, so that's why the captaincy was being taken away." Cole shrugs and somehow I can tell that this isn't even the worst part. I still haven't figured out why Henry is past tense.

"What else happened, Cole?"

"*Someone* told Henry's parents." Cole keeps talking over my gasp. "They disowned him. Kicked him out and refused to pay for anything. Not a cent. He had to drop out of school."

"And..."

"And he left me. Told me I was better off without him, that he was going to bring me more trouble." Cole's voice cracks on the last word. Rushing in, I wrap myself around him as much as I can. My own worries and confusion are forgotten as he cries against my shoulder.

I know I'm only the baby, that I can't do much more than hold on tight, but I will hold onto my brother with everything in me to keep him from cracking apart.

CHAPTER FIFTEEN

Hannah

ON'T CRY.
Don't cry.
Don't cry.

Lisa's hand rubbing up and down my back is nowhere near as calming as my mom's, but I'm glad she's here. The therapist is prodding at my ankle, her fingers searching for any tenderness while her eyes are trained on me, looking for a telltale wince. She keeps poking at me, shifting her hands around my foot and ankle. I fight to keep my face calm and not flinch, scared it's going to hurt each time she presses hard.

None of the spots she presses on the inside of my ankle hurt, there's no pain at all. But when she puts pressure on a spot to the outside of my ankle, right above where my pointe shoe ribbons would wrap around it, I can't stop the hiss of pain that escapes me.

"I take it that spot is tender?" she asks. "What about here?" She presses around the spot, feeling for something and helping me identify how large an area is sore. "Well, young lady, I think we need to get an x-ray, to be safe, but at the very least you're going to have to rest it for a few days. I'm going to arrange with the director to get you the x-ray, but I want you off it for the rest of the weekend, okay?"

"Do you know what it could be?" I ask, my voice wavering.

"Sweetie, I'm not allowed to give you a diagnosis. There are a couple of things it could be, but that tender spot is what's making me cautious. Let's get the x-ray and go from there." I know she's trying to be reassuring but her words aren't doing anything to ease the knot of worry in my gut. "Wait here for a minute while I go get some tape for it." She pats my knee before walking away to rummage in a drawer.

Turning to Lisa, I give her my best smile. "You should go to class, you can still make it if you hurry." We'd headed for the physical therapist's office instead of going to breakfast. Since it's Saturday, our morning classes start at ten instead of nine, which was very helpful for us.

"Are you sure? I can stay and go with you to the x-ray?" Lisa bites her lip. "I don't want you going alone."

"No way, you worked too hard to get permission to come. I'm not making you skip a class to come sit in a waiting room. I'll text Trevor, he should be done soon, he can come with me." Thank goodness his camp only makes them do a short workout on Saturday mornings, he'll be free the rest of the day.

"Are you sure? I don't mind?"

The therapist speaks up from the corner. "Hannah won't be alone, I'll be going with her."

"See? I'll be fine. Now go. Hurry up or you'll be late," I add, pushing her towards the door.

"Text Trevor," Lisa says as she backs out the door, worry written all over her face. I waggle my phone at her so she leaves.

"Is Trevor a friend?" the therapist asks, coming back to sit on the low stool in front of me, two rolls of tape in her hands.

"My boyfriend," I explain, watching as she pulls a long strip of white tape free of the roll. "I thought you'd wrap it?"

"Tape will do for now, love. Besides, someone used the last Ace bandage and didn't replace it." Her casual answer eases a bit of the fear in my chest. Maybe it's not as bad as I thought? "We'll know more once we get the x-rays done. I'm going to go make the phone calls needed. Can you get in touch with your parents for me, please? I need their permission to take you off-campus. Have them call me at this number." She hands me a business card before crossing the room and slipping out the door.

I waffle between texting my parents and looking around the room. We're tucked in the corner of a small gym, a row of cabinets blocking off space for a patient table and her stool, giving us the illusion of privacy. There's a treadmill, a stationary bike, and some free weights along one wall, mirrors along the second and some serious-looking equipment that I've never seen before along the third. A huge rack next to the weights has yoga balls and half balls balanced on it.

I know I'm stalling. I'm terrified of what happens next. The therapist is being so vague, I wish she'd tell me what she thinks is wrong. I wanted to prove to my parents that I was old enough, tough enough, to be out here on my own so I haven't told them anything about my ankle. But I can't put it off any longer. I pull out my phone and start typing.

ME: Hey. So, I've been having some pain in my ankle and the physical therapist here wants to take me to get it x-rayed. Can you please call her at this number?

I type in the number and wait for their response. My phone rings almost immediately.

"Sweetie?" My mom's voice in my ear has my throat closing up. "What's going on? Are you okay?" Swallowing hard, I will myself not to cry.

"So, I've been having some ankle pain off and on. It got bad last night so Lisa and Ms. Parker made me promise to come see the physical therapist here. She wants me to get an x-ray but needs your permission to take me off campus," I blurt out in a rush, trying to get all the words out before I can cry.

"Are you in pain?" My dad's worried voice has tears pricking my eyes but I swallow them down so I can keep talking.

"Not all the time, it's taped for now. It was just kind of achy, it didn't seem like a big deal which is why I didn't say anything before."

"So what happened?" My mom always knows when I'm hiding something.

"It started hurting a lot more once I was rehearsing for Black Swan. Last night it was the worst it's ever been, so now here I am." As I finish explaining, the therapist comes back into the room. "The physical therapist is here, do you want to talk to her?" I look up at her to see what she wants to do.

"Can you have them call that number for me, love? I need it to go through the official channels."

I repeat her instructions to my mom before hanging up. When the phone on the wall rings a moment later, I turn my attention back to my phone.

ME: Therapist wants to take me to get it x-rayed. When are you finished? Think you'd be able to come with me?

While I wait for Trevor's response I scroll through Instagram to see if Martin's posted anything new since yesterday. We've stayed in touch ever since the YIGP finals, sending pictures and comparing notes on the repertoire we're learning, him in New York and me here in Seattle. CBS is doing excerpts from Balanchine's Stars and Stripes for the upper division class's workshop performance. I admit I'm jealous. That ballet has always looked like such fun to dance, especially the sailors, but I wouldn't give up doing Swan Lake for anything. Swan Lake is just so perfect—everything a classical ballet should be.

Martin posted a picture this morning of him and his boy-friend Sammy in Central Park, eating ice cream and looking adorable. Glancing at my messages, I cringe at the double digit on the notifications and close the app, ignoring them for now. I don't get as many messages and follow requests as I did when Martin was posting pictures of us all the time, but it's still more than I can handle.

TREVOR: Finished and showered, I'll be there in a few minutes. And yes of course I'll come with you. Not about to let my girl go through this on her own.

Penelope Freed

ME: Thanks. I didn't want to go alone, but I made Lisa go to class.

Hanging up the phone, the therapist walks back over to the table where I'm sitting. "Okay love, I've squared everything with your parents and have your insurance information. Your mom said you had the card with you?"

"Oh yeah, I do. It's in my room. Should I go get it now?"

"That would be great. Is your boyfriend coming?"

I slide off the table, trying to land gently on my feet. Not that my ankle is hurting all that much right at this moment, but now I'm scared that with every step something is going to go wrong. "Yeah, he's on his way. He'll be here in a few minutes."

"Is he a dancer too?" she asks, curiosity in her tone. "Doesn't he need to be in class?"

I blush. "Oh no. He's attending the runners camp that's sharing the dorms with us."

"Did you meet him this summer then?" She doesn't do much to hide the skepticism in her voice, although if that were the real situation I don't think I'd blame her.

"No, we've known each other for a while. Him being here the same time as me is a coincidence." I make my way to the door, hoping to end the conversation. I don't want to discuss my love life with a stranger. "I'll be right back."

Normally, I'd take the stairs to the third floor where our room is, but something tells me that isn't a good idea so I wait for the elevator to come down.

"Hey beautiful," a familiar voice says as the door opens. Trevor holds the door for me to join him in the elevator. I step inside and immediately wrap my arms around his waist, resting my cheek against his chest. The moment his arms wrap around me I relax.

"Have to get my purse," I mumble against his shirt. He smells clean, making me want to bury my nose in his chest.

"Are you okay?" One of his warm hands strokes the top of my head, his fingers sliding between the strands. Can't I just stay here and forget about my ankle? I'm sure it will be fine. Right?

"Hannah? Is everything okay?" It's the worry in his voice that forces me to speak.

"I'm okay. I'm worried. The therapist won't tell me what she thinks it is until we get the x-ray. But then, she let me walk over here so I guess it can't be that bad, right? Maybe a few days resting it will be all it needs." I know I'm talking fast, but I can't stop myself, all the thoughts in my brain are falling out of my mouth before I can stop them.

Just then the elevator stops, the doors sliding open. Trevor follows me out into the little common area on the floor, his hand sliding down to twine his fingers with mine. "Hey." He tugs me to a stop before I can head down the hall. "It's going to be okay." He smiles crookedly at me, tucking a strand of hair behind my ear, then running his thumb along my jaw to hold my chin, forcing me to meet his eyes. "You got this. Whatever happens, you got this."

The tears I've been fighting all morning spill over and run down my cheeks when I blink. With a choked sob, all the fear I've been pushing aside hits me at once. Trevor's arms are around me, squeezing me tight before I take my next shuddering breath, but my knees don't want to hold me up. Instead of collapsing to the ground in a pile of tears, I find myself being picked up. Instinctually, I wrap my legs around Trevor's waist, burying my face in his neck, holding as tight as I can. He's making shushing noises, his arms wrapped tight around me, holding me close. I feel us move sideways before he leans against something, my knees coming to rest on whatever it is he's half sitting on.

"I'm so scared." I manage to get out. "What if something is really wrong? What if they send me home? I don't want to have a reputation as a fragile dancer, I need to be tough. I haven't even started yet, it can't be over now!" My last word turns into another sob.

Trevor lets me cry for another minute, stroking my hair and murmuring reassurances in my ear. "Hey, we need to get your stuff. Which is your room?" he says with a little twitch of his shoulder to get my attention. "We won't know anything until the x-ray, T. Before you freak out any more, let's get that done. Who knows, maybe it's not that bad?"

Pulling myself upright, I slide my feet to the ground, stepping away from the back of the couch that Trevor is sitting on, and wiping my eyes. My face is hot and gross from all the crying. Oh my god, I can't believe Trevor is seeing me like this. Sniffing, I swallow. "Right…" Crap, I just realized he's not supposed to be here, on our floor. "You wait here, I'll be right back."

Unlocking my door, I grab my purse from the chair I set it on and glance in the mirror. Oh god. My eyes are red and swollen, my cheeks splotchy and my hair is a greasy mess. Why does Trevor only ever see me when I look horrible? I should have showered this morning, but I was in too much of a hurry to get to the therapist so Lisa wasn't late for class.

ME: I'm going to the bathroom, I'll be right back
TREVOR: I'm not going anywhere.

As quick as I can, I splash water on my face, the cold water soothing my puffy eyes. I take a second to let the cold water run over the inside of my wrists while I do my deep-breathing exercise twice. It doesn't make my fear go away, but at least I feel a little calmer. Like maybe I *won't* burst into tears again at any moment.

"Ready?" Trevor asks, holding out his hand to me when I emerge, pressing the call button on the elevator.

I squeeze his hand tight as the doors slide open. "As I'll ever be."

CHAPTER SIXTEEN

Hannah

"*N*OTHING SHOWED up on the x-ray?"

"That's what they said," I repeat, holding my phone out so Lisa and Trevor can hear Mr. Mike's voice as well. We're squished on one of the couches in the lobby, heads together so I don't have to have the volume up too loud. My feet are resting on a coffee table that Trevor pulled close, the ice pack I'd been using abandoned on the table. "I'm supposed to rest it and go back to the therapist on Tuesday to get checked out again. I have my yoga mat and ball ready to go for Monday so I can do floor barre and everything Ms. Parker talked about."

"Good. Will you keep us updated on how it's feeling?"

"I will."

"And promise me you'll rest it today and tomorrow," Ms. Parker chimes in. Lisa chimes in before I can open my mouth.

"I'm keeping an eye on her, Ms. Parker. Don't worry. Between me and Trevor, we'll keep her off her feet."

And that's enough of that. "Bye, Ms. Parker, bye Mr. Mike. I'll keep you updated, promise!" I say, tapping the button to end the call. I do *not* need to talk to Ms. Parker about my love life.

"So…" Trevor drawls, fake yawning and putting his arm around my shoulder. "What do we want to do for the rest of the day? Obviously, we can't go sightseeing anymore." I wince at the reminder that I've upset everyone's plans to go check out the Space Needle and Olympia Park today.

"I'm sorry," I say but am interrupted by Gloria, Uri and the rest of the gang dropping down into the seats around us.

"So, what's the story, Hannah? How bad is it?" Gloria asks.

I look over at Noah apologetically. "They think it might be a strain. Nothing showed up on the x-ray so for now I have to take a few days off and see how it feels on Wednesday."

"Man, I hope it gets better. I had to rehearse Black Swan with Min today," Noah says. "It wasn't awful, but she's not a turner like you so, yeah…that was a bit rough."

Guilt at Noah's words, mixed with jealousy that he rehearsed without me, sours the hope I'd been feeling when nothing bad showed up on the x-ray. A couple days rest and I'll be fine. "You guys don't have to stay here with me, I can go up to my room and watch a movie or something."

"If you think I'm going to pick hanging out with anyone else over you, you're crazy." Trevor kisses the side of my head. "You guys will be fine on your own, right? You can't miss the Space Needle. It's the tall, pointy building."

We're all laughing when Becky and her friends from Six pass us on their way from the elevators. "You know, there are other people who might want to sit in the lobby sometime," she says, with a sneer. "Or did you need all these people to wait on you since you're *injured*. Hope they don't give your solo away." Becky's callus words echo in our shocked silence. "You should do us all a favor and let Min have the part now instead of dragging it out." She looks me up and down, eyes lingering on the bright purple kinesiology tape visible above the tops of my shoes. "You know she does it better than you, anyway," she adds in a sing-song as she walks away.

"Ugh!" Lisa growls from next to me. "I swear she must be long-lost cousins with Allyson," she adds under her breath.

"Lisa?" Thomas gets our attention, leaning on the back of Elena's chair. "Are you going to come with us or stay here with Hannah?"

I pat her on the thigh. "Go, go have fun. Take pictures, you know Katy will kill us if we don't send her something. This is your summer vacation too, you don't have to spend it all with me."

"Are you sure?"

This time Trevor is the one reassuring her. "Go ahead. I think we can manage to entertain ourselves." Laughing and catcalling in an attempt to break the awkward tension Becky's words left behind, Gloria leads the group out the front door. Lisa reaches back for a quick hug before following them out the double doors.

"Behave," she whispers in my ear before pulling away and hurrying to catch up.

"So…" Trevor says, squeezing my shoulder.

"So…" I say back, resting my head on him and closing my eyes.

"I have an idea, if you're up for it."

Without opening my eyes, I smile at the uncertain tone of his voice. "What's your idea?"

"First, tell me how you're feeling. You were really upset this morning, did the doctor help you feel any better?" This time he shifts away from me and I sit up. Trevor faces me, leaning one arm on the back of the couch. He uses the other arm to pull both of my legs across his lap, so I can keep my ankle elevated and face him at the same time. His hand is warm on my skin as he rubs up and down my calf. You would think that after a month of seeing him almost every day I wouldn't still be getting butterflies every time he touched my skin, but you'd be wrong. Apart from our magical first kiss a few weeks ago, we haven't had a moment alone since I've been here.

"I feel a little better. I hope that it just needs some rest. I came here to dance, not to sit and watch. And I definitely don't want them to give my solo away." I mimic his rhythm with the hand I trail along his forearm, grinning and swirling my fingers in a new pattern when goosebumps appear under my fingertips. All this touching is doing a great job of distracting me. "So, what was your idea?"

Trevor's eyes are glued to my hand on his arm for a long second, before he clears his throat and answers. "Um. I was thinking we could go to a movie? We haven't had a chance to go out on a real date yet. My car is here but I haven't used it since we've always been with the group."

I get my own goosebumps thinking about sitting in the dark with him. Unlike the last time we went to a movie altogether—January seems so long ago—this time I won't spend the whole time watching my best friend flirt with his cousin. And I definitely won't ditch him afterwards by faking a headache like I did that night.

He must be thinking along the same lines as me because he squeezes my calf to get my attention. "No running away from me this time, yeah?"

I laugh and lean forward to give him a quick peck on the lips. "I promise, I won't. I couldn't run away tonight if I tried," I add, pointing to my taped up ankle.

Trevor grins and rubs his hands together. "Bwahahaha, you've fallen right into my trap." He swings my legs off his lap and stands, reaching out a hand to pull me up next to him.

"Ugh," Someone says, walking past us, shattering the cozy bubble we've been in.

Looking around, I spot one of the girls from the other day, the ones who'd called me Trevor's boyfriend.

"Ignore them, T, they're not worth getting upset over," Trevor says, a little louder than necessary as he wraps his arm around my waist to lead me outside. Technically, I don't need the help, but I like the excuse to hold onto him, so I don't object.

"Why would you want to date one of those weirdos, Trevor?" the brunette asks. "Seriously? A *ballerina*," she accompanies this with a lame twirl and goofy face. "Bunch of prissy little princesses."

I can't stop my flinch at her words. It wasn't enough to have to deal with Becky and her gang, now I have to deal with these mean girls too? I can't win. "Come on." Not looking back, I walk through the doors, forcing Trevor to come with me since he's still holding onto my shoulders.

"T..." He pulls me to a stop once we're outside, the warm sun settling on my skin.

"Don't, Trevor. It's fine. Let's go."

Trevor insists I wait at the curb while he goes to get his car. I scroll through my phone while I wait, taking the opportunity to catch up on some of my notifications. There's another cute photo from Martin so I leave him a comment.

HANNABANANABALLERINA: NYC looks amazing! Are you dancing the Liberty Bell pas? Future El Capitan?

Scrolling through my feed while I wait to see if Martin responds, I look for anything from Katy. Hiding the pain in my ankle had me hiding from her too, even though I know she's got to be lonely. Hmmm, I wonder if she's managed to get to a ballet class yet? Last time I asked she hadn't and got defensive when I wanted to know why. Nutcracker auditions will be here before we know it and this is the year Lisa and I were hoping to get Dewdrop or Snow Queen. If Katy doesn't take class at all this summer, she's not going to get a lead of her own, I'd hate for that to happen. Ms. Parker tries to be fair, but she expects us to do the work to look good in each part, you don't get cast based on seniority alone.

There's a couple of pictures of her with her brothers, and one of her and Olivia at the outlet mall eating pretzels. I check Oliva's feed to see the same photo, plus lots of her and Tyler. There's one of Olivia, Tyler, and Jack. That gives me an idea, so I check Jack's account, maybe he has more pictures of Katy.

Before I can look for more pictures, a maroon minivan pulls up to the curb. Trevor climbs out and opens the door for me while I stuff my phone back in my pocket. "Your chariot awaits, m'lady." He bows as I climb into the front seat.

We joke the whole way to the movie theater, Trevor quizzing me on the Marvel Universe to make sure I'm up to speed for the movie. My parents would be so proud.

"You're so far away." I laugh at one point, stretching my hand across the space, wiggling my fingers at him. Laughing,

Trevor grabs the tips of my fingers and plants a quick kiss on my knuckles.

"It was my mom's car, but when she got a new one, I inherited it. You'd be amazed at how often it comes in handy to have the van."

"You know...we could have all squished in here," I muse, looking around.

"Maybe. But that first day I wanted to make sure we had an easy out in case we needed it." Trevor shrugs. "Besides, parking downtown is the worst, taking the train was easier anyway."

This car ride is so different to the last time we went to a movie when I'd babbled about my plans, trying to cover my nerves, and hurt at being used by my friend. As we pull into the parking lot ten minutes later, I can't help asking. "Did you ever think, after the first time we met, that we'd end up here?"

Trevor squeezes my fingers before putting both hands on the wheel to maneuver into an empty spot. "Do you want to know what I thought when Tyler told me what the plan was for that night?"

Nervous, I pick at a bit of fringe on my jean shorts. "I don't know. Do I?"

Trevor doesn't answer me right away, just climbs out of the car. He's opening my door before I've had a chance to do more than unbuckle my seat belt. Turning when he opens it, the late afternoon sun behind him casts a shadow on his face, making it hard to read his expression. He pulls my legs until I'm sitting sideways in my seat, facing him, my legs dangling out the car on either side of his. Trevor braces one hand on the back of my seat, the other warm next to my hip.

He leans in, his lips grazing my cheek, before he whispers in my ear. "I was really, really hoping that whoever this Olivia had set me up with would smell good. The bar was pretty low," he adds at my outraged laugh before stealing my breath with a kiss. His kiss is gentle, simply his lips against mine, not urgent but not timid. His kiss is just like him—calm, confident, and comfortable in his own skin. I'm the timid one, unsure, full of doubt that I'm worth the trouble.

When his hand slides behind my neck, pulling me closer, a fire sparks in me. My hands cup his jaw, my fingers tracing the sandpaper of his cheeks before sliding into the soft curls at the back of his neck, pulling him close in return. His tongue sweeps along my lips, with a tiny gasp I let them part. As his tongue lightly toys with mine, a warmth I've never experienced fills me, reaching for him, aching to be closer. My back arches of its own accord, my heart reaching out for his. Our hands tangled in each other's hair and our lips the only points of contact between us. It's not enough.

"Hannah," Trevor pulls back enough to whisper. He peppers small kisses against my temple, my forehead, my nose.

Please don't stop kissing me, I want to beg. I could happily drown in him right now. Can't I forget everything else and live here? In this magical space where it's just us and I don't have to worry about the future or the past or anything in between?

"We should go. Movie starts soon," Trevor says between each press of his lips to my skin.

Blinking, I drag my mind back from its wanderings. Oh my god. Heat rushes to my cheeks the second awareness of where we are comes back to me. "Uh." Actual English words fail me.

Face to Face

Chuckling to himself, Trevor presses his forehead to mine. "Trust me, I could stay here all night making out with you. But I'm pretty sure that security guard over there would ruin the fun in a few minutes anyway." He presses one last kiss to my forehead before straightening up, for the first time I notice that he'd braced one of his knees on the seat next to me.

My cheeks are still hot, but not with embarrassment, although there is some of that. When Trevor pulls back, a piece of my heart goes with him. But now there's a tiny piece of his heart wrapped up in mine. I'll keep his safe and he'll treasure mine. There's something new and tender between us that wasn't there a moment ago. Have I lost my mind? Why do I want to wrap myself as close to him as possible? Not touching him in some way is suddenly unbearable.

"Damn it. I should have dropped you off, then gone and parked." Trevor is eyeing the distance to the movie theater from where we've parked. Turning to me with an apology written on his face. "I'm sorry T, I didn't even think about your ankle."

"It doesn't hurt that much right now, I can walk." I hate the reminder of my injury, I was hoping to forget about it for a while. I slip my hand in his and take a few steps towards the theater, but he doesn't move. Looking back over my shoulder, I catch his eyes moving up my body, a speculative look in them.

Now the heat in my cheeks is from embarrassment. "What?" I ask, trying to hide the nervousness in my tone.

"How about a piggy back ride?"

"You're going to carry me over there?" I lean on my left leg, trying not to make it obvious that I'm easing the pressure on my ankle, ignoring the dull ache those few steps sent through it.

"Well, I could carry you over my shoulder." He grins. "But I didn't think you'd appreciate it." Visions of Tyler scooping Olivia over his shoulder cloud my vision for a moment before I grin back.

I wave to the asphalt in front of me. "Let's go then." Laughing, he bends down in front of me and I climb on, my legs wrapped around his waist, his hands clasped behind his back, supporting my thighs. I'm hyper aware of every inch of my body right now, where we're touching and where we aren't. I can't help wondering if Trevor is feeling the same.

"*F*ROZEN YOGURT? Are you trying to recreate our first date?" I giggle as Trevor deposits me in front of the serve-yourself frozen yogurt chain.

"I figured a do-over was in order." He pulls one of the metal chairs at the outdoor table out for me and waits for me to sit. "Who's that for?" I ask, indicating the third chair he dragged over from the next table.

His answer is to slide his hands along my leg until he picks it up, gently placing my foot on the seat of the chair. "Tell me what flavors you want and I'll bring it out here. Want me to get some ice, too?" At my nod, he goes inside to get our yogurt and some ice.

If you asked me what the movie we just watched was about, I couldn't tell you. Last time we went to a movie I was too busy staring at Olivia and Tyler to pay attention. This time...well, in all honesty we were too busy making out to pay any attention to the movie. What can I say? I'm not sorry.

Face to Face

I can't help grinning to myself as I look through my phone, waiting for Trevor. Giggling, I start typing in my group chat with Lisa and Katy.

ME: So...first real date with Trevor is going very well.

Katy answers right away, I can almost hear her.

KATY: Why are you texting us then?
ME: Trevor is getting us frozen yogurt, I'm sitting outside with my foot up.
LISA: How's the ankle?

We Facetimed with Katy earlier so she already knows about my injury. If one more person yells at me for not saying anything weeks ago, I'm going to say something regrettable right back. I get it. It's fine, it's not that big a deal. A couple days rest, some ibuprofen, and I'll be back to normal.

ME: It's fine. Trevor hasn't let me walk at all. He carried me from the car to the doors of the theater.
KATY: Awwwwwwwwwwwwww!

This is followed by a bunch of gifs of cartoons with hearts in their eyes, making me laugh.

"What's so funny?" Trevor asks, placing two overflowing cups of frozen yogurt on the table in front of me.

"Katy." I flash him the screen so he can see the gifs, before telling the girls he's back and I'll text them later.

"What are you going to do in class on Monday? Obviously tomorrow you're going to rest it some more, but then what happens?"

I take a bite of the chocolate and vanilla swirl, a piece of Reese's' and some strawberry clinging to the spoon as I swirl my tongue around it to catch the drips. Trevor's eyes are glued to me, it takes a moment for me to realize why, but when I do the blush that creeps up my neck and cheeks is instantaneous. I choke on the bite in my mouth, breaking the tension.

"Uh. Um." I cough, trying to dislodge the bit of strawberry that went down the wrong pipe, the sharp cold of the frozen yogurt making it worse. "I'll do floor barre and PBT." I manage to choke out.

"I think I can figure out what floor barre is, but what's PBT?"

Clearing my throat, I explain the basics of the program, Progressing Ballet Technique or PBT. We're the first major summer intensive to offer it, I guess Marco Bethelo spent some time in Australia last year and fell in love with it. He hired someone who learnt it from the woman who developed it down there to teach it here at the intensive. We use large yoga balls to work on pinpointing the specific muscles that ballet dancers need. I've been loving doing it three times a week all summer and can tell how much it's helped, even if my stupid ankle insists on being a problem.

We talk and eat until the sun sets. Okay, I can't lie, we kiss a little more too. Not too much though, we are in public. It's only when the ice that Trevor got for me starts dripping on his shoe through the chair that we look at the time, too wrapped up in each other to look at our phones.

"Shit. We have to go, T, like right now." Trevor says after a glance at his screen, worry furrowing the space between his eyebrows. "If I run to get the car, can you walk to the curb and I'll pick you up? Curfew is in ten minutes." Cursing some more, he takes off at a sprint. Of all the times to finally see him running, I can't even appreciate it because I'm walking so slowly.

Curfew for both our programs means we have to be inside the building by nine thirty. PSB enforces a pretty strict lights out at ten. I don't know if Trevor's running camp does the same thing or not, but if we aren't inside the building in the next ten minutes we're both in trouble.

Trevor pulls up to the curb and I speed up my last few steps to wrench the door open and slip inside, ignoring the twinge in my ankle. We're silent the whole drive back, watching the time tick over, minute by minute. Nine twenty-four. What happens if I'm late? Nine twenty-five. Will I lose my solo? Lose my scholarship? Trevor pulls up to the curb as close to the building as possible. Nine twenty-six. Would they send me home?

"Hop out. I'll go park." Trevor practically pushes me out the car door.

"But—"

Nine twenty-seven. I'm already injured, what if this the last straw?

"Go Hannah. I'll be fine, I promise." He takes off again the second I close the door. Nine twenty-eight. My heart is pounding in my chest and I ignore the pain in my ankle as I speed walk to the front door. I can't stop the worries charging through my head. This isn't like me, I don't get in trouble, period. The lobby of our dorm building glows with a soft yellow light in the dusk, the sun slipping below the horizon. Nine twenty-nine. Shafts of dying sunlight compete with the small lamps on the end tables scattered around the space, I can make out a few packs of people sitting around the lobby. Footsteps pound out behind me, moving fast.

Nine thirty. Oh god.

Hand on the door I wrench it open to slip inside. Breathing heavily, Trevor takes it from me and slides in behind me. A few heads turn our way, curious, but most people ignore us.

Breathing hard, I collapse into the nearest easy chair, head in hand while I take a few deep breaths, trying to slow my racing heart. Trevor's hand drops to my shoulder and squeezes as he perches on the arm of the chair next to me, chuckling between his harsh breaths, heat coming off him. He must have sprinted hard to get to the door behind me.

"Are you okay?" he asks, after a few seconds, amusement lacing his words.

My mouth still dry from the fear of being caught, all I can do is shake my head. What am I doing? I don't go out late and break, okay bend, the rules. Trevor tries wrapping his arm around my shoulder to pull me close, but I hold my spine rigid. Olivia doesn't call me a goody two-shoes for nothing. I'm a rule-follower, I don't do things that might get me in trouble. He tugs a little harder, trying to pull me close, but I stay rooted to the chair.

"Hannah?" Any hint of amusement is gone from his voice now. He slides off the arm of the chair to squat in front of me, peering at my face, worry written all over his. "Beautiful, what's wrong? We made it, it's fine."

"Barely," I manage to whisper. "We barely made it. Trevor, I..." I trail off, not knowing what I was going to say, but knowing I would have regretted it the moment I did.

"What? Talk to me T." His hands on my knees are so warm. Funny how fifteen minutes ago I thought I might wither away if we weren't touching in some way. Now I just want him to go away for a minute so I can think. "Hey, it's okay. We're okay. Look." He nods his head toward the front door where one of the chaperones from my program is locking the door. "See, we made it with a whole minute to spare," he adds with a grin.

Disappointment in myself, and a touch of anger at Trevor, bubbles up in my gut. "We made it because they were late. I can't believe that happened. What if we had hit one more red light? What if there had been traffic? What if being late meant they sent me home? We were already breaking the rules by not having anyone over eighteen with us. Being late guarantees they would have found out." My fears spill over, the word vomit impossible to stop. "I came here to dance, not flirt."

The second the words leave my mouth I want to take them back. Hurt fills Trevor's eyes before he looks away from me, biting his lips for a moment before exhaling heavily. "Trevor, I...I didn't mean it like that." I stumble over the words, not sure what I meant to say.

"Stop, Hannah. I get it. Ballet is the most important thing to you. I knew that already. I'm going to go to bed, before you say something else you might regret in the morning."

Pushing to his feet, Trevor stands in front of me for a moment, those normally warm brown eyes holding my gaze. I hate that the light has dimmed from them. Tears prick at the corner of my own, a lone tear spilling down my cheek. "I'm sorry," I whisper, not bothering to wipe it away.

"I know you are. I'm sorry too, I should have kept a better eye on the time. But I'm still going to bed now." With that he drops a kiss to the top of my head and walks away.

What have I done? Was that our first real fight? How could one of the best nights of my life suddenly taste like ashes in my mouth?

It's only when I walk towards the elevator myself that I notice who else is still in the lobby. That pretty brunette from the running camp is sitting on one of the couches, headphones in, scrolling through her phone. She doesn't say anything as I walk past her, just smirks. At me? At her phone? I have no idea. But it adds yet another thing to my never-ending list of things to worry about.

Getting in trouble for being late.

My reputation.

Will I keep my solo?

The glares and catty remarks.

The fight with Trevor.

My ankle.

So much for a summer of ballet and nothing else.

CHAPTER SEVENTEEN

Katy

"YOU WANT to tell me why you're channeling your inner Cersei today?" JJ drops off the monkey bars next to me, arms crossed over her chest, glaring. I hang from my arms a moment longer, glaring back, enjoying the burn in my shoulders. Swinging my legs up, I wrap my feet around the edge of the monkey bars and pull myself up to straddle them. "Seriously Katy, why are you being such a bitch?"

"I'm not being a bitch, JJ. I'm concentrating." I grind out between my teeth. "I have a lot on my mind, that's all." It's the truth, what else does she want from me? I scramble on hands and feet across the top of the monkey bars to drop down on the other side and sprint my way over to the mini rock-climbing wall going up the side of the play structure. "Shouldn't you be doing this too? The race is this weekend you know."

"Katy."

I ignore her, concentrating on finding the next grip and pushing myself up the wall.

"Katy," JJ calls again.

Okay, it's about five feet off the ground, but I'm using my imagination that it's the twenty feet it'll be this weekend. If I've learned one thing from Hannah it's how to visualize the scene I'm going to perform in. I pull myself over the top of the wall, landing feet first on the platform behind it.

"KATY!"

This time JJ is right in my face, her hand on my upper arm, forcing me to look at her. "What the hell? You've been ignoring me all morning, what's wrong? Did I do something?" Her eyes bore into mine, anger and hurt written all over her face. Normally, right now I would tease her about the halo of curls around her face, or the sweat gathering in her temples and dripping down the sides of her neck.

On a normal day, I wouldn't be wondering what it would be like to trace the path that drop of sweat is taking with my nose, to see if it would give her goosebumps.

I also wouldn't be thinking about Cole and his broken heart and why he's been such a grouch all summer. I wouldn't be worried about Hannah's ankle or Lisa's reaction when she finds out I haven't taken a ballet class all summer.

But mostly, if everything was normal, I wouldn't be sweating my ass off, running next to JJ, working out next to JJ, trying to keep up with JJ, while simultaneously being at total ease and painfully self-conscious about every move I make. All this second-guessing myself has me biting my tongue and silent, instead of my usual chatty self.

"It's not you JJ. I guess I have a lot on my mind." I lie, it is her. It's one hundred percent her, but not in the way she thinks, JJ hasn't done anything wrong, I'm the one who needs to figure myself out.

"Wanna talk about it?"

No. Nope. No, I do not, thank you ma'am. It's not that I'm uncomfortable being attracted to her. But...I didn't know how attracted to her I was until Jack pointed out that she wants to be my friend, or maybe more than a friend. And how the heck do I be *just* friends with someone when I kind of want to kiss her? But also, *do* I want to kiss her? I do. I totally do.

It's like when you're performing a lame skit in class and you don't know what to do with your hands, except instead of my hands I don't know what to do with my heart. Now that I've realized it, I can't un-feel it and I don't know how to act normal around her anymore.

God, I'm a mess.

"Katy?" JJ pokes me in the shoulder and my stomach flutters. "Seriously, what's going on with you? Are you nervous for this weekend? You're gonna be awesome. It'll be fun, I promise."

I go with a half-truth. "Yeah, I guess I am nervous. Last workout nerves, maybe?" We have five days until the terrain race, today is our last real training session so we can be rested and ready on Saturday morning. Hunter and Jack had some top-secret twin business to attend to this morning, so it's just me and JJ. I'm pretty sure they're buying themselves matching outfits for this weekend.

"Are you going to dance today? Or do you want to hang out? We could go catch a movie or something? I need to go back to school shopping, want to come with me?"

"Um, sure, I guess?" After we settle a time for her to pick me up, JJ sprints off to her car, leaving me to walk home alone. Panicking, I text the one person I think may be able to help me.

ME: Help?!
OLIVIA: Do I need to bring a shovel, money, or Starbucks?
ME: JJ wants to go shopping, what do I do?????????
OLIVIA: Um…you go shopping? Why the crisis?

Do I tell her? This is Olivia, she's been my friend for years. This doesn't change anything. Right?

ME: Because Jack pointed out that she might like me. And then I realized that I like her and now I don't know what to do with myself. Do I act normal? Do I flirt? HOW DO I FLIRT?!?!?!?!?!?

I toss my phone from hand to hand while I walk home from the park to shower, waiting for Olivia to answer. The fact that no answer is coming makes me more nervous with each step. It never occurred to me that she would judge, hell, she's the one who openly admits to having a crush on Zendaya.

As I round the corner to my street the reason she hasn't answered is obvious. Olivia's sitting on my front step, waiting for me.

"Hey. It sounded like maybe this emergency needed more than a text." She waves her hand down the street to Tyler's house. "I was at Tyler's anyway."

I can't even fake being cool about any of this anymore. A glance at the driveway reassures me that Jack and Hunter are still out, both of their cars gone. "What do I do?" It's the only question I can ask.

Olivia opens my front door, dragging me inside. "First, you shower. You stink."

Face to Face

An hour later I find myself walking into Target with JJ, freshly showered, boosted by Olivia's pep talk and less frantic about the whole thing. Olivia's advice, shouted through the door as I showered, to "calm the fuck down and go for it," while not exactly on par with Ms. Parker's advice helped more than I would have thought. Or maybe it was the fact that Olivia didn't seem surprised.

I follow JJ to the aisle with all the school supplies, assessing my feelings as she charges through the crowd, intent on finding the exact right set of highlighters. I let her tell me all about the AP Physics class she's taking next year. I'm sure Hunter and Lisa will be in the class with her too, but I'm not ready to think about school starting again. It's the beginning of August, I have a few more weeks until I have to think about it, and I'm determined to enjoy it. I can't help my gut feeling that everything is going to change after this summer.

I don't know how, but I'm sure everything is going to be different.

Squatting down to paw through the bin of highlighter packs at our feet, JJ pokes my butt with her phone. "Are you sure you're okay?"

"Yeah. Sorry. I'm distracted today."

"These highlighters? Or those ones?" JJ points to a different rack.

"I have no idea, aren't they all highlighters?"

JJ eyes me critically, raising goosebumps all over my skin. "Haven't you ever looked at Hunter's notes? I snuck a peak at some of his notes in Chem and I want to do that color thing he does."

I snort, hoping to hide my momentary panic at JJ's admiration for Hunter. She's talking about his notes, quit being an idiot. "Hunter doesn't share his notes. Only with Lisa," I add. Inside, I wince at how possessive I sound. This is JJ, she knows how besotted Hunter is with my best friend, why am I being so defensive? But Lisa doesn't need to put up with any more drama at school next year. Maybe JJ can help me head off the mean girls I know are going to have something to say.

"I know he doesn't. I snuck a peek in class one day. You know, the day Lisa was trying to hide from him by sitting next to me?"

I have no idea what she's talking about, I wasn't exactly gracious about the idea of Hunter and Lisa dating at the time. Don't worry, I've learned my lesson. JJ tells me the whole story while we shop, recounting all the flirting they'd done in class. She must have known Hunter was taken long before I knew there was anything going on. I don't know why that hurts my feelings, but it does.

We bump along through Target, grabbing a bunch of clothes to try on as well. I can't help it, there are dresses with pockets. It's a rule, if you find a dress with pockets you have to try it on to see if you can fit a baby dragon in it. Doesn't everyone have that rule? Just me?

Emerging from my dressing room to model the romper I found, I stick my hands in the giant pockets and lean back, striking a pose for JJ's approval. "You look gorgeous." She claps her hands and grins. "I'm so jealous. I can never find a romper that fits—I'm too tall." JJ steps up next to me, her hip bumping my waist as we look at ourselves in the mirror at the end of the narrow hallway. I meet her eyes in the mirror and for a second, the world fades. My lungs freeze, my heart stops, there's just us, looking into each other's eyes in the mirror.

"You should get it, you look hot," JJ breaks the spell with a grin.

"Yeah?"

"Yeah."

CHAPTER EIGHTEEN

Hannah

THIS SUCKS. Min does the final developpé in second, her leg so high it almost touches her ear. I can never get my leg that high. At this rate I never will. I let myself wallow in the depressing thought while Min and Noah relax and listen to the notes Mr. Bethelo gives them.

"Hannah?" I snap to attention at my name. "Will you come try this part?" Marco indicates I should come join in. Rolling to my feet from my position on the floor, I make my way across the studio to Noah. "Stay flat, but can you do that last developpé for me please?"

I take my position next to Noah, gripping his hand as I draw my left foot from the floor, past my knee and unfold it to my side, my arm mimicking the line it makes. I keep my leg there and undulate my arm, like the flap of a swan's wings.

"Hold it for a moment, please." Marco calls out. "See Min? See how Hannah is matching the line of her leg to her arm? Not whacking it up to her ear, it's two parallel lines." Oh. I guess I won't tell him that I'm getting my leg as high as I can right now. "Now, Min. You try it again."

And once again, I'm replaced.

Angry at being forced to watch, I walk back to my yoga mat and sit down, using the yoga ball for a chair. They can't stop me from working on the upper body. I'm not going to let a bit of rest stop me from improving. Stupid ankle. Aware that I'm being irrational, I can't stop myself from mentally critiquing every move Min makes as they run through the pas de deux with the music one more time, even as I'm busy doing all of the upper body in my corner of the room. She has lovely extensions, but she doesn't have the control she needs for the more difficult turns. Not that I'm perfect, but my struggles have more to do with trusting my partner than control.

I've been a bubbling pot of anger ever since Saturday night. After what should have been a wonderful, sweet date with Trevor, it ended on a sour note and I haven't been able to shake off my anger ever since. I spent all day Sunday in my room, watching Netflix while Lisa worked on some study guide her parents made her promise she would finish by the time she got home. I guess she's been putting it off to hang out with me.

Trevor texted a million times to apologize, I responded, but not very enthusiastically. I know I'm being horrible, but I can't seem to help myself. It got worse when Lisa and I went down to the dining hall for dinner and he was sitting at a table with a bunch of people from his running camp. He looked at ease with them, laughing and talking. Lisa took one look at my face and stuffed me back in the elevator, promising to bring me a sandwich.

What is he even doing with me?

The question has been gnawing at me for the last two days. Combined with my anxiety to get back on my feet, and irritation at my inability to dance right now, I'm a mess.

Finishing the rehearsal, Noah wanders over to me as I tidy up my mess. "Hey, how's the ankle?" I know he wants me to get back on my feet as well. He told me at breakfast that Min is a difficult partner.

"It feels fine today. I didn't want to stop, but Marco made me." I dutifully rested my ankle all day on Sunday, Monday, and Tuesday. This morning I was allowed to take most of our morning ballet class and about half of all the rest of our classes today. I haven't been allowed to jump or put my pointe shoes on yet. My ankle is aching and tired, but I haven't felt a sharp pain all day. I'm not counting the one when I stood up too fast in the contemporary class. Or the one at lunch when I tripped over someone's dance bag between tables. I wasn't dancing, they don't count.

Noah waits until everyone else has left the studio, taking my yoga mat from me before he speaks. "Hey. Do you want to mark through it once with me before we go to dinner? I don't want to forget the way we do it."

I eye the empty space. No teachers to tell me to stop, to take it easy, to rest. Noah grins at me, he gets it. "Give me two minutes to put my pointe shoes on." I say, dropping my bag and everything else to floor.

"Are you sure you should do that?" Noah sounds dubious but I don't care. I need to do this. I need to make sure I still can.

"Heck yes! I'm dying to do it, besides, what's the point of practicing it without my pointe shoes on? You know it's completely different. Go get the music ready." He takes off to plug his phone into the stereo system. "And Noah—don't you dare tell anyone. Lisa would freak if she knew."

He grins at me from across the studio, taking his place on stage left while I take my place opposite on stage right, ready to come flying in on the music, the sly, seductive Odile, imitating the shy and sad Odette. "My lips are sealed." With that he presses play and we take off. I ignore the ache in my ankle as I land the first jump, instead focusing on the power in my legs and the sharpness of my movements. The whole first section is on my good foot, I brush my leg back behind me in attitude with a sharp cock of my head, reveling in the almost satirical imitation of Odette's movements. As much as I love the soft and desperate movements of the White Swan, Odile's attitude matches my own anger and frustration right now.

As we run through, it becomes clear that there are two spots that are going to give me trouble on my bad foot. There is a series of saut de basques from either corner that mean on one side I'll have to jump off my bad foot while brushing the other and turning in the air. The other is the supported fouetté sauté we had trouble with when this all began.

"Hey Noah?" I stop dancing halfway through, letting the music play on. "What if we switched the fouetté to the other side? Then I would be taking off from my good foot." Noah jogs over to pause the music while I work backwards from the starting point of that section to see if we would need to adjust anything else to make it happen.

"Do you think we can?" he asks, walking back.

I shrug. "Why not? Professionals change little things all the time to suit their strengths. That just happens to be my strength right now. It would be super easy, I think. We would have to run to the right instead of the left to start, it's an easy fix. Come on."

I pull him to the opposite corner and we walk through it, figuring out which hands to hold and which way we're turning and lifting. "Hey, that's easier for me with that arm," Noah says after we try one of the supported jumps. "It feels more coordinated too. That is so much better." We slap our hands together in a high-five. "Teamwork makes the dreamwork, baby!"

Laughing, I head to the starting position so we can try the new side with the music. Noah cues up the music, then heads back over to me. "Okay, once with the music then we need to go. I'm starving." Laughing, we hit our mark and let the music catch up. We pull it off without a hitch. Jumping off of my good leg is so much easier, I go flying up into the air, Noah's hand holding mine secure, his other hand pushing up against my hip. For a moment I'm weightless, the anger I've been tamping down floating away.

Grinning, we collect up our stuff, turning off the lights as we leave. I leave my yoga mat and ball in the studio since we'll be back there for our first class in the morning. Walking down the dark hallway with Noah has me nervous about getting in trouble, but no one notices us. We slip into the dining room and grab some food, thankfully no one passes by to make any snide comments. Feeling a little more like myself, I follow Noah to the table where our friends are already sitting, plates empty.

"How was rehearsal?" Lisa asks as I sit opposite her.

"Good." I shovel a bite of food in my mouth so I don't have to give any details. Looking around the table, the person I wanted to see the most is conspicuously absent.

Swallowing, I ask, "Where's Trevor?"

Lisa grimaces and points to a table behind me. Trevor has his back to me, sitting at a table full of guys I don't recognize. "He saw you weren't here and decided to go sit with them." Lisa shrugs. "I'm sorry."

"It's okay. It's my own fault. I need to talk to him, but I'm nervous," I admit. "How was your rehearsal?" Lisa's been called to almost as many extra rehearsals as Noah and I have, the difficult Cygnets dance proving to be a challenge. After all the pros and cons lists we made, neither of us considered that we'd be put in one of the highest levels of the intensive and all the extra dancing it would mean. It would have gone on our pro list, for sure.

I keep eating while Lisa fills me in on her own rehearsal. It sounds like a real struggle with the Cygnets, trying to get everyone to remember all the precise heads. I'm glad I only have myself and Noah to worry about. She's in the middle of telling me what went wrong on their last run though when her eyes go wide and she stops speaking.

"What?" She shakes her head. "Lisa? What's wrong?" I follow her gaze over my shoulder and turn to see what has her so flustered. A group of girls has descended on the table where Trevor was sitting and are busy squishing themselves into the group. Since there isn't a lot of space, half of them are sitting on the laps of the boys.

Including Trevor.

Every ounce of happiness I had mustered from dancing with Noah vanishes. My heart cracks as the girl sitting on him flips her long, carefully curled brown hair over her shoulder, her hand resting on his shoulder. I see all this in a moment before tears fill my eyes and I push to my feet. I have to go. I have to get out of here.

Half blind, I grab my bag and start walking towards the elevators. I can't look. I should have expected something like this. I knew everything was too good to be true. Trevor belongs with someone like that, someone who understands his world better than I do. Someone who is here, not a thousand miles away.

"Hannah!" Lisa rushes up behind me. "Hannah, wait. Maybe it's not—"

"Lisa. I can't right now. Not with everything else. I need to go." The elevator doors open right away and I step inside. I risk one more glance across the foyer towards the dining area. Trevor is on his feet, jogging towards me, but I let the doors close before he can get there.

My phone buzzes before the elevator can get to the third floor. It keeps buzzing as I walk to my room, but I refuse to look. Not until I'm safely hidden away in my room. I slip inside the door, throwing my bag on a chair and myself on my bed, face buried in my pillow as hot tears soak into it. Why is everything falling apart now?

I let myself cry for a moment before digging my phone out of my pocket to see the messages I know are from Trevor.

TREVOR: Hannah, it wasn't what it looked like, I promise. I swear, I don't know that girl.

TREVOR: TT, please talk to me. Please. I'm so sorry about everything, you have to believe me. Those girls appeared out of nowhere. I told her to move, I didn't want her touching me, I promise.

TREVOR: I'm not going to stop texting you until you respond. I let you have space after Saturday, I knew you were upset, but I miss you. I need to see you, I need to talk to you. Please.
TREVOR: Come on Hannah, please talk to me. Tell me what's going on. Talk to me, that's what we do, right?

Fingers shaking, I ignore Trevor's messages for a minute and call someone who isn't going to ask me about my ankle, who isn't going to look at me with sad eyes and definitely isn't going to ask me about Trevor.

"Hi!" Katy's voice in my ear is so normal. I pull a deep breath into my lungs so I can speak.

"Hey," I manage to sound almost okay.

"What's up? I was about to call Lisa and see how your day went."

I grab a tissue and try to silently blow my nose. "It was okay. They let me do barre and part of class today. Did you go to class today?" I've been bugging Katy about going to class since she got back from her big trip. I'm sure Ms. Parker wants her there.

"I didn't," she sighs. "Don't yell at me." I let Katy's voice wash over me explaining about some workout she did with JJ, willing myself to calm down, to pretend I didn't see what I saw, to ignore the buzzing of my phone against my ear. I'm sure it's more texts from Trevor but right now, I can't deal with it.

"Katy?" I interrupt. "What is more important than going to class? You're not pulling an Olivia and doing nothing are you?" I'd much rather focus on being annoyed with Katy than upset over Trevor and my ankle.

There's a pause on the other end of the call, accompanied by another buzz against my ear of incoming texts. "Um, excuse me?

I was *just* telling you what I was doing. And for your information, there are plenty of things in life as important as going to class. It's ballet. It's not life or death. Geez." Great, now I managed to piss off Katy. I can't win tonight.

"Sorry, I didn't mean it like that, Katy. It's been a rough day." I sigh, swinging one leg up in the air while I speak, enjoying the stretch in my hamstring.

"You called me," she points out. "You want to talk about it?"

"Not really." I'm about to elaborate when there's a knock on my door. "Hey, someone's at my door, I gotta go. Talk to you later?"

Katy heaves a sigh. "Yeah, I'll call Lisa. Bye."

Swinging my legs off the bed, I make my way over to the door. That can't be Trevor can it? He's not allowed on my floor. I know he came with me the other day, but he wouldn't do that again. Would he? Especially when everyone is around after dinner? Who else would it be? Gloria?

I pull the door open, not sure who's going to be on the other side. A brunette I don't recognize is standing there, hand on hip, looking smug. There are more girls I don't recognize with her. "Um, can I help you?"

"Are you Hannah? The one who's dating Trevor Stanley?" Who is this girl and how does she know who I am? Movement down the hallway catches my eye, I glance over in time to see Becky disappear around the corner.

"Yeah..." I draw the word out. "Why?"

"I thought you'd want to see this." She holds out her phone to me, a picture on the screen. Lisa and Trevor are sitting next to each other on one of the couches in the lobby, Trevor's head on her shoulder. "I guess even the picture perfect ballerina can't keep her friend from stealing her man. What a pity." She smirks before tucking her phone away. "I just thought you'd want to know."

Um, what the heck is going on? "Why are you telling me this? I don't know you."

"Oh, I thought, you know, girl to girl, you'd want to know. I mean, if *my* boyfriend were cuddling up to some other girl and letting other girls sit on his lap, I would hope that *someone* would be kind enough to tell *me*." Her saccharin-sweet tone and exaggerated words should make me want to laugh, but the razor's edge I've been balanced on all week, trying to keep calm and focused instead of freaking out about my ankle, has left me with zero ability to laugh this off.

"What the hell is your problem? Did I do something to you?" I snap. Between my ankle, Trevor, fighting with Katy and now this, I'm done. There isn't one drop of patience left in me for this kind of pettiness, I don't even know this girl's name.

The brunette turns back, smirk still in place. "Trevor should be with someone like me, not some prissy little good girl. You'll never understand him in the way that I could, you have nothing in common. Quit taking our boys and stick to your own kind. That is, if you can find one who likes boobs instead of balls." I'm numb with shock at the venom coming out of this girl's mouth. "Or do you even have boobs?" She eyes my chest while the rest of her gang titters behind her. I recognize her now as the girl who made the awful homophobic comment the other day. Did they set this whole thing up on purpose? "Maybe you'll be fine, since you don't have boobs anyway."

Her words are so unexpected that she's walking away before I can formulate a response.

"Hey!" I call down the hall. The whole gang of them turns back to look at me. The sight of their beautiful, flowing hair swinging as they turn in a group, a flock of swans ready to protect their queen, has me shrinking back against the frame of my door. I can't compete with that. Maybe they're right, maybe Trevor should be with someone like her. Didn't I just think that earlier today?

"What?" The leader stares me down from the hallway, daring me to talk back. The fight goes out of me in an instant. Deflated, I slip inside my room and shut the door on their laughter. It doesn't matter if they set the whole thing up to mess with me, I have nothing left to fight with.

Flopping back onto my bed, feet up on the wall, I catch a whiff of myself. Nose wrinkling, I should shower, but instead I unlock my phone.

> **LISA:** Hannah, nothing happened with Trevor and that girl. I saw the whole thing, he pushed her off a second after you saw it. He didn't even know you saw until then. He's really upset down here, I think you should come talk to him.
> **TREVOR:** TT, please, I'm begging you, come talk to me.

There are a couple more texts along the same lines, but they all boil down to Trevor begging me to come downstairs and talk to him, and Lisa letting me know she's staying in the lobby with him for a while, hoping I'll come down too.

I should go talk to him. Set up or not, I owe him an apology. But first I need to clean up. I can't eat humble pie smelling like a locker room.

REVOR DOESN'T notice me at first, his head down looking at something on his phone screen. Lisa is the one who looks up from her phone and sees me first. "Hey," she says, nudging Trevor with her elbow. "I guess I'll go upstairs?"

"Yeah, we're good. I'll be up later," I tell her, eyes glued to Trevor's. He reaches out to take my hand, running his thumb across my knuckles. I suppress the shiver it sends down my spine, doing my best not to melt into a puddle on the floor. "You want to go outside?" I nod my head towards the main doors. I don't want to have this conversation out here in public, not with all these groups of people scattered around. Who knows who they are and who they might talk to?

"Of course, whatever you want, Han." Trevor keeps hold of my hand as he gets to his feet. Giving me time to pull away, he loops his arm over my shoulder, pulling me into his side. His sigh of relief against my side would be funny if I wasn't such a wreck from tonight's emotional rollercoaster. I slide my arm around his waist to take the weight off my ankle as we walk, hoping he doesn't notice. Maybe running the whole pas full out wasn't the smartest move, but it felt so good to be able to dance again that I don't care.

Silent, we step outside into the warm air, the setting sun casting golden light across both our faces. "Hannah, I'm—"

"Trevor, I'm—"

As our words crash, we freeze. Trevor clears his throat, pulls me two steps away from the door to a patch of dying sunlight and turns me to face him, hands on my shoulders. "Han, do you believe me that nothing happened? I promise, nothing did. And I'm so sorry about Saturday night." I'm mesmerized by the pleading in his brown eyes, the sharp line of his jaw and straight nose. The light catching the different tones of brown and gold in his curls. He's studying my face the same way I'm studying his.

I don't want to tell him about my confrontation with the girls from his program. Am I afraid that he'll believe them? A little. Am I worried that he'll say something to them and make it worse? Definitely. Am I terrified, deep down in a dark little space in my heart, they're right and he would be better off with someone who understands his world better? Absolutely.

Do I have the strength to push him away? Not a chance.

"I believe you. And I'm sorry for overreacting on Saturday. We didn't get in trouble. Getting mad at you for something that might have happened, but didn't, is silly." The moment the words are out of my mouth Trevor has me crushed against his chest. I slip my hands around his waist and let him take tonight's worries away. They won't be gone forever, but for tonight, I'm content to let him hold me and chase my anxious thoughts away.

I try to lean subtly to my left, to take my weight off my right ankle, but he's paying too close attention to let me get away with it. "Is your ankle bothering you?" When I don't answer, he swings me up in his arms and carries me back inside, depositing me on one of the couches with instructions to stay there while he gets some ice.

As we sit together in one of the overstuffed armchairs, watching videos on his phone, do I notice the looks from the other girls hanging around the lobby? Yes. Am I going to say anything about it? Nope. Hoping they'll go away if I ignore them, I snuggle into my boyfriend's side and tune them out.

CHAPTER NINETEEN

Katy

ME: You're sure it's not hurting you?

HANNAH: I promise, it's fine. I'm allowed to rehearse my pas, but staying flat so it's just the lifts. Which is probably a good thing since that's what I was having the hardest time with.

I DON'T KNOW how much I believe Hannah, but I haven't been able to get her or Lisa on the phone or Facetime tonight so texting will have to do. I let myself stay mad at Hannah for twenty-four hours, but after she apologized and Lisa filled me in on the drama they've been having with the track girls, I decided to take the high road and let it go. Yawning, I pull my clean clothes out of the dryer to take them back to my room.

ME: are the other girls still giving you a hard time? Do I need to come up there and bust some heads in? Say the word and I'll get my gang together.

I debate between sending a gif of Taylor Swift's Bad Blood video or a pack of hunting lionesses before sending the lionesses.

The last two days have been a blur of running in the mornings with the boys, swimming with JJ in the afternoons, and going to dance with Olivia in the evenings—Ms. Parker was happy I finally made it to a ballet class. She didn't say a word about me not being there all summer which made me feel worse, but by the end of class I remembered why I love it.

> **HANNAH:** they still suck, but whatever. What can they do? At least they've stopped adjusting their bras every time I walk past them.
> **ME:** they seriously did that? Wow, and I thought the plastics here were petty!
> **HANNAH:** Hahaha. Yeah, Lisa noticed it first, but after the fifth time I got the message. But then Noah, bless him, asked one of them if they dropped crumbs down there. It was pretty great.

I laugh to myself, picturing the scene. I don't want to be there for all the classes, god I'm so glad I'm not, but I wish I could be there for all the other stuff. Their little gang of new friends sounds so cool, I'm sad I'll never get to meet them.

> **ME:** Noah sounds like a hoot. I think he and I would get along.
> **LISA:** You and Noah would definitely get along. If he and Jack were ever in the same state I'm not sure we'd all survive.

Face to Face

Dumping the clean clothes on my bed, I load up the next pile and take it to the garage to throw in the washing machine, my phone tucked inside the waistband of my pajama shorts.

> **HANNAH:** Yeah, he's not on the same level as Jack, but he has the same vibe. We miss you, can't wait to see you guys. Lisa is dying to see Hunter again. Are you ready for your race? We need pictures!
>
> **LISA:** Can you blame me? Five weeks is a long time.

An idea starts building at Hannah's words. I wonder...

> **ME:** I'm sure I'll have pictures, my parents are coming and you know my dad will take a ton. My mom is too worried. Pray that I don't die. I'm going to eat all of my favorite foods in the next 24 hours, in case it's my last chance.

Ha! I crack myself up sometimes. A half-formed idea starts to take shape in my mind. I'd have to talk to my parents, and probably convince Cole to come too. I should convince Cole first, then my parents might not say no. The gif of a woman stuffing her face with food Hannah sends has me giggling as I move a load of wet clothes from the washer to the dryer, pulling out the leotards and hanging them up to dry.

> **ME:** Did I tell you that Cole decided to join us?

I'm taking full credit for the fact that Cole has been much less grumpy since we talked. He even played Quinn Ball with us yesterday. The whole gang was over, the football team, the cheerleaders—minus the bitch squad—me, Cole, JJ, and a few other people. Without the mean girls around, I actually had a great time. Maybe it was because I knew I had Olivia and JJ in my corner, maybe it was because for once I didn't care about what anyone else thought of me.

> **HANNAH:** That's good, did you ever figure out what was wrong?

I'm not going to out my brother so I hedge my answer.

> **ME:** He's been having issues with his teammates. I guess some of the guys on his team are super toxic and homophobic.

Hannah takes a while to write her answer, I'm hoping that means she has a juicy story to share, not that she's weirded out by my answer. You'd have to be a particularly horrible kind of person to be immersed in the ballet world and have an issue with anyone being queer.

> **HANNAH:** That's awful Katy, I'm sorry. Do you ever forget that people like that exist? I kind of did. Sharing the dorm building with them has been interesting. I never realized how sheltered I was until I came here. It's so different from home.
> **LISA:** Agreed. I never realized just how white everywhere else is compared to home.
> **LISA:** I miss my mom's rice balls.

She's not wrong. Our safe little suburb has Korean, Persian, Ethiopian, and any other kind of food you could ever want on every corner. And a ballet teacher who never comments on our weight, yells at us, or compares us to each other? Yeah, you could say our lives have been sheltered, but not sheltered from experiences, sheltered from some of the ugliness of the world.

HANNAH: It doesn't matter how "cool" you are in PSB, like Gloria and Uri, the runners will always see all of us as dorks. Trevor is the only one who's made friends with any of the dancers. And the other runners give him a hard time about it. It doesn't matter that Uri drives a motorcycle back home in Israel, or that Noah is also on his school's varsity baseball team. It doesn't matter that Elena is from freaking Cuba.

LISA: We're all ballet nerds to the runners. And the gay comments? They're like a Lifetime movie or something. I didn't think people like that were real.

Cole's face when he told me about Henry flashes in my mind. I hate this Marcus dude, I hope I never meet him because it will be ugly if I do. JJ's face flashes in my mind too. I should tell my friends about her—I don't know why I haven't. But I've never talked about my crushes before, at least not the ones on people we actually know. Hannah's "no boys" rule squashing the odd discussion. I debate how to bring it up as I carry a load of clean clothes up to my room.

HANNAH: I can see why Cole would be grumpy with a team of people like that. Your family is so awesome it would be hard to go from that to being surrounded by a bunch of toxic dudes all day long. Did I tell you Trevor yelled at a bunch of them when they called Gloria a beard behind her back? And before you say anything, yes I realize how great he is and that I was dumb for being mad.

Respect for Trevor floods through me. I guess I have to like him now, no more teasing Hannah about his habit of sending her a hundred texts in a row.

ME: I'm going to go then so you can go hang out with your amazing boyfriend. I'll send you guys updates so you know when to come to my funeral.
LISA: You better!
HANNAH: Night!

"Hey Bug?" Jack sticks his head in my room, as I'm dumping my clean laundry on the bed to fold it and put it away.

"What's up?" I look up from sorting the multiple shirts and socks in my hands.

"Just checking on you. Are you nervous for the race?" Jack leans in the doorway, watching me refold the tank in my hand.

Am I nervous? "I'm not nervous about the race. I think we're going to kick ass." I leave it at that, hoping Jack won't be like he always is and get in my business. He's the nosiest person I know.

"So, what *are* you nervous about then?" Damnit.

"Who says I'm nervous?"

"You folded the same shirt three times in a row," he points out.

With a sigh, I put down that shirt and start rolling up a pair of tights. Finally going back to a ballet class the other day reminded me how much I love it. I'm planning to get to at least a couple more classes before summer is over. If nothing else, it's a couple of hours that forces me to stop thinking about JJ. "Honestly? I don't know why I'm nervous."

"Katy Bug, it's going to be fine. We got you. You know Cole, Hunter, and I won't let anything happen to you." Right. Dingbat here doesn't believe that I'm not nervous about the race.

"Jack, I'm not nervous about the race. I promise."

Jack watches me pair up some socks in silence. "Is it JJ?"

I freeze, my heart racing in my chest. Deliberately, I pick up another pair of socks and roll them up. "Why do you ask?" Meeting his eyes, I have to know. "Do *you* like her? Is that why you're so determined for us to be friends?"

"What? No." Jack starts to explain. "She's cool, I like her, but I don't *like* her, like her. She's like a sister to me, or one of your ballet buddies. I thought you would need a friend since Hannah and Lisa were going to be gone all summer."

"Like a sister?" I can't help asking.

"Yeah, Bug. Like a sister. Besides, I know for a fact she's not interested in me that way."

I toss the leggings I was folding in a pile, frustrated. "Why do you and Hunter keep hinting that you know something I don't? It's so annoying. Both of you keep acting like you know some secret about whoever it is that JJ is interested in. All these stupid hints and insinuations, like I'm supposed to trust that for once in my life a girl might want me more than you two? I'm not stupid, I know that's not true." My voice is getting louder, a tight sensation in my throat warning me that tears are coming any minute. "Stop, whatever it is you think you're hinting at please stop. I'm just the goofy sidekick in everyone else's story. And it's fine. Really."

I turn my back on Jack, shoving the folded laundry into my dresser drawer, not bothering to separate it. A sniff escapes me before I can stop it, wiping the lone tear that rolls down my cheek.

"Bug, I—"

"Go. Please." I don't turn around, listening for the sound of Jack's footsteps retreating. He closes my door with a quiet snick as he walks away. I throw myself down on my bed, hugging one of my giant pillows to my chest, willing myself not to break down crying. Why do I even want to cry? This is so stupid. I have nothing to cry about. I just miss my friends, right?

They're off meeting all these interesting new people, getting to do pas de deux and learn all these cool dances and I'm stuck here with the boys, trying to fill up the days of nothing with meaningless time killers. I suppose it hasn't been nothing, the training sessions with JJ have been fun, I'm probably in the best shape I've ever been in, the definition in my arm muscles is pretty amazing.

JJ called them Michelle Obama arms. Which is badass.

So why am I so upset? What am I even upset about?

I ignore the voice in the back of my head that desperately wants to know which mysterious person JJ has a crush on. It's not me, so why does it matter? My little crush on her doesn't change the fact that she has to be interested in someone way cooler and smarter than me.

Not wanting to be in my own head anymore, I pull out my phone to distract myself. For a split second. I wish I had some kind of homework to do, something that I needed to get done so that I was forced to stop thinking the same things over and over again. But only for a second, I don't really want to do homework.

Face to Face

Unlocking my phone, I ignore all the notifications and start scrolling through my apps, looking for something to keep my attention. A soft knock sounds on my door before it opens to admit my mom. "Mija?"

I pat the bed beside me and scoot over to make room for her. "Hi Mom." She sits down next to me, holding up her arm for me to curl under. Yes, I'm sixteen and I still cuddle with my mom. It's our thing, you can't shame me into not enjoying it. When I was little, this was our nightly ritual, after my brothers were in bed, my mom would come sit on the bed with me, cuddled up. At first she would read me a story or two before tucking me in and saying goodnight, but as I got older it started to become the easiest time to talk, just the two of us. Two women in this house full of testosterone.

I don't know if any of my friends realize how much of their lives my mom knows from our late-night chats, or how much of my advice for them is really from her, from the good advice she gives me to pass along. "I noticed Cole has been much more cheerful the last couple of days."

I sigh, of course, she wants to talk about my brothers. I shouldn't be upset, our chats have always included comparing notes on the boys, but tonight, I'm tired of being in everybody's shadow.

"Yeah," I hedge, not sure how much my mom knows. She always finds ways to get our secrets out of us. It's magic. "He was telling me about some of his teammates the other day."

"Me too. I met that Marcus boy after one of their games. I didn't like him."

I smile, it sounds like she may know almost as much as me.

"Yeah." I flex my bicep. "He better hope he never meets me and my new guns in a dark alley." Getting a laugh from my mom is the best. So many of my best jokes have been met with a smile, even though her eyes sparkle in amusement, getting a full laugh from her is an accomplishment. "Did he tell you about Henry?"

Her chest lifts and drops in a sad sigh under my head. "Yes. I hope that they can reconnect. I told him that his Henry would always be welcome here." She squeezes me tight. "All my children are always welcome in my home, no matter what. We have space. And if we run out of space, we can make more space."

"I'm going to miss him when he goes back to school," I say, knowing my mom feels the same way.

"Me too, Mija. Me too." We sit in silence for a long moment before she speaks again. "It's been a long summer for you without Lisa and Hannah here. Do you miss them?"

How does she read my mind like that? Silent, I nod my head against her. "It's been cool hanging out with the boys so much, but yeah. I miss them."

"You've had JJ and Olivia. But it's not the same, right?"

"Right." She doesn't say anything, so I keep talking. "It's been fun trying something new, something that's not ballet. I like all the training with JJ. But then, once I went back to class again this week, I realized how much I loved doing that too."

"You can love more than one thing." My mom's voice is gentle. "You don't have to do one or the other. You can do both."

Her words explode like a bomb in my mind. Is it that simple? That I can just do both? I can workout like I did with JJ because it feels good? And I can also dance and enjoy class and seeing my friends, because it feels good too?

"You don't think that Hannah and Lisa would be mad at me? We weren't exactly nice to Olivia when she joined the cheer squad." Thinking back to how we'd excluded Olivia from the group isn't pleasant. I know things are fine now, but I'm still ashamed of how I treated her.

My mom strokes my hair for a moment, her fingers soothing away my worries. "I think you've all grown up a bit since then, yes? I don't think they would be mad at you. None of you are the same people you were six months ago. I think you should give your friends more credit than that. True friends will be happy for you as long as you're happy."

"I don't want to quit dance." I need to make sure she understands that. "I don't want you to think you wasted your money or anything all those years."

"Mija, it made you happy, that's all that matters." My mom chuckles. "We don't expect your brothers to be professional football players or basketball players do we? Those are the things that made you who you are, our wonderful children. They taught you things that are important, they gave you friendships that have changed your life. All this is true, right?"

"Of course Mom. But—"

"You've never said you wanted to be a dancer. So, what do you think you want to do?" I'm surprised by my mom's next words. "I saw that you weren't very interested in the dance programs when we toured the colleges. If not dance, then what are you thinking?"

"Physical therapy, maybe," I say quickly. "Maybe. I'm not sure. It's a lot of school."

Mom squeezes my shoulders and kisses the top of my head. "I think that would be wonderful, if that's what you want. You've seen your brothers and your friends get injured, I can see you being very good at it one day. But you don't have to decide today."

"Thanks Mom."

She squeezes me once more before swinging her legs off the side of my bed. "Goodnight, love you."

"Love you too."

CHAPTER TWENTY

Hannah

*S*HAKING THE bottle as silently as I can, I spill four little brown pills into the palm of my hand, popping them into my mouth as quickly as I can, hoping no one notices. I wash them down with a sip of water before tying the ribbons on my pointe shoe. The dull throbbing in my ankle barely registers in my mind, it's the sharp stab of pain I can't ignore as I roll my feet in circles, waiting for everyone else to get their shoes on. Lisa is in the middle of the studio, rehearsing one of the trickier transitions in this contemporary piece with her partner.

"You ready?" Noah appears in front of me, holding a hand out to help me to my feet. "How's the—"

"It's fine, I'm fine." I force myself not to snap at him. If one more person asks me how my ankle feels I might lose it. All I want is to dance. Dancing is the only time I'm not thinking about it. Praying that the ibuprofen I took kicks in soon, I follow Noah to the middle of the studio and wait for everyone else. We're rehearsing the contemporary octet, it's me and Noah plus Lisa and her partner James, and then two couples from Eight. Marco Bethelo himself choreographed it to Philip Glass' *String Quartet No. 3*, and it's one of the most beautiful things I've ever learned.

The eight of us slide and wash across the stage, getting closer and farther apart with each step. The little trills of quick violin notes match the thrill in my soul as I spin across the stage or in Noah's grasp. The smooth ebb and flow of the notes as I'm lifted high in the air in an arabesque by Noah and James, floating above the world before I come spinning and falling down, caught in the cradle of Noah's arms.

He told us there is no story to this dance, but between the music and the movement I like to imagine we are the embodiment of all the times your soul wants to explode from your body—it doesn't matter if it's from happiness or sadness. Those days you can't keep everything locked inside anymore and it has to come out somehow. Maybe it's a day you stay in bed and cry under the covers, or when you smile so big it hurts, screaming in pain or screaming in laughter, it doesn't matter. As I twist and spin and step and leap through this music with everyone else, making and breaking beautiful shapes, I let all of those feelings wash through me.

Trevor's fingers brushing over my cheeks as I look into his eyes.

Fear overwhelming me before getting the x-ray on my ankle.

Butterflies in my belly standing in the wings in New York, Martin by my side.

A dark cloud descending on me after the competition, not wanting to dance, not wanting to do anything.

Landing that perfect pirouette.

My brain racing off into a million anxious, fragmented thoughts.

The feeling that I'm an imposter, looming over me every time I step into an audition.

Seeing my name next to the Black Swan pas de deux, knowing I earned the chance to dance it.

Shock at the venom spat at me by the athlete girls, for doing nothing except being in their way.

Each time we run through the dance I go to that place in my mind, letting it all leak back out through each sweep of my fingers, the placement of my head, and trust in my partners. If nothing else, it pushes the pain in my ankle to the back of my mind, a place I can ignore it, pretend it doesn't exist.

"Lisa!" Marco calls out in the middle of our third run-through. "Really let yourself fall back here, James will catch you." She's held straight up in one of the boy's arms, James behind her, and throws herself backwards, falling into a catch and a spin, her legs piking up, then opening into a split as James spins her. They finish spinning with a slide to the ground, rolling past each other before standing and joining the rest of us at the back of the studio. It's one of my favorite parts. I wish Hunter could see it, he'd be so proud to see how many times she's being featured in different dances.

A week from now we'll be doing this on stage, no more rehearsing. One more week to soak in every bit of this experience I can. To learn everything I can, to pray that they ask me to stay for the year-round program. One more week with Trevor. Is it terrible that I'm not sure which I'll miss more? Dancing here or seeing Trevor every day?

The final notes fade out at the end of this run through as we spin off the stage. "Good," Marco calls out, the signal we can relax and catch our breath. "Hannah, can I speak to you for a moment?"

I look at Lisa, panic clawing at me. She gives me a small smile and a jerk of her chin. Walking over to Marco, I pull a deep breath into my lungs, still winded from dancing.

"How's your ankle feeling?" he asks, eyeing it. "I noticed you didn't mark anything today. Is it strong enough for that?"

"It's fine. A little sore." I downplay the pain, no way am I telling Marco that it hurts the same as it did last Saturday. It did feel better after the days I rested it, but since I've started dancing again, it's back to the constant dull ache, especially at night. The throbbing makes it hard to fall asleep, but I'm managing. "I'm good to keep dancing, I promise." I can ignore the occasional sharp pangs. Maybe a little more than 'occasional' at this point. The rest is background noise.

"Hannah, you don't need to be a martyr, you have a whole career to think about. Wrecking your ankle now for a summer workshop isn't worth risking the rest of your future." Marco looks around to make sure no one else is listening in to our conversation, everyone else is busy chatting or getting a sip of water. "I promised Leslie I'd keep an eye on you, are you sure you're okay?"

Under any other circumstance, I would be thrilled that Marco freaking Bethelo was taking such a keen interest in my well-being, I'd even be thrilled that he talked to Ms. Parker about me. But not when it comes to babying me and running the risk of him sidelining me now. Since there's no classes on Sundays, I'll rest it again tomorrow, but I only have six more days of dancing left. There will be plenty of time to rest my ankle once I get home to California. "I'm fine, I promise," is all I trust myself to say without sounding like I have an attitude.

Marco starts to walk away from me, letting me off the hook with a brief check in, but he turns back after a step or two. "Hannah, there could be a spot for you here in the fall. *If* you're in good enough shape to take it." With that bombshell he walks away, leaving me stunned.

Noah sneaks up behind me and grabs my hand to twirl me under his arm. "What was that all about?" I pull my hand back and step away. I never would have imagined it, but the closer Trevor and I have gotten, the easier time I've had in pas de deux class. Maybe because I can feel how different it is when Trevor touches me versus when Noah or any of the other guys do. Or maybe it's that I've gotten more comfortable in my own skin. But right now, I don't want to celebrate anything with Noah. Marco is dangling a chance to stay here year round like a fat carrot in front of me. I have to show him that I'm serious about my dancing, that I won't let anything distract me from it. Not pain, not classmates, nothing.

"Nothing, he was checking in to see how my ankle was feeling. I'm fine, before you ask." I poke his side. "You asked me five minutes ago, it was fine then and it's fine now."

Fortunately, we only have a few minutes of rehearsal time left, just enough to practice one or two small things, before we're dismissed. "Ugh, I need a shower so bad," I tell Lisa as we pack up and head out the door. "Are you going to stay or are you going to go out with the gang?"

"Actually, I think I'll stay here, I'm exhausted. Want to call Katy in a bit and see how the race went today? I'll text Hunter and see if she's awake from her nap yet." Laughing, I follow her to the elevator, pulling my phone out of my pocket as I walk to check for messages.

As much as I was hoping for a message or two from Trevor, I'm not surprised when there aren't any. Since the running camp is finishing this weekend, they're holding a mock meet to test their progress from the last four weeks. Luckily for me, it's open to the public for observation so that's where I'll be spending my day tomorrow. I'll have to take a lesson from Katy on how to cheer for my boyfriend.

There are some pictures from Martin of him in his El Capitan costume. CBS is having their end of workshop performances this weekend. I send him back an encouraging message. I know he's hoping to be invited to stay here in the US as badly as I want to be invited to stay here in the fall.

Lisa drags me to the elevator. "Come on slowpoke, quit looking for texts from your boy, let's go shower and call Katy."

CHAPTER TWENTY-ONE

Katy

M Y STOMACH churns as I follow my brothers through the crowd, sweat trickling down my back, dust and dirt tickling my nose. The sun is already beating down on us, already almost ninety degrees. JJ walks besides me, her quiet and calm attitude keeping me from puking in the nearest trash can.

Bless my parents for getting up at five this morning to drive us, we all slept the two hour drive to get here. JJ's shoulder is surprisingly comfortable. "Did he ever respond to your message?" She leans in to whisper in my ear, careful to make sure my brothers don't hear us.

Grinning, I nod my head. "Yesterday. He couldn't promise, but he said he'd try. Don't say anything." I mime zipping my own lips, and in a moment of bravery, I mime zipping JJ's as well. My fingers barely brush her lips but even that sends sparkles of excitement through me. JJ's eyes open wide at my action, for a split second I could have sworn she started to purse her lips. No, that's just wishful thinking. She does grin and poke me in the stomach, her fingers toying with the knotted strips of fabric at the side of my shirt.

"Come on slow pokes," Jack calls, the three of them a dozen yards ahead of us. Jogging to catch up, we take spots in the little space they cleared. "Does anyone know what time it is?"

Instinctively, I reach into my pocket, but of course it's empty. None of us have our phones on us since we'll be getting wet and muddy as soon as we start the race. JJ glances at her wrist, she's got one of those heavy-duty running watches. "It's seven fifty-three. We have time." Our heat doesn't start until eight fifteen so we take the time to stretch and warm up while we wait for the groups before us to get lined up and sent on their way.

I adjust the wristband with my number on it and pull my socks up more securely. I know how to prepare for a show—perfecting my makeup, smoothing back my hair, getting pointe shoe ribbons tied. Those are the things that calm my nerves, the routine of preparation, the comfort of finding something to use as a barre and going through plies and tendus, swinging my legs and stretching. All of this is similar and yet so different. It's close enough to my normal to feel manageable, but different enough to have me second-guessing everything I'm doing.

Were the double French braids a good idea? What about my socks, what if they slip inside my shoes as I run? The underwear and sports bra I'm wearing feel wrong—my brain is used to feeling this kind of pressure when I'm wearing tights and a leotard, not somewhat normal clothes. Looking at my brothers and JJ, we're all dressed in old clothes, with the exception of the bright pink matching shirts Jack and Hunter organized for us, even my parents are wearing them. When they pulled them out to show us, JJ and I burst out laughing at the hot pink color. "We wanted you to be comfortable," Hunter had said, with a wink. "Besides, I think we're all secure enough in our masculinity to wear a hot pink shirt." Again, I'd laughed, even if I couldn't help glancing at Cole. His genuine grin as he pulled the shirt on reassured me that he was in on the joke as much as anyone. I still catch him looking sad when he thinks no one is looking, which is what prompted my top-secret plan, but at least he isn't quite so grumpy these days.

Finally, it's time to line up with the rest of our heat, there's maybe fifty people corralled between temporary fencing, a big sign ahead of us proclaiming this the starting line. Glancing around, I spot my parents standing on the hill to our left, they won't be able to watch the whole race, it winds through and around this wide open space, but they'll watch as much as they can and meet us at the finish line. My mom gives me a thumbs up, ready to play her part in the plan.

"Okay gang, are we ready?" Cole's voice breaks through my nerves. "We stick together, we get through this as a team, right? Agony of De Feet forever!" He finishes his pep talk with a deep roar, Jack and Hunter joining him, JJ and I adding our own yells to the mix. Jostling in the crowd, Cole maneuvers behind us, sandwiching JJ and I between him and the twins.

As I scream, my heart thumps and heat rushes through me. I bounce up and down, shaking my hands and pumping my elbows. Suddenly, I don't miss all the prim and proper whispers of backstage. I add a few more whoops to the noise of the crowd as the race announcer gets us ready to begin. Someone slaps my butt. Turning to glare at Cole, he holds his hands up and mouths "wasn't me" before grinning and nodding his head towards JJ.

I slap her butt in return and earn myself a grin and a wink as the announcer starts his countdown. "Three…two…one…GO!" The crowd shuffles forward at a slow jog, with the exception of a few guys at the front of the crowd who take off at a sprint. The cloud of dust kicked up by the runners in front of us has a fine layer of dirt already sticking to my sunscreen-tacky skin.

"Let's go!" JJ shouts in my ear, before darting into an opening beside Hunter, taking the lead from him. Laughing, I follow, grinning to myself at the chorus of protests from my brothers. They can be as protective as they want, but JJ and I got this. I chase her to the first obstacle, a giant set of monkey bars, suspended over a muddy pit. JJ climbs up next to me and we take off, swinging from bar to bar. My hands burn from gripping the metal, my shoulders pulling and stretching as I shift my weight from one arm to the other. I pump my legs to help gain momentum near the end, my lungs burning in my chest. People are shouting encouragement to us from the other side, even as other racers fall into the mud beside and behind us. I tune out the distracting grunts and splashes, focusing on my goal of making it to the other side.

With a triumphant yell, I swing my legs forward to set my toes on the bar at the finish. JJ is already there, waiting for me, hand held up waiting for my high five. Looking back, Jack and Hunter are already swinging across, grinning, and yelling encouragement to each other. "Should we wait for them?" I ask, nodding my head in their direction. Cole is following behind Hunter on the monkey bars, a streak of mud already decorating one cheek.

JJ watches them for a moment. "Nah. They'll catch up. Come on!" Jumping down off the bars she reaches a hand back for me. Taking it, I jump down and run with her past the slower racers ahead of us. My heart pounds in my chest, my lungs burn, and the hot August sun beats down on my skin. I'm a warrior, a hunter, Diana loping with her hounds through the forest, JJ by my side.

Army crawling beneath a field of ropes, we grit our teeth against the mud being kicked up by the racers in front of us. Swinging across a water filled trench on a rope, my hands and shoulders strain from the effort to hold on until I'm across. Carrying a bucket filled with rocks for twenty-five feet slows us down enough for the boys to catch up. JJ's crow of triumph at seeing the buckets of rocks has me reaching out for her before I know what I'm doing. At the last second, I turn it into a high five, instead of whatever else my heart wanted to do in the split second I wasn't thinking.

"Hey Bug, you got a little mud on you," Jack's voice interrupts our groans as we put the heavy buckets down on the other side of the marked area. Casually setting his bucket next to mine, he has my head locked under his elbow before I can get away. Fighting to get loose, I push and tug at the thick bicep curled around my head as the sound of footsteps gets closer. A yelp from Jack as he lets go tells me that JJ at least has my back against these overgrown boys.

"Took you long enough, I thought you boys would never catch up," JJ teases as Cole and Hunter stride over to us, wiping their dirty hands off on their shorts. "Are we ready for this one?" She points at the twenty foot wall and suspended rope climb looming ahead.

"Hell yeah!" Jack lets go so he can lead the way, the rest of us falling in line behind. I'm wet, exhausted and have mud in places it definitely shouldn't be, but I'm having the time of my life. The rest of the race is a blur of burning arms and legs, hauling myself over obstacles, pulling JJ or my brothers after me and splashing our way through the course.

"Come on," I shout as we clear the last hurdle. All that stands between us and finishing is a few dozen yards and a narrow trench full of water. Laughing, I grab JJ's hand and pull her with me, leaping over the trench with an awkward grand jete as she long jumps over it beside me. Jack, Hunter, and Cole are waiting for us on the other side, hands held out so we can all cross together. I don't even care how ridiculous we must look, holding hands as we cross the finish line together like a freeze-frame ending from a made-for-tv movie. I've never felt this satisfied or alive.

Sucking air into my lungs, I walk a few steps forward so I'm not blocking the finish line, but not paying attention to where I'm going. It's only when someone grabs my shoulders and spins me around that I notice the medals hanging around my brothers necks. JJ is the one who turned me, a medal hanging around her own neck as she grins at me. "You forgot the best part," she says, holding out the medal hanging from her hand. "Come here."

I duck down so she can loop the ribbon over my head. As I straighten up, she leans forward and presses a kiss to my lips. It happens so fast, if I didn't catch the shock on her face matching my own, I wouldn't believe it happened. Neither of us has a chance to say anything before Jack and Hunter are pulling us away from the finish line and towards our parents.

What just happened?

Whatever it was, I want more.

I don't have a chance to dwell on it before my parents come into view, grinning and clapping. But it isn't my parents that my eyes fixate on. It's the tall black man standing behind them, a shy smile on his face. An anguished cry of "Henry?" from behind me is the only warning I get before I'm pushed to the side in Cole's hurry to get to him. I can only look for a moment before the raw emotion on both their faces has tears blurring my vision and a blush heating my cheeks.

"You did good, Mija." My mom gingerly kisses my temple, one of the few spots on my face that *doesn't* have mud on it. "Here." She hands me and JJ each a wipe from the pack of baby wipes in her hand before going off to fuss over Hunter and Jack.

"Here, let me do it," JJ says, taking the wipe from my hand before I've had a chance to do more than swipe it down one cheek. Tenderly, she cleans the mud off my face, holding my chin with one hand, her fingers burning my skin. Or maybe that's my own blood boiling at her touch. Or maybe it's the really, really hot weather. My eyes closed, I let myself drift in the sensation of her touching my face, my hands floating up to hold onto JJ's waist, not caring who might be looking or what it might mean. All I know is, the butterflies in my stomach are the best kind and I don't want her to stop.

"Fuck yeah, now that's a finish line I'd like to see!" JJ freezes at the crude words and accompanying whistles coming from behind us. Whirling, I spot a group of twenty-something guys coming up the finishers chute behind us, fist-bumping each other and leering at us. Before I can formulate a response, I'm shoved behind the wall of my brother's backs.

"Are you serious, asshole? They're in high school," Cole yells, menace lacing every word. "I dare you to say One. More. Word." Cole punctuates each word with a menacing step towards the group of guys who throw their hands up and back away, muttering.

Embarrassment floods through me and I stumble away from JJ, retreating to the safety of my parents. The next few minutes are a jumble of awkward apologies and clearing throats while we decide what happens next. Jack saves us all by declaring he's starving and if he doesn't get fed soon, we'll all be sorry. Knowing that isn't an empty threat, we head to the car to grab the change of clothes we each packed so we can go get some brunch.

By the time we're cleaned up, changed, and driving to the nearby diner for a big greasy breakfast, a silence has fallen between us that I don't know how to break. Cole rides with Henry, leaving an empty seat between JJ and I in the back row. It might as well be the Grand Canyon for all I know how to reach across it.

I let the chatter in the car fill the silence between JJ and me. It's not until we're all sitting at the booth, menus in hand and the conversation turns that I speak up. "Hunter, did you talk to Lisa yet?"

"Not yet. They have rehearsal for another couple of hours." It's easy to tell from the way he's memorized their schedule how much he misses her. I mean, I miss them too, Hannah and Lisa, but I don't think it's been quite the same.

"I wish I could see their workshop performance," I tell him, as the waitress places waters in front of all of us. The sight of the ice-cold water has me reaching for it and gulping it down. All four of us are too busy chugging the water down to keep talking.

"Why can't you see it?" Henry asks as we drink. "Are they not allowed to have an audience?"

"They're up in Seattle," I say, shrugging.

"Sounds like a perfect reason for a road trip, if you ask me." Henry bumps shoulders with Cole, both of them grinning. They haven't been more than three feet apart since we finished the race. When I managed to sneak his number out of Cole's phone last week I'd hoped that Henry still felt the same way as Cole, but it wasn't until he agreed to come to the race before I'd even finished my sentence that I knew I'd done the right thing.

"Another road trip?" Jack piped up from his end of the booth.

"I don't know boys, I can't take any more time off work…" My dad, ever the voice of reason.

"Cole and Henry are technically adults," Hunter points out.

"How far is it to Seattle?" JJ asks, scrunching her face over the menu.

"It's a two-day drive," I add. "Well, eighteen hours, give ot take."

"Please Mom?" Hunter asks, knowing who we really need to win over.

"Please?" Jack and I chime in.

"I'll think about it." Looking up at the waitress hovering over our table. "First we need to order."

CHAPTER TWENTY-TWO

Hannah

"HANNAH YOU can't dance on that." Trevor stares down at me, arms crossed over his chest. "I can see the bruise from here. I'm worried, what's if it's more serious than you thought?"

I shift the ice pack a little farther over my ankle. "That's not a bruise, it's red from the cold." I glare right back from the deep seat of the armchair. "I *can* dance on it and I will. You're not a dancer, Trevor. You're not a doctor either, you don't get it."

Trevor flinches at my words but doesn't relent. "I don't get it? Pretty sure I do, T." We've had the same argument every night this week. I know he's worried about me, but he doesn't understand. I'm tough, I can handle the pain. Besides, I just have to get through this afternoon's dress rehearsal and the performances tomorrow and then I'll be able to rest it for at least a few weeks. But I have to dance tonight and tomorrow. This is my last chance to prove to Mr. Bethelo and the other teachers that I deserve a place here year-round.

"I'll ice it again tonight, I promise." Trevor drove over to have lunch with me today since I won't see him tonight. With his camp over, we haven't seen each other quite as much, but he's been coming over in the evenings to hang out and have dinner with us. "It's *fine*."

The only people I've told about my conversation with Marco are my parents. I was worried about having the privacy to tell them without Lisa hearing, but since she didn't come with me on Sunday morning to cheer Trevor on at his final mock meet, I had the chance to tell them without her overhearing. They're arriving late tonight so they can watch tomorrow's show before they drive Lisa and I home. My mom said we can talk it over once we're home, which wasn't a yes…but it wasn't a no either so I'm hopeful.

Trevor drops into a squat in front of me, reaching out for my hand. "Hannah, your ankle isn't getting better. You can't deny it." His thumb brushes across my knuckles, warming my skin. "I don't want to see you hurting." The worry in his eyes chips at the anger that's built up around my heart.

"I know. But you have to trust me, Trev. It's my body, I know what I'm doing. I'll be fine, I promise." I need him to drop it so we can stop arguing over it. He studies me for a few moments. I'm starting to squirm under his gaze when he sighs and moves to sit next to me on the chair. I scoot over to make space for him but instead of squishing me, he picks me up, turning so he's sitting in the chair and I'm draped across his lap, my feet resting next to him on the arm of the chair. Trevor resettles the ice pack around my ankle, pressing a kiss to my shin when he's done.

"How long do we have before you need to leave?" he asks, letting the argument go.

"About half an hour. All my stuff is packed and ready to go." I wave to my dance bag on the floor next to me. "I was prepared." I add with a wink.

"Good." Trevor grins and pulls out his phone and earbuds. We each put one in and settle in. We're in the middle of an episode of Teen Titans, one of Trevor's favorite cartoons, when Lisa appears, her dance bag in hand.

"Ready?" A glance at the time has me swinging my legs to the ground.

Trevor doesn't let me go right away. "You sure you're okay?" At my nod, he peers around me to Lisa. They share a look, to my annoyance.

"Guys, I'm right here. Don't do that." I wave at their faces. "I know what I'm doing, no ganging up on me." With that I drop a kiss on Trevor's cheek and stalk out the door, trusting Lisa to follow. I focus on walking without a limp as we head over to the theater on campus, even if my ankle is shouting at me with every step.

I'll rest it soon, I swear.

THERE'S AN older Asian woman we've never seen waiting in the lobby when we get back to the dorms. She's peering at each group of dancers entering the building. Something about her sets my heart racing.

"Do you know Hannah O'Brian?" she says to Gloria as we follow her inside the building. My ankle is hot and achy, but not as bad as I feared it would feel after the dress rehearsal. Since there are so many groups who all have to dance, I had a long time to rest between dances, which helped. It was easier than an afternoon of rehearsals would have been.

Gloria points over her shoulder with her thumb. "That's her, with the red hair."

The woman looks up and meets my eyes. Panic overwhelms me. Oh my god, did something happen to my parents? I haven't heard from them in a couple of hours, they've been driving through the mountains of Oregon and I haven't looked at my phone for a while. "Hannah?"

I swallow, struggling to find my voice. Lisa grips my hand tight, picking up on my fear. "Yeah? Is something wrong?"

"Is there somewhere we can sit and talk? In private?"

I look around the lobby, full of dancers wandering into the building from the theater. "I guess the dining hall is pretty clear right now?" Lisa squeezes my hand again, forcing me to look at her.

"Do you want me to hang around?" she whispers. At my nod, she heads over to one of the couches by the elevators. I lead the way, walking slowly. I only take a few steps before I can't take it any longer. "My parents are okay, right?"

Surprise replaces the stern look on the woman's face. "Oh goodness, yes. This isn't about them. I'm sorry if I scared you, that wasn't my intention."

We find an empty table and sit on either side, facing each other. Clasping my hands on the table, my brain goes into overdrive. What does she want? Am I in trouble? My leg jiggles under the table as I wrack my brain for some other reason she might have to be looking for me.

"Before you get any more worked up, you're not in trouble." The woman reassures me, reaching across the table to rest her hand on top of my own, stilling the nervous twisting I hadn't even noticed. "I'm Dr. Alicia Lee, I'm one of the sports therapists for the PSB school."

I sag in my chair, relief, exhaustion, and worry fighting for dominance in my chest. "Um, nice to meet you. What did you need to talk to me about?"

Dr. Lee takes the time to look me up and down, her dark eyes assessing me. I'm thankful my legs are hidden under the table so she doesn't see the KT tape on my ankle. "Well, I've been asked by the staff to assess your injury and your general health. My apologies for getting to you this late, I was out of town until this morning."

"Um, I'm good." I draw out the words, not sure what she wants to know.

She pulls a sheaf of papers out of her bag and lays them on the table in front of me. "I'm not going to do an assessment right now, although I do have some questions about your recent injury. Mostly I need to go over these forms with you. Some of these are forms for your parents and you to fill out and there's one your primary care doctor back home needs to sign before you come back in September."

Come back in September?

She's talking about…

"Oh my god!" I squeal at the top of my lungs, shooting up out of my chair. "Are they…I'm coming…are you saying what I think you're saying?" I can't finish the thoughts or the words tumbling out of my mouth.

Dr. Lee is taken aback for a moment at my reaction "Didn't anyone tell you the decision had been made?" When I shake my head she snorts. "Well, I guess it's understandable, it's been a busy day, right?"

Taking a deep breath, I settle back into my chair, my leg jiggling under the table for an entirely different reason. "So these are medical clearance forms?" I ask, trying to sound calmer than I feel. This is it. Oh my god. This is it, everything I've been dreaming of. I fire off a text to Lisa, letting her know she doesn't have to wait for me.

"Well, yes. But before I can give them to you, there have been some concerns raised about your injury. I would like to do a quick examination now, if you don't mind." She gestures to my ankle, hidden under the table.

"Did someone say something about my dancing tonight?" I ask as I slip my shoe off and place my ankle on the chair Dr. Lee's pulled over. She starts running her hands along my foot and ankle. She's a brave woman touching my foot after I've danced on it for the last three hours. I cringe when she bends down to look closer.

"I was told someone called the front office and left a message with the admin there." Dr. Lee doesn't look at me as she speaks, concentrating on my ankle instead.

It takes all my self-control not to jerk my foot out of her hands. Someone called and left an anonymous message that my ankle was hurt? Fury at whoever tried to sabotage my chances of staying rolls through me, leaving me a seething mass of rage. I bet it was that girl, the one from Trevor's camp. She kept eyeing me when I was there to cheer Trevor on Sunday. I wouldn't put it past her.

Or maybe it was Becky? She and the other Six girls have had it out for me from the beginning. And they were the ones who wanted me to let Min have the Black Swan pas. The more I think about it, the more convinced I am it must have been her.

Who else has the most to gain from taking me out of the show at the last minute?

Lucky for me, I'm so distracted by trying to figure out who could have called in a concern about my injury that I'm tuning out the way Dr. Lee is prodding around my ankle. I almost flinch when she presses a particularly painful spot, but I manage to hold myself still. One more day, then I'll be home to rest it for a while.

Speaking of. "When would I need to have everything signed by? I don't know when the new year starts."

Dr. Lee prods a few more spots before she answers. "The new fall session begins the Tuesday after Labor Day, so you would have about three weeks or so to get everything taken care of." She looks up, patting my ankle. "You're sure there aren't any tender spots? It's a little warm to the touch in places. I need you to be honest with me about how it's feeling. We want you to be healthy and ready to dance in September."

I nod my head. "It's fine. It's a little sore tonight after all the dancing this week, but it's not bad." I don't lie and say it doesn't hurt at all, but I'm not going to tell her the truth either.

"I can't tell if that's bruising right here." She points to a spot above my ankle bone, halfway between the side of my calf and my Achilles tendon, around the edges of the KT tape. "Or if it's the light in here."

"I'm sure it's just the light." I say quickly. Maybe too quickly, judging by Dr. Lee's raised eyebrow. "I haven't noticed any bruising," I add. I can't meet her eyes at my outright lie. I noticed the bruising this morning as I got out of the shower and deliberately covered it with the KT tape so Lisa wouldn't see it. Did I feel guilty while I did it? Yes, I did. But nothing is going to stop me from my goal when I'm so close.

We finish up, Dr. Lee explaining all the different kinds of paperwork and who needs to sign off on what. I force myself to pay attention, but the whole time I'm turning over in my mind who could have tried to get me out of tomorrow's show.

"Thank you," I say, standing up as we finish. Dr. Lee leaves me and I pull out my phone and check for messages. It's almost ten o'clock, I'll have to hurry to get upstairs before lights out. There's a text from my parents letting me know they checked into the hotel and were going to sleep soon. They sent it ten minutes ago so I hit the button to call my mom's phone, hoping they haven't gone to bed yet. I know I'm supposed to go to my room, but I won't be able to sleep without telling my parents the news.

"Hi sweetie!" My mom's voice has my throat closing up. "How was dress rehearsal?"

I swallow hard, confused by the overwhelming sadness and homesickness that washes over me at her words. "Um, good. It was good. So, I have some news."

There's a shuffling and some whispers before my mom's voice comes through again. "I put you on speaker so Dad can hear too. What's up?"

I have to swallow again to get the words out. "Well. Um. They offered me a spot here in the fall."

There's silence on the other end of the line for a long moment before my dad's voice comes on. "Wow pumpkin, that's amazing. How do you feel about it?"

Duh. "I'm so happy I could cry," I say honestly. "Um, I have a bunch of paperwork and medical forms for you guys to look through. I'll pack them in my bag tonight so it doesn't get lost." And also so Lisa doesn't see it. I don't know how I'm going to tell her. She's going to be devastated. We've always dreamed of dancing together, even if deep down neither of us was sure her parents would ever agree.

We chat some more as I ride the elevator up to my room, hanging up as the door opens on my floor. It's past lights out and I don't want to wake anyone up, so I tiptoe down the hallway. A door at the end of my hall opens and someone peers out. I can just make out Becky's sneering face in the dim lighting.

"Hmph. Not enough to be the flavor of the summer, now the rules don't apply to you?" She mutters as I pass her on the way to my room. That last bit of venom is more than I can take.

"I know it was you who called the front office about my injury. Do you think I would let a little something like that stop me from performing tomorrow?" I snap at her.

"Call the office? I don't know what you're talking about."

"Don't lie to me Becky, I know it was you."

"You're delusional. I never called anyone. I have better things to do with my time that obsess over a red-headed, skinny bitch who couldn't pull off Odile to save her life," Becky sneers before closing her door.

I don't want to believe her. I want to think that it was her who called the office. But she looked genuinely surprised at my accusation. Maybe it wasn't her?

It couldn't have been Lisa. Could it? She wouldn't do that to me, would she?

Opening our door as quietly as I can, Lisa's worried face is the first thing I see. "Is everything okay?" she asks the second I'm inside.

I lock it behind me and toss my phone and the stack of papers from Dr. Lee on my bed, sitting with a sigh. 'Yeah. That was one of the school therapists, she wanted to check my ankle again before tomorrow." Guilt at not telling her the whole story eats at me, but I need to know if it was her.

"Well that's good that they're making sure you're okay. You are okay, right?"

"Yes, I'm fine. All checked out." Do I take a shower now or in the morning? I'm so sweaty from rehearsal, but I'm so tired.

"What's with the papers? Is that some kind of physical therapy thing?" She starts to reach for the stack, but I twitch it out of her way, shoving it into a zippered pocket on the outside of my suitcase.

"Something like that yeah." I'll shower in the morning. Sleep is what I need. "Did you talk to Hunter or Katy?"

"It was so weird, I tried to Facetime both of them but neither one would pick up. Hunter called me back but it sounded like he was downstairs watching tv with Jack and Cole so we didn't talk long. Katy never picked up her phone."

Speaking of phones. I check mine to see if I have any texts from Trevor. Of course there's a few. "I'm going to go to sleep. Night Hannah." Lisa reaches up to turn off her light. In the almost darkness, I take my phone into the bathroom to read my texts while I wash my face and change.

> **TREVOR:** Hey beautiful, wanted to see how dress rehearsal went. How's the ankle holding up?
>
> **TREVOR:** I'll be up late so feel free to respond. Any news?
>
> **TREVOR:** Did you know that stress fractures can get misdiagnosed as a sprain or a strain? I've spent way too long on the internet searching for this kind of stuff. Please tell me to stop looking up symptoms. According to all of these websites you're probably dying.

TREVOR: TT, I hope they did a good x-ray on your ankle. Also, the internet is a dark and scary place. Will you hold my hand?

Normally, I would get a warm fuzzy from his texts, but tonight I don't have the patience for them. My mind turns over all the possibilities as I get ready for bed. Someone made a phone call to the front office trying to get me pulled from the performance tomorrow. If it wasn't Becky, who was it?

CHAPTER TWENTY-THREE

Katy

*E*VERYTHING IS so green here, it's like the Emerald City. And the trees are so tall. It makes me feel claustrophobic, the way they loom over the road. We stopped for lunch in Portland an hour ago. Cole and Henry are in the front seat of Mom's Suburban, taking turns driving. Well, everyone except me has taken a turn at driving. Even though I got my license last week, none of the boys will let me take a turn.

I guess I should say that JJ hasn't driven either. But then, it's not her mom's car so it doesn't count. Although they let Henry drive, so what do I know? Everyone who *can* take a turn at driving has. Except me. Just another one of those "Katy is the baby" annoyances. But I can't help squirming with happiness as we pass a sign saying "Seattle–47 miles." So close.

After days of working on our parents, we came up with a plan they would agree to. Cole, Henry, Jack, Hunter, JJ and I piled into the Suburban after dinner last night and headed up the Five freeway, destination: Seattle. We all took naps on Friday afternoon

248

so we could drive through the night and get to Seattle around two in the afternoon. Mr. and Mrs. O'Brian already helped my parents reserve two rooms for us up there—one for the girls and one for the boys. Hannah and Lisa don't know it yet but they're going to come stay with me and JJ after the performance before we all drive back home on Sunday.

I thought we were going to get caught out when Lisa kept trying to Facetime both me and Hunter. Luckily, Hunter called her back later, when we stopped for snacks and gas in the middle of Central California. I didn't trust myself not to give something away, so I didn't answer. She'll forgive me tomorrow, I'm sure of it.

JJ and I have been relegated to the back row for the whole trip and I'm dying a painful death from the awkwardness. I'm in a constant state of not knowing what to do with myself when I'm around her. We haven't talked about what happened at the race last weekend at all. Just gone back to hanging out like we have all summer.

Even if I can't stop myself from staring at her when I think she isn't looking.

And my fingers itch to touch her.

And as excited as I am to be going on this road trip with my brothers in order to surprise Lisa and Hannah by being at their show, I'm equally excited because I'm getting to take this road trip with JJ. Lisa and Hannah are still my best friends, they always will be. But JJ is too. I have no idea how I'm going to juggle everything once the summer is over—Lisa, Hannah and ballet have always been my whole life, but that's not what I want anymore. I need them to like JJ, I need them to understand that me wanting to do other things won't make me any less their friend.

JJ and I have been dozing off and on since about one in the morning, but now I'm awake and staring out the window while my brothers talk basketball stats with Cole and Henry. All those numbers are more than my short-circuiting brain can manage, so staring out the window it is.

"Katy?" Hunter's voice breaks through the jumbled thoughts in my brain.

"What's up?" He's turned back over the bench seat in front of me, his phone in hand. "You should at least text Lisa, she's worried about you."

With a sigh, I lean back in my seat, arms crossed over my chest. "Don't tell me how to be Lisa's friend. She was my friend for *years* before she was your girlfriend." I can't hide the annoyance in my tone. I'm so sick of him and Lisa relaying messages to each other through me. I'm not their freaking secretary.

"Sorry," Hunter starts to say before JJ interrupts him.

"Hunter? I think what Katy means is that she appreciates you wanting to pass on the message, but she'd like to have her own friendship with Lisa, and her own relationship with you, and not be in this weird three-way thing that's happened." JJ looks at me for confirmation. At my nod, she grins and pats my knee, jerking her head towards Hunter.

Sitting up straight, I lean my arms on the back of the seat in front of me, so I don't have to shout. Irritated at the scowl on his face, I want to let all my sleep-deprived grumpiness out, but she's right. "What I'm trying to say, Hunter, is that I love you and Lisa. But I am not your secretary and I hate it when you guys pass messages to each other through me, or when you use each other to tell me things instead of telling me yourself."

I flop back in my seat, hands in my lap, relieved that I said something. Hunter eyes me for a long moment. "I guess you have a point, Bug. I'll do my best." He looks down at the phone in his hand. "But you should text her, she needs to talk to you." With that he turns around and joins back in on the boys' conversation.

"Thank you," I say, turning to look at JJ. I grab her hand and squeeze, needing the reassurance. When she flips her hand to twine her fingers with mine, my stomach bottoms out and my heart catches in my throat. I stare at our linked hands, her long slim fingers, tanned and golden from a summer spent outdoors, next to my stubbier ones, the bronze of my skin complimenting hers. She has two thin gold rings on her middle finger. One has a twisted band with a little red stone nestled in the curve, the other is shaped into an open heart. An open heart, like hers. From the start, JJ's been the one working to be my friend. I was suspicious and stand-offish, and then I was confused and afraid. JJ was brave enough to fight through my three over-protective brothers to get to me, not to mention my own stubborn belief that she was using me to get to them. Maybe it's time I stepped up and was brave enough to show her what's in my heart too.

Silent, I stare at our hands, a slow smile creeping across my face. Giving her time to see what I'm planning, and pull away if she wants, I bring our joined hands up to my lips, before placing a gentle kiss on her knuckles.

JJ tugs at our hands, forcing me to look up at her face. A question sits in her eyes, but whatever is on my face must answer it because it disappears, an answering grin blooming across hers. When she smiles at me like that, I can hardly breathe, she's so beautiful. The moment is broken when we hit a rough patch of highway, everyone in the car crying out at the bumps. But JJ and I don't let go, squeezing our clasped hands before joining in with the conversation.

I have no idea what any of us talk about for the rest of the drive, all of my attention focused on the beautiful girl holding my hand, brushing her thumb across it. At some point, JJ slides into the middle seat, her hip pressing against mine, our arms twined as she leans up to whisper in my ear.

"Hey," her soft voice sends shivers down my spine.

"Hey," I whisper back, letting myself linger a little in the crook of her neck, until a bump in the road jolts me back.

Once the road smooths out again and we're nearing the campus where Hannah and Lisa have spent the whole summer, JJ leans back in to whisper again. "So, are you *finally* convinced I was never interested in your brothers?" Her nose brushes the shell of my ear and I stifle a gasp. The hard finger she pokes into my side surprises a squawk out of me, getting the attention of all three of my brothers, plus Henry. Cole eyes me in the rear-view mirror.

"No flirting in the back seat." He winks before looking back at the road.

Instead of protesting, I stick my tongue out at him. "Too late."

Hunter and Jack's smirks earn them each a flick on the forehead from JJ. "Mind your own business." And with that, she loops her arm over my head, tucking me into her side. Jack reaches out like he's going to high-five her but then pulls back.

Pasting a glare on his face he growls instead. "Break her heart and I'll break your face." Then he grins, reaching out for the aborted high-five. "God, I've been waiting to use that line for years."

Hannah

"MAYBE IT was Min?" Lisa says, placing a stack of leotards in her suitcase. I shrug, I wouldn't put it past her. We're busy packing up our stuff before the show tonight. We could stay in the dorms tonight, but we decided to sleep in the hotel with my parents instead.

I hadn't been able to keep my secret from her for long. When I kept swiveling my head around at breakfast, eyeing every person who walked in the door, she refused to let it drop until I told her what was wrong. I may have left out the little tidbit about being asked to come back in the fall. I don't know how to tell her and dropping that bomb on her at breakfast seemed cruel.

But she was incensed at the idea that someone may have tried to get me out of the show by exaggerating my ankle injury to the staff. My phone buzzes against my desk at the same time as Lisa's. Since my arms are full of clothes, Lisa picks up her phone to check. "It's Katy."

Lisa reads silently for a few seconds while I shove the clothes in my suitcase, grabbing a stray sock off the floor to toss it on top. Her happy squeal startles me into stubbing my toe on the bed. "What?"

"They're here!" Lisa turns her phone to show me a photo on her screen. The picture was taken in front of the dorms, Katy, her brothers, and JJ grinning.

"Oh my god!" I grab my own phone to check that I got the same photo. There it is. Our best friend somehow managed to get all the way up here to see our performance? "When did they? How did they?" I can't formulate all the questions running through my mind.

"Hunter and Katy. You know how persuasive they can be." Lisa grins, typing away at her phone. I start typing away at mine too.

> **ME:** Hey, Katy and her brothers drove up for the show. Want me to introduce you? Now or after the show?

It only takes a moment for him to respond.

> **TREVOR:** I can head over now, I'm not doing anything at home. I kind of feel like I already know them all anyway.
> **TREVOR:** See you in thirty?

I send him a kissy face gif.

> **TREVOR:** Got it. How's the ankle? Are you ok to dance today?
> **ME:** Ankle is fine. I'm fine. I'm great. Hurry up and get here.

Face to Face

A thought occurs to me right after I hit send on that text.

ME: Ummmmmmm, hope you're ok with meeting my parents. They're supposed to be here soon.

TREVOR: Parents love me. I'm very non-threatening.

Stuffing my phone in my pocket, I follow Lisa out the door, struggling to keep up with her pace. We giggle the whole elevator ride down, Lisa barely able to contain herself until the doors open. "Oh my god, just go!" I laugh, shoving her in front of me when she pauses to wait for me. Hunter and Katy are peering through the glass wall of the lobby, the grins on their faces bright as the sun shining in the sky.

Lisa bolts out the door and throws herself at Hunter, jumping into his arms as I step outside behind her. "You're here! You're really here" She's laughing and hugging him as he spins them around for a second. Seeing her this happy has me grinning as Katy launches herself at me.

"Surprise!"

Hugging her tight, I can hardly believe they're here. "How did you guys pull this off?" I ask.

Katy grins that mischievous grin. "It took a lot of begging and promising to be careful. If Cole and Henry hadn't agreed to come it wouldn't have happened," she adds, pointing at her brother and the very tall man standing next to him, Jack hovering nearby.

I wave and they wave back before going back to their own conversation. Katy keeps talking, her eyes sparkling. "We left after dinner last night and drove straight through. We're staying in the same hotel as your parents so we're having an epic girl's night in our room tonight."

"We are?" Katy nods. "Hi JJ," I add, waving at her. "How did Katy rope you into coming?"

JJ laughs, taking Katy's hand. "I was promised VooDoo donuts."

Laughing, I grin before looking around for Lisa. She and Hunter are deep in conversation on one of the benches. "We're not going to get either of them to pay attention to us for the next twenty minutes at least. Want to come help me pack until Trevor gets here?"

Katy and JJ come help me get our room packed up, packing up Lisa's things for her while I finish shoving my own stuff in my suitcase, only keeping out what I need for tonight's show. We're almost done when my phone buzzes.

> **TREVOR:** I'm here. I'm going to go ahead and assume that the guy making out with Lisa is Hunter and the matching dudes nearby are Jack and Cole?
>
> **ME:** That would be correct. Just make sure they come up for air at some point. Lisa still has to dance tonight. We're almost done, I'll be down in a bit.
>
> **TREVOR:** Take your time, I'm not going anywhere.

CHAPTER TWENTY-FIVE

Katy

"I ASSUME FROM the stupid smile on your face that's Trevor?" I tease Hannah, tucking Lisa's laptop into its case while JJ wraps the cords up.

She nods. "Pretty sure your face matches mine." She nods her head at JJ who grins and gives me a thumbs up in response. "You guys are cute together." I don't know why her words are as reassuring as they are, but hearing them releases the last tiny bit of tension in my shoulders. I knew Hannah wouldn't judge, in theory. But having everything out in the open is a weight off my heart.

Finishing up, Hannah takes a last look around the room. I can't read the expression on her face but I do my own survey for anything of Lisa's that might have been left behind. Spying a hairband and some bobby pins on the windowsill, I reach for the nearest bag to slip them in the outside pocket.

"Wait!" Hannah's sharp tone freezes me in my tracks, outside pocket of her suitcase unzipped. "Um, hang on. Don't put those in there." A guilty look flashes across her face for a second before being hidden behind a smile. Instead, she pulls out a small toiletry bag from her large dance bag. "Put them in here, we'll need them tonight."

"Ready?" JJ asks, breaking the awkward moment. She grabs one of Lisa's bags, slinging it over her shoulder, and the handle of another, hauling them toward the door. I grab the handle of Hannah's biggest suitcase and a reusable grocery bag stuffed full and follow her.

"Okay, maybe there's something to be said for whatever you've been doing all summer," Hannah says, awe in her voice. "You guys have way more upper body strength than me." She grabs her own dance bag and the smallest of the suitcases, straining to carry it all.

"We aren't going to have to worry about not having any boys this year, I can pick you all up. Maybe I'll audition for Cavalier this Nutcracker." I laugh as we head down the hallway toward the elevator. Hannah doesn't answer, just gives me a tight smile. Weird, I thought that was pretty funny. JJ laughed. As we pass the last door it cracks open and a brunette sticks her head out, looking rumpled.

"Do you mind? I was taking a nap." The second she lays eyes on Hannah, her face scrunches in distaste. "Of course," she mutters before closing the door again.

I pin Hannah with a look. "Was that the infamous Becky?" At her nod, I'm tempted to go back and bang on the door, give that little bitch a piece of my mind, but Hannah marches on, digging her finger into the elevator button.

The door opens with a ding and we pull everything inside, Hannah struggling to get her smaller suitcase over the gap while

JJ and I easily lift the bigger bags into the space. I flex my arms as the door slides closed. "That's right, check out these guns." JJ joins me which gets Hannah laughing.

"Oh my god, I missed you," she manages to get out as the elevator comes to a stop. "I take back everything I said, you obviously stayed in excellent shape, even if you weren't in class."

I shrug. "Well, you did kind of have a point. I didn't realize how much I missed being in class until I went back. But I did also have a ton of fun doing other things." I hesitate, not sure if right now is the time to bring this up, but I plow on anyway. Might as well get it over with. "I'm not sure that I'll be there as much next year. I think I might cut back on my classes. It is Junior year you know, and I want to be able to spend time with JJ and doing other stuff."

Hannah's back goes stiff as she pulls her suitcase out of the elevator. "Is that what you want?" she asks quietly. "I know you've never been as obsessed with ballet the same way Lisa and I have. But…" Hannah shakes her head like she's changing her mind about her next words. "Everyone will miss you in class."

Okay, that was kind of weird. She didn't say *she* would miss me in class. I don't have time to dig into her words before Lisa and the boys come wandering over, a tall, lean guy I recognize from Hannah's pictures holding the door open for us. "Thanks," I say. "Trevor, right?"

"At your service." He tips an imaginary hat in my direction. "You must be the famous Katy. It's nice to meet you in person."

"Same. This is my," I glance at JJ unsure of what to say. We haven't had a chance to discuss anything since the car. Is she my girlfriend? I fumble for the right word.

"I'm JJ, Katy's girlfriend," JJ answers for me, setting down her bags to shake Trevor's hand. I don't know if that's a blush creeping up my cheeks or the sun shining on me, but her words send a happy glow through my whole body. I sneak a glance over at JJ and catch her radiant smile. She winks and starts chatting with Trevor as I hunt down Lisa.

I find her tucked into Hunter's lap on one of the nearby benches. "Think you can come up for air long enough to make sure we packed everything of yours?" I kick Hunter's foot, dislodging her. Grinning like the rest of us, Lisa swings her legs down, dropping a kiss on Hunter's cheek before she stands up.

"Will you come with me? I want to hear about everything." She nods her head at JJ before pulling me towards the doors. "We'll be back!" Lisa calls over her shoulder.

I follow her through the doors and back up to their room, filling her in on everything that's happened with JJ and I in the past few days. She doesn't seem surprised when I tell her we're official now, in fact she just smiles to herself. "Did everyone call this before me?" I ask, slightly put out.

"Oh babe," Lisa pats my shoulder. "JJ told Hunter and Jack she had a crush on you weeks ago. In fact, that's why Hunter invited her to your house that first time, she'd said something about you to him at track. They've been trying to set you up all summer."

What? My dopey brothers have been trying to get us together all summer? "Seriously? The whole time I've been trying to figure out if she was using me to get to them." I shake my head at the idiocy of it all. Who knew that for once in my life it was the opposite? She was using my brothers to get to me? We walk into the bare room and Lisa starts opening and closing drawers, checking to make sure nothing got left behind.

"Hey," Lisa interrupts my musing. "I know you just got here, but does Hannah seem…weird to you? She's hiding something and I don't know what. I know her ankle isn't okay, but it feels like it's more than that."

I step into their bathroom and start looking around for anything left behind. Grabbing the can of hairspray I find tucked in the corner of a shelf, I bring it back out. "Maybe? I can't tell. She was kind of squirrely when I tried to put something in her bag, but it could be nothing. Maybe she had a love note from Trevor in there or something."

Lisa smirks, taking the hairspray from me and setting it on the bed with the book in her hands. "Maybe. God Katy, they're so cute together. I'm already heartbroken for them, who knows when they'll get to see each other again."

"Good thing he has family nearby. And Christmas isn't that far away." I sit on the bed next to her. "Maybe that's all it was. I kind of got the feeling she was hiding something, but it's also possible I've been spending too much time with my brothers and their stupid secrets so I could be wrong."

Lisa pokes into a few more drawers before looking satisfied. "Hey, thanks for packing up for me," she says, picking up the book and hairspray.

"You know I'd do anything for you," I tell her. "Even pack up your stinky pointe shoes." Laughing, I follow Lisa out the door and down the hall, grateful my parents let us come. I missed my best friend.

CHAPTER TWENTY-SIX

Hannah

ISA AND I finish doing our makeup and start doing our hair. We've been told to wear it in a high bun for the entire show so I sweep my hair up into a high ponytail and secure it tight before twisting and pinning it against my head.

The dressing room is noisy with a dozen different conversations, people flitting around, getting dressed, borrowing cans of hairspray, stealing a hairpin, or sharing a nice red lipstick. There's a mix of Six, Seven, and Eight girls in this dressing room, all of us gathering with the people we've become closest to over our time here. Elena and Gloria are sharing the mirror next to us. Gloria has a bag of gummy bears out on the counter, sharing with all of us.

"Did you hear anything?" Gloria is asking as I steal another gummy bear.

"Hear about what?" Lisa asks.

"If they asked anyone to stay for the fall? It's always a big secret. They don't post a list or make an announcement or anything. I think it's lame to make it so secret. CBS announces it all on stage at the end of the workshop, which I think is way better. Can you imagine? I would pee my pants on stage!" Gloria snorts with laughter at her own joke.

My stomach flops in a mix of nerves and excitement. It never occurred to me that they might make an announcement onstage after the performance. That was a close one.

"They don't tell anyone here?" I ask, wanting to be sure.

"Nope. It's all very hush, hush. Last year they asked my roommate to stay and I never knew until she posted a picture of her first day in September! Can you believe it? So rude." Gloria pointedly pokes at Elena before they both collapse in a fit of giggles. We all know there's no way Elena would stay here for the fall. She has to stay at her school in Cuba until she graduates, there's some government reason why. Since she's Cuban, getting a visa to study in the US would be difficult for her.

Besides, being here in the summer was too cold for her, I can't imagine how she would survive a winter. My phone buzzes again and I glance down to see a text from Trevor.

> **TREVOR:** Merde beautiful. I'm so excited to see you dance in person! Kick ass!

I have to laugh at his version of an encouraging message. I guess it works though, since I'm ready to tackle Black Swan and everything else, my ankle forgotten in the excitement and adrenaline of the looming performance.

The eight ibuprofen I took twenty minutes ago is probably helping too.

*E*VERYTHING WAS fine until the contemporary piece.
Black Swan?
Nailed it.

Noah and I hit every single turn, lift, and balance. He threw me into the air in the big fouetté lift and I swear I heard the audience gasp. I was on cloud nine going into the contemporary piece. If I could have planned a perfect performance, it would have felt like this. No rush to change costumes, plenty of time to catch my breath between pieces, everything going off without a hitch.

Standing in the wings with Lisa before the contemporary piece, our long black dresses sweeping the floor and swishing around our legs as we moved, I almost told her—that I was invited to come back in the fall. That my dream was coming true. How could I be anything but ecstatic today?

Katy and her brothers are here to surprise us, my parents are here, and my amazing boyfriend is here. Okay, true he's been a pain in my butt about my ankle this week, but it's only because he cares.

I'm dancing the best I ever have in my life, and that's with this stupid ankle. I can't imagine how much better it's going to be once I've rested it. When I come back in September, I'm sure I'll be even better.

Right now, in this moment, this is all I want in my life. Dancing. Performing. Getting on stage and creating beauty. Nothing else matters.

Okay, I don't know how I feel yet about the reality of living up here on my own. And I don't know how school works up here, will I have to enroll in a public high school? And where will I live? What about my parents? They haven't actually said yes yet. And I know I'll miss Ms. Parker and her advice.

And then there's Lisa—how can I move up here and have it all, when she'll have to go back home? That's what stops me from blurting out my news to her right then and there. Instead, I lock my joy down tight and prepare for one last chance to perform with her, in this amazing piece.

And that's when everything goes wrong.

The second I come leaping out of the wings with her, something in my ankle catches and pulls. I don't let the sharp pain stop me from jumping as high as I always do, but landing is another matter. I can't stop the gasp of pain that escapes me as I move into the next step. Noah shoots me a worried look as I go into our first lift, spinning me around with him, my legs mimicking a walking action as he suspends me above the ground.

"Are you okay?" he grinds out through clenched teeth, never stopping his movement. I curl up, letting him support my knees, echoing Lisa and her partner, as my arm sweeps overhead and I curve my spine towards him,

"Just a twinge, caught me by surprise. I'm good," I mutter in his ear.

And I am until the very end of the piece—moving and swirling along with everyone else, ignoring the stabbing pain with each step. Everything is becoming more and more of a blur, but I am determined to finish strong. I am *not* going to let this summer end with a fizzle.

I just have to get through one last bit. All four of us girls are lined up across the back of the stage, holding still while the boys weave and swirl, leaping and rolling between, behind, under and over each other. One last chance for us to suck in a breath before the race to the finish.

As the last rush of music begins building to the end, we run straight at our partners and leap before being carried off the stage in different positions. Lisa leaps over her partner as he rolls under her before dragging her off, legs open to the side, his arms wrapped behind her back. One of the level eight girls is carried off on her partner's back after he swings her around his body. The other couple do the opposite of Lisa and James, she rolls and he leaps over her before dragging her backwards off stage.

Noah is supposed to catch me mid-air. I run and jump, twisting in the air so I land on my back in his arms, arms overhead, reaching for the audience, before he spins us off into the wings. As I take off for my jump, an excruciating pain sears up the side of my leg, radiating from my ankle. I bite off the cry that tries to escape me as Noah's arms hold me but I can't stop the tears that leak from my eyes or my ragged gasps for breath. Noah's arms tighten around me as he spins us off the stage, fear in his eyes.

"What happened? Are you okay?" he asks the second we're out of sight of the audience. There's a flock of dancers in the wings, waiting for us to finish so they can go onstage for the final piece. Each class comes back on one more time for a final bow. For sure I'm going to miss it, there's no way I can go back onstage like this.

"No. No. Don't put me down." I manage to gasp out. "It's my ankle. Oh god, it hurts." I cry. Tears are streaming down my face and I don't care. The pain is unbearable, throbbing and pulsing with each thud of my heart. I can't think.

Music starts playing from somewhere and the wing empties a little.

"Here, put her here." Lisa takes command of the situation. "I'll get the stage manager." Noah sets me down on a chair, my foot balanced on the prop table next to it. My pointe shoe ribbons cut into the skin around my ankle as it starts to swell.

"Someone get her pointe shoe off," a stern voice says above me. I can't see who it is through the tears, but gentle fingers start plucking at the knot in my ribbons. I bite my lips to hold in the whimpers that threaten to escape me as each movement sends more pain through my ankle. "This is going to be unpleasant, I'm sorry," that same stern voice says before grasping the toe of my shoe and the heel, slipping it off. The elastic around my ankle pulls tight, sending another shot of pain through my leg. I gasp, hiccupping and crying with it, almost choking on my own breath, then my shoe is off and someone is squatting next to me.

"Hannah? Hannah, can you tell me what happened?" I know that calm voice.

Wiping my eyes with the heels of my hands I turn to see Dr. Lee next to me. "It...I..." I suck in another breath and start over, trying to speak. "When I took off for the last jump, something snapped," I manage to get out.

I spot someone hovering out of the corner of my eye. "Go, don't miss your entrance, Lisa." I say, nodding my head.

"No, it's okay. I don't want to leave you," Lisa answers, worry painted on her face.

"Lisa. Go. I'll be okay." She hesitates. "Go." The pain makes me snap the word out, eyes wide, Lisa scurries away. Groaning, I let my head fall back.

"Okay, Hannah. Take a deep breath for me. I thought I felt a tender spot last night. We need to go get this x-rayed again." She pulls her phone out of her pocket. "Are your parents here?"

Biting my lips, I nod. The tears I thought I'd stuffed down overwhelm me again and I can't stop the sob that explodes from my ribs. The movement jars my foot, sending another wave of pain through me. In response to Dr. Lee's question, I dial my mom's cell phone, praying they pick up. When she doesn't answer I send her a text from the number.

The moment it registers as 'read' Dr. Lee's phone rings. I hand it over so she can talk to my mom, taking slow breaths to keep myself calm while I wait. Briefly, I turn my head to watch everyone on stage, but the sight of Lisa, Noah, and the rest of my class running out of the wings and into the bright lights without me is too much. With a sob, my heart breaking, I close my eyes and wait for Dr. Lee to come back.

In a haze of pain and heartache, I let the music wash over me, floating in and out of conscious thought. A wave of applause follows the last note. Eyes still closed, I feel the rush of bodies as a crowd of dancers leaves the stage. It's finished. Everything's done.

Am I done?

"Hannah?" My mom's worried voice breaks through the fog I've been floating in. I snap my eyes open to find her and my dad kneeling next to me. I glance behind them and spot Trevor and Lisa, hovering in the doorway.

"Hey, Mom." I try to smile, but it's watery and pitiful. The moment her arms wrap around me, pulling me tight against her chest I lose it. Does a tiny part of me cringe that Trevor is watching me sob like a baby against my mom? Absolutely. Am I in too much pain to care? One hundred percent.

"I have a connection at the local urgent care, they'll rush us in for an x-ray," Dr. Lee is telling my dad. She gives him an address, which he types into his phone. "Can you walk Hannah?"

In response, I swing my legs down to the ground, but the second I try to put any weight on my right foot I know I'm not walking anywhere. Shaking my head, I sit back in the chair. "I can carry her," Trevor offers, stepping forward. "Uh, if that's okay?"

I let my dad, Trevor, and Dr. Lee figure out a plan to get me to the car and off for x-rays. "Hannah?" Lisa is standing next to my mom, talking quietly. "I'll pack up all your stuff here and take it to our room, okay? Will you keep me posted?"

"I will," Trevor volunteers for me. "Go, Katy and Hunter may tear down a door or two to get back here if one of us doesn't let them know what's happening soon. Green and purple are not Hunter's colors." I crack a smile at Trevor's words, remembering that first awful date when I had no idea who he was referencing.

"Ready?" My dad is standing by the door with Dr. Lee.

Trevor steps in close, sliding one arm behind my knees and the other behind my back. "I'm so sorry," he whispers and he lifts me. The motion sends another sharp pain through my ankle, but I clench my teeth and manage not to cry as he carries me out of the theater and to my parents' car. As he's setting me in the back seat, Lisa comes running out with my dance bag.

"Here, I thought you'd want your clothes and your phone." she says, handing it to Trevor to put in the car.

"Thanks," I manage. "Are you coming?" I look up, directing my question to Trevor.

"Of course. But I'm going to drive my car and meet you there. Your dad gave me the address already." With that, he leans down to press a kiss to the top of my head before closing the door.

Urgent care is a blur of waiting rooms, flipping through magazines without seeing them, Dr. Lee's incessant clicking of her pen and the never-ending replay in my mind of the moment it happened. The pop, the pain, the way I knew in that split second something was very wrong.

"Well Hannah," Dr. Lee regards me with a sad smile. "I have good news and bad news." I grab my mom's hand and squeeze.

"The bad news is that it looks like you have a fibular fracture." She gestures to the x-ray held up to the light box on the wall. "If you look at the x-ray, you can see right here"—she points to a faint line on the thinner of the two bones in the picture—"there's a pretty clear fracture." She points to a second x-ray. "This is the one from a few weeks ago, see how there's no line, but now that we know where to look, there's the tiniest hint of darkness there?"

I peer at the two pictures. The line on the x-ray from tonight is faint but distinct. I can't see anything on the other x-ray and say so.

"It's very difficult to see unless you know what you're looking for, it's a very common mis-diagnosis. My guess is that you've had a stress fracture back there for quite a while, but because it didn't show up on the x-ray, the other therapist assumed it was a soft-tissue injury. When you kept dancing on it, that soft spot in the bone turned into a proper fracture."

I take a deep breath. A fracture. That's bad. That's really bad, right? "How long will it take to heal?" I ask at the same time my mom asks, "What's the good news?"

Dr. Lee smiles at us. "Well, the answer to your question Hannah is the good news. A fracture like this has a tendency to heal with less complications down the road, as long as you give it the time it needs to heal. You'll have to be in a boot, in fact I'll want you on crutches for a week or two, but once it's healed, it should heal cleanly with no scar tissue. It will be a matter of building strength more than anything else. Rehabilitation from a break or a fracture can be much easier and less complicated than a sprain."

"How long will it take?" I ask. "Do you think I'll be ready to come back for the fall term?"

"You're going to have to work with your doctor at home to determine that. Based on past experience, I'm sure they will hold your place in the fall unless it looks like it's going to be longer to recover than anticipated. But that will be up to Mr. Bethelo and the staff to decide. My job is to weigh in on whether I think a dancer is physically healthy enough to continue in the program."

Immediately, determination to be ready for the fall term fills me. I may not be at one hundred percent on September first, but I'm determined to get back on my feet as soon as possible. "I'll be ready. What can I do? How do I make sure I'm healing as fast as possible?"

"For starters, you're going to be *honest* with your doctor at home about what kind of pain you're feeling." Dr. Lee glares at me. "If I'd had a chance to look at these x-rays before I saw you last night, I might have made a different decision. I definitely wouldn't have believed your stoic expression when you insisted you weren't hurting."

Dr. Lee turns to my parents. "Do you know a good sports medicine practitioner back home? Someone familiar with dancers?"

"Oh yes," Mom answers. "Her dance teacher is married to one. All our girls go to him."

"Oh? What's his name?" Dr. Lee looks curious.

"Michael Brooks. He's married to Leslie Parker."

At the mention of Ms. Parker's name Dr. Lee's face clears. "Oh, I've heard wonderful things about how he helped her. Well, that makes me feel much better, knowing she'll be in good hands back home."

Dr. Lee has the urgent care nurse get me set up with a boot and crutches before I follow my parents out of the exam room, struggling to coordinate getting through the door with my added accessories. Trevor jumps up from one of the chairs in the waiting room as we emerge.

"Hey, do you need help?" He reaches for me, unsure of what to do or how to help.

"I'm fine." I grunt when one of my crutches hits a chair as I swing it forward.

"So?"

My parents are with the receptionist dealing with the insurance billing so I go to sit down.

"It's a fracture. Dr. Lee thinks there was probably a stress fracture there the whole time, but when I didn't stop dancing it developed into a full one." Trevor sits next to me, taking my hand in his. I haven't been alone with him since everything happened last night. I haven't even had a chance to tell him about Dr. Lee's visit or being invited to come back in the fall.

"The doctor couldn't tell when she checked you out last night?"

I freeze at his words.

I never told Trevor about Dr. Lee paying me a visit last night. "Did Lisa say something to you?"

"No. I only saw her when we were getting you from backstage. Why?"

A sick feeling slides through me. All this time I was blaming one of the other dancers for ratting me out.

I turn to look him in the eye, praying that my suspicions are wrong. Please be wrong. "Are you the one who called the front office about my injury?"

My face must give away the fury that's boiling inside me because Trevor goes pale. "Um." He swallows. "I was worried about you," he says so quietly I almost miss it.

"I told you I had it under control," I hiss back. "How could you do that to me?"

Now it's Trevor's turn to be angry. "Well, obviously you *didn't* have it under control, did you? You were dancing on a fracture waiting to happen. What part of that is under control?" His normally warm voice crackles with ice.

"That wasn't your decision to make, Trevor." I can't stop myself from growling at him. "It's not your life, it's not your dream, it's not your body. You don't get to make that kind of decision for me."

"I thought…"

"You thought what? That you'd tell the front office and they'd magically make it better? Tell me to be careful? Do you know what really would have happened?" I lower my voice when I catch my mom looking over her shoulder at us. "You almost cost me the chance to do Black Swan, to do a solo. To guarantee my spot here in the fall."

Trevor's eyes go wide at my words. "A spot here in the fall?"

I don't want to make him feel better. He betrayed me by going to the front office like that. What if they hadn't let me dance? Sure, I was hurting now, and this fracture sucks, but at least I had a chance to perform tonight. At least I got the thrill of being on stage, of doing what I love best, and doing it well, before it happened.

"Yeah, Trevor. They offered me a spot in the fall. No thanks to your meddling. You could have made them rethink it, you know. No one wants to deal with a helicopter parent…or boyfriend." I can't let go of the anger. The betrayal that he thought he knew my own body better than I do cuts deep. If I know anything, I *know* my body. I know what it can do and what it can't.

"Hey, is everything okay?" My mom hurries over as my voice gets louder and louder. "You ready to go home?"

"Yeah. I'm done here." I say, my heart cracking at the double meaning of my words.

Trevor must hear it in my voice because he looks up sharply. "Done?"

Tears fill my eyes at the pain etched on his face. "Yeah," I whisper, pulling myself to my feet and tucking the crutches under my arms so I can follow my parents out the door. "We're done."

CHAPTER TWENTY-SEVEN

Trevor

NO. NO, no, no, no, no, no. That can't be it. My heart in my throat, Hannah limps away from me, her head bowed under the weight of her words. Her beautiful fire-red hair is still pulled up in a bun from her performance, exposing the long line of her throat. I'm rooted to the spot as she walks away.

Don't leave me.

I wanted to help.

You don't understand why I was so scared.

Let me explain.

Come back.

Thoughts race through my mind but for once in my life I say none of them out loud. Instead, I watch through the window as her mom helps her climb into the car, sliding the crutches in after her.

All I wanted was to take care of her. I swear. What have I done?

Hannah's words rattle around in my head. She said they offered her a spot to come back in the fall. That means she'll be here, in Seattle. A few miles from me instead of the thousand-mile distance I've been trying to navigate since January. Slowly, a plan forms in my mind. Where's JARVIS when I need him?

I'm no Tony Stark, but I'm no slouch in the brains department, I know I can come up with a plan to fix this. Because I have to fix this. Hannah is the most amazing person I've ever met, I'm not going to lose her over this.

Step one—get to California.

Not Quite The End

Hannah's story concludes in *Heart to Heart,* available for pre-order now.

Want to keep up to date with all of Penelope's releases? Sign up for Penelope's newsletter

https://sendfox.com/penelopefreedbooks

If you enjoyed this book, the best way to thank the author is to leave a review. Thank you!

ACKNOWLEDGEMENTS

I'M SORRY! I know that cliffhanger is terrible! But I'm sorry, it had to be done, Hannah and Trevor aren't ready to get their Happily Ever After. They have a little growing up to do first. Just hang on, *Heart to Heart* is coming soon and hopefully will make up for the awful way I left you hanging.

When I was planning out this series, I had a big blank next to book 3. I knew it was going to be Katy's story, I knew what Hannah and Lisa were going to be up to. I even knew how that cliffhanger was going to play out. But Katy was holding out on me. I knew she always felt like she was in the shadow of someone—either her brothers or her friends—and I know from firsthand experience how that feels. But I didn't know what she needed.

It wasn't until I got to the end of *Head to Head* and JJ came waltzing into the Quinn's backyard that I knew what was going to turn Katy's world on its head. I'm going to admit something, Katy and Cole's story are a big middle finger to the world on behalf of everyone who's ever been told that who they love is wrong. Love is love, and the more of it in the world the better.

Face to Face

If you think that having not just one, but two, coming out stories in a YA romance is wrong, or ruins it for the genre, or makes you uncomfortable, guess what? I don't care. And if you think that both of them being accepted by their family and friends without a second thought is unrealistic, that it's not how the world works? Too bad. It's how the world SHOULD work. It's how *my* world works.

It shouldn't matter who you love as long as they treat you with kindness and respect. If you need someone to talk to or help you deal with family or friends who don't support you, listed below are some great resources to get support.

But know this—I see you, I love you, and you matter to me. Stay. It gets better.

THE TREVOR PROJECT:
thetrevorproject.org

LGBT NATIONAL YOUTH HOTLINE:
https://www.glbthotline.org/talkline.html

PFLAG HOTLINE LINKS:
https://pflag.org/hotlines

Thanks as always to my amazing editor, Cate, you make me look good.

Lasairiona, thank you for cheering me on when I was nervous about this book and for making me do the big scary things. And also for holding my hand while I freak out about the million tiny things.

Norma and Patti, my amazing betas, I'm sorry! I'm so, so sorry. You've had to wait the longest of anyone to know what happens next and you've borne it with utmost patience. I'll never be able to make it up to you!

Melissa, the best bestie in the world. Thank you for checking on me, cheering me on, and being the one to make sure I take care of myself, not just everyone around me.

My mini-me, thank you for being my inspiration as always. I'm not ready for you to do the grown-up things. Stay little forever, please?

And always, my #1 fan. Thank you for doing the dishes when I don't want to, for not getting mad when I forget to put your laundry in the dryer, and for always having dinner ready on Monday nights. Love you!

ABOUT THE AUTHOR

Penelope Freed lives in the Pacific Northwest where you can find her learning how to drive in the rain, walking her dog and making a mess in the kitchen. Her husband and daughter think she's a little bit bonkers and really hate it when she dances embarrassingly in public.

Which she does, often.

After a lifetime in the ballet world, Penelope decided to start writing down the stories in her head instead of narrating her ballet classes with them—her former students are very thankful for this decision. Now, Penelope writes stories about dreamers, just like she is, who are willing to do whatever it takes to make those dreams come true.

Made in the USA
Monee, IL
11 October 2021